# PINING & LOVING

## EMMA STERNER-RADLEY

# SIGN UP

Firstly, thank you for purchasing Pining & Loving.

I frequently hold flash sales, competitions, giveaways and lots more.

To find out more about these great deals you will need to sign up to my mailing list by clicking on the link below:

http://tiny.cc/pining

# REVIEWS

I sincerely hope you will enjoy reading Pining & Loving.

If you did, I would greatly appreciate a short review on your favourite book website.

Reviews are crucial for any author, and even just a line or two can make a huge difference

# DEDICATION

*For Malin -*

*You taught me what battling mental illness looked like, explained how it felt, and fought bravely until the day it won. Throughout all of that you prepared me for my own smaller battle and made me able to write a character like Gwen.*

# ACKNOWLEDGMENTS

The first thank you goes to my wife Amanda for beta-reading and making sure the story made sense to a reader without mental illness.

Huge thanks to my editor Jessica Hatch and my proof-reader Cheri Fuller. You were both understanding and very open with me on this project and as always, I cannot thank you enough!

Thank you to two artists on Tumblr for answering some of my research questions: jengrayart (Jen Gray) and awanqi.

The final thanks goes to my lovely family for putting up with a writer who buries herself in her books and is thereby useless to her relatives. Also, many thanks for taking the journey with me through the ups and downs of mental illness that our family have lived through.

Caveat for readers - The mentions of The Tragedy of Lord George is not an advertisement, I'm not even a fan of it. So hey, if you want to buy me a present or bribe me for a sequel, message me to ask what scent I'd like! Or just buy me a coffee.

In memory of
Malin Sterner
1973-2011
Jag saknar dig.

## Chapter One

# GWEN DAVIES

Gwen could think of a million better ways to spend a rainy Saturday afternoon. Well, at least three. One, drinking warming tea with a dollop of macadamia honey. Two, reading a good book. Three, daydreaming about a certain older woman who set hearts and private parts ablaze with one confident wink.

Instead, Gwen was stuck here, glaring at a bland picture of a bridge over still waters. The quote, "Be not wishing and pining but thankfully content. For it is a short bridge between wanting and regret," was written over it. Why did so many therapists have this sort of thing on their walls?

Of course, she shouldn't judge all therapists by Edward. He was the dullest, most unimaginative one she'd ever met.

She frowned at him. Being boring wasn't the worst thing about him. No, that had to be the fact he insisted on wearing his socks over his jeans. Who the hell tucked their jeans into their socks? How was she meant to trust her mental stability to a man who did that? Not that

1

she'd been all that unstable these past few years. Between therapy, antidepressants, and every trick in the mental hygiene books, she was keeping her depression to a minimum.

Or she had been.

Subtle signs of her brain chemistry getting wonky again had been creeping up in the past week. Some listlessness. More fatigue. Perhaps this period of her brain getting enough serotonin and dopamine was ending.

Still, his socks—today a white pair of tattered tennis socks—pulled over the jeans drove her even crazier than any upcoming depressive period might. She'd rather look at the clichéd motivational poster than them.

"I see you're admiring my new wall decoration," Edward said, interrupting her thoughts.

"Yeah. It's, um, a pretty bridge."

He gave her a stern look. "The bridge isn't the significant part. The quote is. And it actually ties in with what we're meant to be discussing today, your infatuation with this woman who comes to your café."

Gwen tilted her head. "How does that tie in? I don't know if she likes bridges. I guess most people like bridges. They're harmless at worst and helpful at best. Like if you want to cross bodies of water without getting your feet wet. Don't you hate getting wet feet?"

"Stop trying to change the subject," Edward said. "You know I meant the part about pining. Ever since your exgirlfriend ended your relationship last year, you've appeared to obsess over this woman, pining over this stranger."

"First of all, Sarah wasn't just my girlfriend, she was my damn fiancée. And she ended our three-year-long *engagement*. Secondly, I wouldn't say that I'm pining,"

Gwen replied, her voice armoured. "Mocha inspires me to draw, and she makes me happy when I see her. Also, she's not a stranger. I serve her every morning."

He picked up his notepad and flipped back a few pages. "Ah, yes, she always orders a mocha?"

"Mm."

"Which is why you call her Mocha?"

Gwen tapped her foot against the outdated carpet, keeping time with the rain against the window. "Yes. What about it?"

"Well, doesn't the fact that you don't know her real name make you think she's a stranger?"

Her foot tapped faster. "No, not really. Loads of my friendships are with people online. Several of them I know as their usernames, not their given names. That doesn't make them strangers; I know them really well."

"Be that as it may, Gwen, my point still stands. You don't know this woman other than the brief interactions you have with her every morning."

He was right, of course. She didn't know Mocha, despite seeing her every day. They would make small talk about the weather, new haircuts, current news. Sometimes, if Mocha wanted an extra shot of espresso in her drink, they might talk about how much sleep they had missed last night. That was it.

Still, something about this woman touched the very core of Gwen, not just in the sexual and physical sense, but the very core of her heart and mind. Mocha was unique. Her way of moving, talking, and even how she looked at people, as if they were the most interesting thing in the universe. She was polite but always in control, powerful but never in a cruel way. She seemed to have everything together, always knowing what to do and say.

Perfect figure. Perfect speech. Perfect sense of humour. Perfect interest in, and knowledge of, the world around her. Even her clothes were perfect, down to her vintage, mocha-coloured suede coat. Yep, her signature coat matched her signature drink. She was *that* well put together.

Gwen stopped tapping her foot. The only way out of Edward telling her things she didn't want to hear was to change the topic.

"Sorry if I'm testy. I'm having trouble sleeping again."

He put his pad down. "Insomnia?"

"Some. But mainly it's intense nightmares."

His dull eyes lit up. "Insomnia *and* nightmares? That sounds like symptoms of your depression worsening. Tell me about these dreams."

There. Topic changed. Gwen fascinated him by launching into a long tirade about dreams with sugar-spun moons and strange things lurking in labyrinthine basements. She'd always been able to chat herself out of anything she wanted to avoid. Well, except those socks over the jeans. No chat in the world could make that go away.

## Chapter Two

# AYA LAWSON

Aya gave the punching bag another smack. She wasn't keeping to proper form, just punching wildly, and she knew she was going to get told off for it. She might not be fighting competitively anymore, but that didn't mean she should punch randomly like some street thug. But she was so *furious*. So angry at herself for ruining everything in her life. She grunted as she pounded the punching bag with such force it made her ponytail smack against her shoulder.

"Hey! What in the name of Pete do ya think you're doing?" Bill groused. Her former coach, now mentor and friend, loomed over her with a disappointed look on his wrinkled face.

Aya lowered her arms. "No need to tell me off. I'm just… venting."

"Well, vent without breaking my equipment, will ya?" Bill said, his accent coming out even more through his annoyance. It always stuck out in this Stoke-on-Trent gym, filled with British Midlanders, when Bill spoke like the American old-timer he was. Never mind that he had lived in England for the past two decades, his accent was still as strong as his beaten-up body.

Bill stood to his full height, which meant something as he was one of the tallest men she had ever seen – a stark contrast to how short she was. They were both built with the sort of muscle that boxing gave a fighter. They had that, and a certain grumpy air, in common. Otherwise they were opposites. Bill was an extrovert while she was an introvert. Bill liked a good chat; she was quiet. He was a pessimist, and Aya Lawson was an optimist at heart.

Or, at least, she used to be. At the moment it was hard to see anything bright on her horizon. All she saw were the jobs she was turned down for and the job interviews she didn't even get called to, her lack of a social life; both when it came to friends and lovers, and her career as a boxer behind her.

At least that last point wasn't due to what she'd like to call her awkwardness. Her last girlfriend, whom she'd been with sometime back in the Ice Age, had chosen to call it her social anxiety. No, the end of her career as a boxer had come when she'd taken a particularly bad blow to the head during a match. She'd been so panicked by the lingering effects and hospital stay that she quit.

The other two things, however—the non-existent social life and her current lack of a job—came down to the fact that Aya couldn't open her mouth without saying something people found weird, offensive, or that they didn't understand. Sometimes she wondered if it was a self-fulfilling prophecy that she ended up saying the most random stuff. She often found herself trying so hard to find the right things to say, trying to find something to say that made her sound smart, funny, or interesting. Or, at the very least, kind and polite.

Whatever the cause was, the terrible consequences still showed up in every failed job interview she had endured over the last three months and on every disastrous date she'd slogged through for the last four years. Most times, she didn't even get to the date stage. Take, for example, every time she tried to talk to the gorgeous blonde in the gym's self-defence class. Sometimes Aya would help the instructor, pitching in when she was ill or by acting the 'attacker' so the instructor could show where kicks, blows, and shoves should land. This meant Aya had seen quite a lot of the blonde and had gotten many chances to talk to her after class. Yet, every time she tried, she'd either start stuttering and have to leave or not be able to get a single syllable out of her useless mouth.

Bill snapped his fingers. "Hey, daydreamer. You awake? Why are you just standing there staring at my punching bag?"

"Sorry, I have a lot on my mind," she mumbled.

He put his huge hand on her shoulder and squeezed. "Yeah, well, box or let someone else have a go at the bag, will ya? I don't keep the doors to this place open for people to stand around and stare, kid."

He walked off and Aya smiled after him. *Kid.* She'd turned twenty-seven last month. Still, she figured she would always be a child in Bill's eyes. She had come to his boxing gym, Muscles & Mitts, when she was fifteen. Her dad had caught her punching one of their sofa cushions after a confrontation with some school bullies. He sent her to her room, and when she was allowed out again, he and her mum told her to go with her father's co-worker to a local boxing gym. They had no idea what that entailed or that she would love it so much that she'd pursue as a career. In fact, part of her wondered if they saw her frustration but didn't know what to do about it, so they wanted her and her noise out of the house. Her parents loved her but never understood her. Or seemed very comfortable in her presence.

Either way, her dad's workmate had taken her to Muscles & Mitts. She had stared up at the words on a simple sign on the top half of a pebble-dashed building with a nail salon on the first floor. Aya remembered wondering what winter gloves had to do with muscles and then, that very evening, learning what a pair of punching mitts were. It was hard not to when Bill had rushed over, given this surly, little black-haired and equally black-eyed teenager the onceover, and then bellowed, "Yes! Finally, someone who isn't a huge testosterone-fuelled meat bag wanting to be tough. You, kid, I can work with!"

And he had. He had been her coach, suffering through every strenuous workout and every action-packed match with her, unlike her parents, who never came to anything. Sadly, though, Bill couldn't help her now. Aya had mediocre grades from a lacklustre school, no special qualities that fit in work applications, and no charisma to use on employers. All she could do was box. And say the wrong thing.

Bill couldn't help her figure out how to charm women either, though that wasn't to say he hadn't tried a few times. After all, what had brought him here was falling in love with an Englishwoman. However, these days, dating took more than having an exotic American accent and offering to make a lady the best milkshake she'd ever tried with the secret ingredient of marshmallow fluff. Aya was pretty sure that wasn't going to work for her.

She gave the punching bag another echoingly loud thwack.

## Chapter Three

# MOCHA

Coffee4You was a dingy café close to Stoke library. It was also where Gwen had been working for the last few years.

On good days, she liked her job well enough. It gave her a chance to talk to people and keep the demons in her mind at bay by staying busy. Moreover, it helped that the couple who owned it were understanding when she needed some time off or to take a break to go to therapy. When she was kind to herself, she understood that this was because she took initiative, worked hard, and gladly took extra shifts whenever she was able. It didn't hurt that the customers loved her sense of humour.

On bad days, though, she wondered how long she'd be able to keep up with the pace without taking too many sick days. Also, on bad days she wondered what was wrong with people. Like the person in front of her now, who always tried to pay with a grocery store loyalty card and blamed it getting declined on magnetic disturbances in the air. The sad part was that he wasn't strangest customer she had served today. That pride of place went to the woman wearing a shower cap and screaming at her for not selling carrots.

The man mumbling about magnetic disturbances finally located a five-pound note and paid with that. Gwen gave a sigh of relief.

He left with his oatcake, his takeaway mug, his change, and, of course, his loyalty card, holding the door open for another customer as he did so. Gwen somehow knew who the other customer would be before she saw her. Mocha. The older woman strode toward the counter with confident steps and a winning smile. She moved with such speed that her coat billowed behind her. Her long hair followed suit, turning her smooth tresses into a veil.

The few people currently in the café moved aside, not because Mocha seemed as if she would bump into them, but simply to watch her float past. At least, Gwen assumed that was why they stepped back and eyed the unearthly beauty who now graced this boring place.

Gwen forced herself to breathe normally and to ignore the sensation of Mocha arriving and filling this black-and-white place with sparkling colour. It was ridiculous just how much her day improved with one glance into Mocha's eyes, which refracted into emerald greens and navy blues in the morning sunlight.

"Ay up, me duck," Mocha said, using the classic Stoke-on-Trent greeting even though she didn't have a Midlands accent. No, she had more of a Southern accent. From Surrey or Kent maybe? Somewhere posh, anyway.

"Hi!" Gwen said, resisting the urge to run and check her make-up and hair in the bathroom.

Mocha put one hand on the counter, leaning but still keeping perfect posture. "I'm so glad you're working today. Yesterday morning I had to be without my dose of blue."

She was referring to Gwen's hair, of course. It was cut asymmetrically and platinum blonde everywhere but the long bit where the tips, currently tickling her jawline, were tinted sapphire blue to match her eyes.

Being thirty-three years old meant that she wasn't expected to have unnatural colours in her hair anymore. Gwen didn't care. She did, however, worry that her fun-loving but non-neurotypical personality, matched with the unusual hair, made her fit the cliché of a Manic Pixie Dream Girl. Not that she was manic or would ever be some passive dream girl to help an immature artistic man discover himself. Or a man in general. Still, her self-loathing mind got hung up on stuff like that, second-guessing every instinct, thought, and emotion. She didn't worry about what others thought of her; she was too busy with how badly she thought of herself.

Anyway, she had to take joy wherever she could find it, and the blue in her hair cheered her up. She focused back on Mocha and the conversation.

"Hm. Weird that I didn't see you. I was working yesterday. You must've come in right when I was on my break," Gwen surmised.

"True, I was a little bit early, as I had a morning meet-ing. I'll have to make sure to not be that early again, right Gwen?"

Normally when customers read her nametag and used her first name, it freaked her out. Somehow, though, Mocha made it natural. Comfortable. More than that, the way she said her name was downright *sexy*. She took Gwen's commonplace Welsh name and made it sound like the term for a perfume or a dessert.

Gwen had to, once again, remind herself to breathe. Mocha wasn't really flirting. She was like this with everyone in the café, at least everyone who was respectful. Gwen had seen her snap at people who pushed in front of her in line or who were rude to Gwen. The tendency to not put up with nonsense just made her even more attractive.

Gwen remembered that she hadn't answered. "Um. Uh. Yes. I mean, that would be nice!"

*Smooth,* she berated herself. *You sound like a teenager with a crush.*

"I'm glad we agree." Mocha retrieved her hand from the counter and buttoned up her gorgeous coat with a wink. "Now, I'm afraid I'm in urgent need of my sugar and caffeine fix."

Gwen snapped to it. "Sure! One large mocha dusted with chocolate powder coming up!"

No matter how Gwen dragged out the process, Mocha always had her drink far too quickly and was on her way out. Gwen watched her leave, a sense of loss thrumming in the pit of her stomach. Edward the sock-over-jeans therapist was right. She knew nothing about this woman. But if Mocha brightened up a day like this, did it really matter? After all, a woman like that could never be interested in a mere mortal like Gwen. Hell, Mocha was probably straight as an arrow. It was harmless desiring her from afar.

Just then, Gwen's annoying co-worker Dave appeared. He carried a tray with a full mug on it but focused more on the flashing phone in his other hand. He elbowed her and said, "Could you take this coffee over to the table in the corner?"

She peered over to the three occupied tables in the corner. "I could. If you told me which one you meant."

Dave was tapping his mobile onehandedly, clicking away the flashing call. "Huh?"

"Focus, please, Dave. Which corner table? Or rather, which customer?"

He pulled his gaze from the screen to the tables for the briefest moment. "Oh, it's for the foreign-looking woman. Like she's a tiny bit Chinese or Japanese or something?"

He missed Gwen rolling her eyes at him. The woman in question was wearing a bright saffron hoodie. He could've said 'the woman in yellow' or 'in orange'. Or maybe 'the woman with long black hair'. Instead he had to go straight for the fact that she might have Asian descent.

Gwen shouldn't have been surprised. Dave reacted like this to anything outside of his straight, able-bodied, cis-gendered, middleclass, white existence. She'd noticed that first-hand when she came out to him. In the blink of an eye, she'd gone from being a regular co-worker to being the only non-straight person he knew. This led to constant inappropriate questions and so-called jokes. He treated her as if she were some sort of animal at the zoo to be studied and giggled at. It had gotten worse when he found out she had clinical depression.

Gwen was overcome by the need to get rid of him. "Sure, I'll take the coffee over to her. You can go check your phone in the back and then come back and restock the pastries."

He looked up at her with raised eyebrows. "What? You're the boss now?"

She put herself in his personal space, loathsome as it was. "Hey, I said you could check your phone. If I were your boss I wouldn't be saying that, I'd be firing your useless bum."

He sniffed and slunk off to the backroom in a sulk.

Gwen sighed and gazed out the window as she lifted the tray. The sun had retreated behind dark clouds, which seemed fitting. Mocha had left, and Gwen was stuck here with Dave all day. Bloody marvellous.

She took the coffee over to the woman in the saffron hoodie. She had graceful features, despite the deep scowl on them, but serious stay-away body language.

"Looks like the weather is turning for the worse," Gwen said conversationally.

The other woman accepted the coffee and said, "Yeah." She snapped her mouth shut as if that was all she was going to say about it but then added, "About right for a day like this," before going back to whatever she was doing on her battered laptop.

Gwen walked back to the counter, her shoulders slumping. Then it occurred to her: on rainy days Mocha sometimes came in for a treat lunch and an extra mocha with whipped cream.

Gwen turned to the window, wishing those dark clouds would bring rain. What was more, she noticed her reflection in the glass was smiling.

## Chapter Four

# SELF-DEFENCE

It was time for another self-defence class, and Aya had once more been roped in to help. Not that she minded. It gave her a sense of purpose and, of course, a chance to see that hot blonde again.

Aya stretched while waiting for the instructor to finish greeting the group. She breathed deep, enjoying the gym's familiar scent of leather and the menthol cleaning products that Bill used to mask the smell of sweat. Though the salty tang of sweat was gone from the air, Aya felt as if it were embedded in the building's materials and the equipment. All the people who had expelled so much effort, ambition, and fighting spirit between these walls had left an echo of raw power that still pulsated all around her. She tapped into that atmosphere of strength and endurance, flexing her arm and shoulder muscles—visible through the tight T-shirt she wore tonight for that very purpose—and then, in slow motion, pounced on the class instructor.

The instructor moved aside, spun, and pretended to jab her fingers into Aya's eyes before kneeing her in the crotch. As Aya theatrically bent forward, cupping her groin, she caught a glimpse of the mysterious blonde. She let her gaze linger. The blonde wasn't as fit as Aya but quite a lot taller, with a posture so impeccable she looked unreal. What had caught Aya's eye the first time she saw the blonde was the way she held herself. It was just as impressive now.

The class carried on, giving Aya plenty of chances to not only get a small confidence boost by showing her physical prowess, but to help the group learn how to defend themselves and understand the power of their bodies. She also got plenty of chances to watch the sexy blonde practise the moves. Aya had to learn her name. Even if she didn't dare to talk to her or, god forbid, brave asking her out.

As soon as class ended and the participants milled out, Aya stopped the instructor and blurted, "Can I ask you something?"

"Sorry, I didn't quite hear that?"

"I wondered if I could ask you something," Aya repeated more slowly, trying to sound normal and confident.

"Sure! You can ask anything, considering I owe you for helping out with this class."

Aya waved that away. "Don't mention it. I like helping, and I think everyone should learn to defend themselves, especially women." She adjusted her ponytail, wishing this conversation would go faster so she could run out. "So, um, I wanted to ask if you know the name of the blonde in the dark red leggings?"

"Hm," the instructor said, tapping her hand on her thigh as she pondered. "Oh yes, I'm pretty sure her name is Susannah. She's lovely. Always helps the others out and always good for a laugh. Why?"

Panic rose in Aya. She hadn't considered that there would be follow-up questions if she started asking around about people. "Um, I just thought I knew her from somewhere. I must've been wrong. Thanks. See you next time."

Aya hurried off before the instructor could reply.

*Susannah. Pretty name. Unusual around here, although not as much as mine, of course.*

As she walked down the corridor, gaze fixed on the ground, she said the name out loud, liking the warm sound of it. "Susannah."

"Yes?"

Aya nearly swallowed her tongue. In front of her was the blonde. Responding to her name, which Aya, like a creepy person, had just said out loud.

*Bollocks!*

Their eyes met. Up close, Aya saw fine lines by Susannah's eyes and full lips. Aya swallowed hard. What the hell was she going to do? How could she get out of this?

"I… um…" Her heart was pounding hard enough that it could shatter her ribcage.

"Well, there's a coincidence," said the instructor from somewhere behind them. "Aya here was just asking about your name, Susannah. She thought she knew you, but it turns out she was mistaken."

Aya said a silent thanks to all the heroes who helped tongue-tied people out.

Susannah's eyes twinkled. "I see. That's a shame, you know. You've struck me as a person worth knowing."

"I have?" Aya croaked. "I mean, uh, I didn't think you'd have noticed me."

What a ridiculous thing to say! Of course Susannah would've noticed her; she'd stood in front with the instructor during most of the classes.

"Who wouldn't notice you? That muscular body and the confidence you have in it. Not to mention your glossy, midnight-black hair. Simply stunning."

Midnight-black. Glossy. Such classy words to describe what Aya thought of as regular, black, flat hair. How did people have that kind of way with words? How did someone just say stuff like that without having to plan it in advance?

Aya shuffled her feet. "T-thank you."

"Anyway, I came back in because I must've left my phone in here somewhere," Susannah said while scanning the room.

This was Aya's big chance. She could be the hero. The charmer. She could find the phone, or at least say something helpful. Her brain raced, trying to find the right words and the right action.

She opened her mouth and said, "Lost your phone? That's bad of you. No! I mean bad *for* you." She snapped her fingers as if looking for the right words. "I mean, um, it's always a bad thing to lose stuff—I mean, like, not that it was bad of you to lose your phone. That happens to me. I mean that happens to everyone. Right? I mean, right?!"

She stared wide-eyed at Susannah, wondering if she had blinked at all during that pathetic monologue.

The instructor broke the confused silence by clearing her throat and saying, "I think I saw a phone on the shelf by the left wall. Could that be it?"

"Oh, yes, that was where I put it," Susannah confirmed. "Great. I'll just go get it. Thank you."

She went into the room and soon came out with a sleek, posh-looking phone held aloft in victory. She walked past them with a "thank you again" to the instructor and a "nice to meet you" in Aya's direction.

She opened the door, letting the noises of people boxing flood into the tiny hallway that bridged the classroom and the boxing gym.

Just like that, Susannah was out of Aya's life again.

The instructor patted her on the shoulder and walked out with a sympathetic "see you soon."

Aya stayed there. Alone. Clenching her fists. Wishing she was anyone but herself.

## Chapter Five

# PINING FOR MOCHA

A piercing, white-grey morning illuminated Stoke-on-Trent, making Gwen squint at the sharp light streaming in from the window. Her customers had so far been the usual Stokies: friendly, funny, down to earth, and tough enough to be suited for this underprivileged but stout city. So far, there'd been no strange customers and minimal amounts of nonsense from Dave. In short, it had been a good morning despite another night of sleeplessness and the severe, cloud-filtered light hurting her eyes.

She fetched a cloth and wiped down the counter. She daydreamed about Mocha, about laying in summer sunshine on a picnic blanket and kissing to be exact, while keeping an eye on the door.

She didn't have to wait long for a new customer. It was a woman about her own age, maybe a little younger. She carried a rolled-up magazine and had her gaze set on her feet. Something about her was familiar. When she unzipped her canvas jacket to reveal a saffron hoodie underneath, Gwen recognised her as the coffee drinker from yesterday.

"Hello again," she said with her customer-facing smile. "Another grey day, huh?"

The other woman glanced up from her magazine, showing Gwen a flawlessly sharp jawline and a puzzled look. "Um, yeah, I suppose it is. Can I get a large, black filter coffee, please?"

"Of course." Gwen checked the coffeemaker. "The pot is nearly empty, though. Can you wait while I brew more?"

"Sure, duck. I'm in no rush." The customer leaned against the nearest wall and returned to her magazine.

"Great," Gwen replied, putting on a fresh pot. While her back was turned, she heard the bell above the door and peered over her shoulder to greet the new customer. Mocha! Gwen checked her watch. She was early again. Thank goodness she wasn't on break this time.

Mocha strode up to the counter, adjusting her coat collar with her usual elegant, confident movements. "Gwen! Phew, you're here. I worried I'd miss you since I had to come in early again. How are you, my lovely?"

A flutter of gossamer wings filled Gwen's chest. "I'm good. How are you?"

Mocha wasn't making eye contact anymore. She now perused the pastries and sandwiches in the glass cabinet next to the till.

"I'm well. Now. I have a long day ahead, so I'll have to force down some breakfast. Does the pesto and mozzarella on sourdough there have pine nuts?"

Gwen went through the ingredients in her mind. "Um, nope. Are you allergic?"

"No. I just cannot stand them. Vile little things." Mocha winked.

Gwen laughed. "I see. Well, I'm 100% sure that there are no pine nuts in that or any of our sandwiches."

"Excellent. Get me one of those, then. I'll have my usual drink."

"Of course," Gwen said, already picking up the take-away cup for the large mocha. "So, you said you have a long day ahead?"

Mocha groaned. "Bloody hell, that's an understate-ment. I have masses of projects to finish up before I leave."

"Oh, going on holiday?" Gwen paused the espresso machine so she could hear the answer.

Mocha was reading something on her phone and glanced up distractedly. "Sorry, what was that?"

Gwen kicked herself for disturbing her. "I only asked if you were going on holiday?"

"I wish," Mocha drawled. "No, I'm being transferred to my company's head office today. They need me there ASAP. Ruddy nuisance as it is, it's a much better job, and I'll be moving into a much nicer house, too."

The bottom fell out of Gwen's world. Mocha was leaving Stoke? She swallowed and finished making the drink before saying, "I see. Where is this head office, then?" She managed to sound normal, but her hands trembled around the takeaway cup.

Mocha tapped her screen and then put the phone in one of the pockets of her stylish, mocha-coloured coat. "It's over in Chester, so only around an hour by car."

"Okay," Gwen said, holding out the cup. "Well, that's good, I suppose. Not too long a drive for the move."

"No, and since I don't have much to pack, mainly souvenirs from travels and my clothes, the move should be done with rather quick. I plan to be settled and ready for work before sunset."

"Great!" Gwen said, forcing what she hoped resembled a smile and not a death spasm.

"Absolutely. Then I need to search out a café that makes mochas the way I like them and employs a charming server like you." Mocha tapped her mug and gave her a conspiratorial wink.

Gwen didn't feel like she was in on the chummy banter. She didn't want Mocha to find another barista. Or to move at all.

She put the sandwich in a paper bag and gave it to Mocha.

"Ah, thank you. Can I get a napkin as well?"

Gwen stared at her in confusion for a moment. Who had time for napkins when one of the biggest bright points of her life was moving to bloody Chester?

She snapped out of it. "Yes, of course."

As she handed over two napkins, she noticed that her hands were still shaking. Trying to make them stop made her fumble so the napkins didn't quite make into Mocha's outstretched hand. They fell, but before they hit the floor, they were picked up by the coffee drinker in the saffron hoodie.

"You, uh, dropped these," she said to Mocha.

That obviously wasn't true. Mocha was too in control of her body to be dropping things like that.

Nevertheless, Mocha took them and without a glance at the stranger thanked her before leaving the café. "Thanks for the great service, and good luck in future," she said over her shoulder to Gwen.

Then she was gone. Just like that.

Like it hadn't been an important part of her day coming in here every morning for small talk, semi-flirting, and a mocha. Well, it probably hadn't.

It had been to Gwen, though.

She grabbed the counter. The sensation of her blood pulsing slower in her veins overtook her, making her feel dejected as well as dizzy. Everything was colourless again. No more anticipation of seeing Mocha to get her out of bed each morning. No more glimpses of Mocha to fuel endless, vivid daydreaming.

What would be the new highlight of her day be? Maybe she could buy a pet? Or start every day with a call to her best friend? No, Charlotte was busy in the mornings.

*Besides, no one deserves the pain of hearing your depressive whinging every damn day.*

Gwen surveyed the café and spotted the chocolate éclairs. Maybe she should start eating chocolate in the morning? No, maintaining her blood sugar levels helped her keep on top of her depression, and she already had to factor in the honey in her tea. She wouldn't get a hobby, considering she already had drawing characters from TV shows and books for commissions on social media to fill that slot. No, she'd need another sort of kick, but what the hell would give her the same sort of adrenaline rush as seeing Mocha every day?

Feeling despondent, she scanned the café further. The paint peeling on the walls and the constant smell of sugar and coffee, which she'd loved at first, were suddenly unbearable.

The woman in the hoodie ambled over. Gwen mechanically poured her some coffee and took payment, her brain busily searching for a plan. Maybe she could somehow keep seeing Mocha. If only she had gotten her real name. Or an email or something. Then she could have contacted her and stayed in touch.

Gwen groaned inwardly. How? And what would be the point? Not only did they not know each other, but this woman was so far out of her league that it was hilarious. The two of them becoming some sort of weird pen pals would be like an impeccably cut diamond hanging out with a commonplace pebble. In her mind's eye, she saw a flawless diamond in a little mocha coat and a grimy pebble with a bit of blonde and blue hair stuck on top. She covered her eyes and sniggered under her breath. The snigger soon died away. She couldn't even rely on her weird sense of humour to get her through this.

Gwen regarded the door which had ushered Mocha out of her life. What was stopping her from going out that door, too? Right this minute? She didn't much like this job. Nor her flat. Nor her therapist. She could just leave Stoke.

Slowly, common sense began trickling back into her mind. This job wasn't perfect, but she liked it well enough and the pay was pretty good. She couldn't risk losing it. *Especially not if you really are at the start of another severe depression period. You might not be able to work soon*, she reminded herself. *Not the time to take risks.*

She couldn't leave Charlotte behind either. Her best friend had saved her life and was her rock, just as Gwen was hers. They needed each other.

Despite that, Gwen's gaze kept returning to the door. Maybe she shouldn't walk out on her life because her crush was moving, but she could take some of her vacation days. That would give her a chance to think things through. Maybe, just maybe, she could find Mocha and talk to her again. Just some small talk. That would give her inspiration for her art as well as her daily dose of serotonin.

She put her hand above her left breast, a soothing

gesture to feel her heartbeat, as she kept thinking. Even if she didn't find Mocha, at least she would get to see Chester. She'd been told it was a real tourist destination with its Roman walls and unique architecture. She didn't have a car, but there were plenty of trains. She chewed her lip and tapped her hand on her chest in time to her heartbeats. This was the sort of decision she usually spent a lot of time pondering, weighing the pros and cons, perhaps even talking it over with her therapist. But where had that sort of caution gotten her? Her life wasn't very exciting, was it? Maybe that was why she craved the pick-me-up that seeing Mocha gave her. Why she needed the daydreams.

In her mind's eye she saw Mocha. That smile. That walk. That flirtatious tone in her voice. Her heartbeat picked up under her hand. Energy fizzed in her blood, and she breathed in so deeply that her chest and belly filled with the coffee-scented air.

She slammed her palm down on the counter.

Yes. She'd take a quick trip to Chester.

She called the café's owners, certain that they'd let her take a couple of days' leave despite the short notice. They owed her that much for all the extra responsibility and time she put in. Oh, and for putting up with Dave, who incidentally would love taking some extra shifts to pay for booze.

As the dial tone on her mobile sounded, Gwen was deciding whether to ask for one day off or two. Either way, she was taking the train to Chester first thing tomorrow.

*Chapter Six*

# SHOWER DECISIONS

It was late at night, and Aya was at home, enjoying a hot, muscle-relaxing shower after a long run. She wasn't enjoying her thoughts, though.

The job search was still a bust. She had been on a call this afternoon, for a waitress job she didn't even want, and had been told at the end of it that they needed someone a little more 'bubbly'. Her meagre savings from her old career were spent, so now she had to be on benefits until she found a new job.

Still, while rinsing all the shampoo out of her long hair, Aya dredged up some of her past optimism. She was a fighter; she'd get up and try again. There must be loads of jobs out there. Maybe she should widen her search, apply for positions in admin perhaps? The worst that could happen was that they would say she was under-qualified.

There was a knock on the door. "Aya, are you almost done?" her mum called, impatience in every syllable.

A fresh wave of exasperation hit Aya, this time at

living with her parents. Moving out hadn't been a priority when she boxed and travelled from match to match. Now that she was home all the time, she needed her own place. She needed time to herself. Actually, if she was honest with herself, what she needed first was some socialising and some fun. Maybe even to get laid, if she could remember how to talk to women without sounding weird. But how was she meant to do that in her parents' house in Stoke? There was nothing but the lukewarm, stale sense of failure surrounding her. How was she meant to keep up her usual optimism when everything here dragged her down?

She watched the shampoo foam slide down her body and gather at her feet.

"Did you hear me?" her mum called.

She snapped out of her reverie. "Yes, Mum. I'll hurry up."

"Good. Your dad and I have had long days at work. We'd both like to take a shower before we have to go to bed to soon get up for another long day of work, you know!"

"I know. I'll be out soon."

Aya's frustration made way for shame. *Your dad and I have had long days at work.* Another jab from her parents, who believed that solid work was all there was to life. Another reminder that she wasn't working, wasn't paying her way. That she kept failing.

As she grabbed the conditioner bottle, she had all but decided. She didn't dwell on decisions and trusted her gut when it gave her an impulse. The impulse now was to leave all this failure and shame in Stoke for a while, to breathe other air.

*A chance to get out of the bloody house and out of Stoke. To see something new.*

Yep, she'd give herself a quick reset through a getaway. She'd start the drive right after breakfast tomorrow.

## Chapter Seven

# A RUDE KNIGHT IN SHINING ARMOUR

Gwen hadn't eaten breakfast. She'd woken up with intrusive, depressive thoughts and that dull, deadening ache in her chest. Trying to combat that had taken all morning, resulting in having to get ready and dressed in far too much of hurry. The panicked stress still buzzed in her body, making her uncomfortable and frazzled.

Although, between sleepless tossing and the occasional nightmare last night, the cruel sleep gods had allowed her a wet dream about Mocha. She focused on that. Her dream had given her a vivid account of how it might feel to run her hands over Mocha's hourglass body and kiss the lipstick off those vermillion lips. Half distracted, Gwen snatched up her shoes and then had to laugh. She'd put on mismatched socks in her hurry. One navy blue and one black.

*Well, at least I didn't pull them over my jeans like good old Edward.*

She chuckled as she pulled her shoes on, but her brain kept whirring, ruining her attempt at humour.

*Wait. Did I take my antidepressants? Yes, I did. I*

*should've eaten something with them, though. Bollocks. I don't think a gulp of coconut milk counts.*

She grabbed her jacket and left her flat. Standing in the slowly moving lift, she ran her fingers through her hair.

*Man, I hope I look okay. I should've done my hair and make-up. Great. Now I'm useless AND ugly.*

When she passed Stoke Minster, she checked her watch. She was late now. Very late. It was about a seven-minute walk from here to the train station. Her train left in five. She took off running. About a year ago she'd started to take brisk walks every day to help her mental health, but sprinting was a whole other thing, especially in her current state. She was out of breath in seconds, her legs trembling and a serious stitch in her side.

She had to slow down to a walk, and by the time she was ready to start sprinting again, she was at the station and had to wait for the ticketing gates to scan her ticket and open. When she'd located her track and rushed to it, the train was pulling away.

She dropped her hands to her sides. "Come back," she whimpered. The train just kept chugging down the tracks. Mocking her.

Gwen was exhausted from lack of sleep and her rough morning. Not to mention the lack of breakfast, the physical exhaustion of the run, and, of course, the fact that she'd bought a ticket for that specific train and would now have to buy a new one. She slumped on the nearest bench and fought back tears.

When she noticed people around her giving her strange looks, she forced herself up and back out through the ticket gates. She wished she could ignore what others thought of her, the way she did most of the time. Now however, she felt their staring and their judgement like pinpricks on her skin. She needed to get away from prying eyes and walk a little to collect her thoughts. She knew that she should get some breakfast and then buy a ticket for the next train. That was the sensible next step. That was what a non-mentally ill person would do. Right now, though, that felt as impossible to Gwen as single-handedly draining a lake.

The tears welled up in her eyes. She blinked them away as best she could, furious with her uncooperative mind and body.

*Thank goodness I didn't have time to put mascara on this morning. I'd look like a melodramatic raccoon by now.*

She saw another bench and sank down on that, watching cars whizz by on their way to work. The drivers all seemed so in control of their fates. So aware of what they needed to do and how to do it. So disciplined and energetic and—she let the tears fall freely now— so in control. They just did things, without having to fight every demon their brains could conjure to simply be able to take a deep breath. Or another step. It wasn't fair.

A Nissan sped past, hitting a puddle and spraying water up the pavement and onto Gwen's shoes. They were soaked. Of course. Obviously, anything that could go wrong today would do so. With bells on.

She closed her eyes to slow the tears soaking her cheeks. She sniffled, part of her wondering if she had tissues in her bag, the rest of her mind arguing that it didn't matter if she was snotty and people saw it. That last thought was frightening. This meltdown was okay; Gwen could handle sadness and dejection. She worried more about what might come next. She could end up in one of the worst stages of depression: the vast, dark ocean of nothingness where there were no emotions, no energy, no point to anything. This horrible day might undo the work she'd been doing for so long, the work of staying above the surface and not letting depression drown her. What if it dragged her all the way down?

She leaned forward, hugging her arms around herself. Her eyes were still closed, but she heard a car pull up.

*No, don't help, please don't ask me how I'm doing. I can't pretend to be okay. And you can't help me. We will both feel worse if you try*, she mentally told the stranger.

She opened her puffy eyes and saw a pair of scuffed leather boots. She followed them up a short pair of thin, muscular legs in tight jeans. Then there was a grey, long-sleeved top with a print reading "Muscles & Mitts" hugging a slender waist, the rounding of breasts and brawny shoulders and arms. When Gwen got as far as the face, she realised it was one she'd seen before. But where? Gwen's brain was sluggish, and her eyes weren't much sharper through this damn veil of tears. The buff woman took off a pair of aviator sunglasses, the kind whose mirror-like lenses always reminded Gwen of shiny armour.

The part of her that was still above the surface of the sea of depression was mortified that someone who knew her was seeing her as this ugly, crying mess. She might not care much about the opinion of others but even she wouldn't let people see her like this.

The rest of her mind just didn't care, though. Because what was the point? What was the point of anything?

The stranger fiddled with her sunglasses. "Um. Hi. Are you all right?"

"Sure. I'm having the time of my life," Gwen said in what she hoped was a jokey tone.

"Uh-huh. Do you need me to, I don't know, call someone or something?"

"No. Ignore this. I suffer from depression, and I'm having a bit of a breakdown. It'll pass." Gwen had given this speech so many times in her life that it just rolled off her tongue.

"Okay," the other woman muttered.

She didn't get back into her car, though. Instead she put the sunglasses back on. Then took them off again, fidgeted with them, then put them on again. Finally, she sighed and groused, "Look, I'm not good with people or stuff like this, but I don't think I should leave you here. Not in your state. Can I at least give you a lift somewhere?"

Gwen gave a hollow laugh. "Sure, how about Chester? That was where I was going before I missed my sodding train."

The stranger put her hands on her hips. Then she frowned and hummed pensively.

Gwen saw her own reflection in the mirror-armour of the sunglasses and quickly fished a Coffee4U napkin out of her jacket pocket to blow her nose. Sadly, there was nothing she could do about her swollen eyes or the dark circles under them. When she'd blown her nose, the black-haired woman was still looking like she was actually considering the joke about driving to Chester. Gwen had to say something.

"You *do* know I was just kidding? I don't expect you to drive an hour to Chester for me. You're probably going to work, right? I bet I've already made you late. I'm so sorry about that."

"No," the stranger snapped. "I don't have a bloody job."

"Oh, okay," Gwen said, silently agreeing with this woman's earlier statement that she wasn't great with people.

A muscle bounced in the stranger's cheek, and then her hands dropped from her hips. "Look, I don't mind driving an hour to anywhere. It's just that I'm not used to having people in my Jeep, especially not strangers. Crying strangers at that. But I don't want to be rude and you clearly need help. So…" She fell silent.

Gwen said nothing, waiting for the rest of the sentence. When it was clear that nothing else was forthcoming, she prompted, "Wait, you're actually offering to drive me to Chester? I can't inconvenience you like that."

The muscly woman appeared confused, or maybe conflicted, for second. "Yeah. Bugger it. Get in."

Gwen glanced from the car, which looked to her like one of those little army jeeps from old movies, to its owner. Sure, this woman was helpful. And attractive. Not to mention familiar. But she was also quite rude. Was a rude stranger really what Gwen needed when she was so emotionally fragile and had a place to get to? Did she want to spend her precious day off with this person?

She remembered the napkin in her hand. She wasn't crying anymore. Nor had she fallen into that bottomless ocean where she felt nothing. In fact, she was curious about this woman and maybe a little bit insulted at the rudeness.

That was feeling something. Even better, it was something that wasn't sadness, dejection, or self-loathing. She took that as a sign and stood up. On wobbly legs, she walked over to the Jeep and got in.

## Chapter Eight

# JANET ON THE M6

Aya squeezed the steering wheel. She'd picked up a hitch-hiker. An upset one. Who would need comforting. What the hell had she been thinking?! This was so far out of her wheelhouse, not to mention her comfort zone, that it was ridiculous.

She loosened her grip a little to allow blood flow to her fingers. If she thought about it, it was obvious why she had offered. Firstly, this woman needed help. Secondly, Aya had decided she needed to be more social. Thirdly, they were going to the same place.

As if reading her mind, the sniffling woman asked, "So, where were you heading to?"

"Chester."

Out of the corner of Aya's eye, she could see her passenger smile a little.

"Yeah, I know that's where you're going now. I meant where were you driving to before you picked me up?"

"Chester."

"You were actually going there as well? That's… quite the coincidence."

Aya rolled her eyes at herself, glad it couldn't be seen through her sunglasses. *Great. Now she thinks I'm some kind of crazy person who's making stuff up or stalking her or something. Well, that normal behaviour lasted shorter than usual.*

"Well, I was going to Chester," Aya said, trying not to sound petulant.

"I believe you. Just a funny coincidence," her passenger replied before blowing her nose again.

They were silent for a while. All that could be heard was the jeep going over a few potholes on its way out of Stoke-on-Trent.

Suddenly, the blonde with the blue streaks in her hair said, "I've seen you before."

Aya flinched. "I'm not stalking you or anything, but yeah, you do seem familiar."

"Let's see. Where can we have met? I don't go out much these days, so it shouldn't be too hard to pinpoint. You wouldn't happen to have therapy with Edward Smith, do you?"

"Nope, I don't go to therapy. Do you ever work out at Muscles & Mitts?"

The other woman snorted out a laugh. "Hardly. My only exercise is daily walks down by Caldon Canal and the occasional attempt at yoga in front of the telly. Hm, where else? Well, there's the obvious place, I'm a barista at Coffee4You, the café by Stoke library."

Aya took one hand off the steering wheel long enough to snap her fingers. "That's it! I've been there twice, and I think you served me both times. Yesterday, I picked up the napkins you dropped when you handed them to…" She hesitated, again feeling like she was coming off stalkerish. "A customer."

It still bothered her that Susannah hadn't looked at her that day. She'd just taken the damned napkins and left.

"Aha," her passenger exclaimed. "You're the woman in the saffron hoodie. I couldn't place you because you were in such different surroundings and I'm in a complete state today. So, you were there when Mocha said she was moving to Chester. Was that what gave you the inspiration for a day trip to Ye Olde Roman Township?"

"Mocha?" Aya queried.

"Oh, that's what I call that customer. You know, the striking and ever-so-poised blonde in the *mocha-coloured* coat."

"You nickname people after what clothes they wear?"

The barista squirmed in an insulted manner. "Not always. Although I'll admit to having thought of you as the woman in the saffron hoodie. I love that hoodie, by the way. Such a great colour, and it fits you really nicely. I like that it doesn't have any print on it. So many hoodies have text or images on them now. Why aren't you wearing it today?"

Aya struggled to keep up. This woman spoke so fast and so damn much. "Hang on, saffron? That hoodie is like a light orange."

"More like an orangey yellow. Saffron, to be exact."

"If you say so," Aya said sceptically. "It's in the wash. It's an unusually warm morning for September. Why would I wear a thick, hooded jumper anyway?" She cast a glance over at her passenger. "And why are you wearing a leather jacket?"

The taller woman ran her hand through her hair, smoothing the blue streaks down with a chuckle. "You know, that's a good point. Overheating is the last thing I need today." She took her jacket off and mumbled, "Thanks."

Despite her expression of gratitude and the fact that she'd laughed, she still seemed upset somehow. Not just from her crying fit, but there was still a tense air about her.

Aya steeled herself, came right out and asked, "Did I say or do something to upset you? I do that. Which is why I avoid talking to people. Actually, it's why I avoid even being around people if possible. So, you know, if I did do something rubbish, sorry."

The other woman watched her, with what from Aya's limited view since she didn't want to take her eyes off the road, looked like fascination. "You know, I think that was the longest I've heard you speak."

Aya only scoffed in reply.

Her passenger added in kind tones, "For what it's worth, as the crying mess who needed rescuing back there, I think I'm the one who should be apologising. Anyway, thanks for telling me. Now I'll try to not take it personally if you say something that sounds off or if you're short with me."

"Short with you? Was that meant to be a joke about the fact that you're taller than me?" Aya remembered to add a smile to show that she was teasing.

The other woman chuckled again. She had a nice laugh; in fact, she had a nice voice, a little raspy but soft. "No, it wasn't, but I'll try to squeeze in plenty of height jokes from now on, Tiny Tim."

Aya sucked her teeth. "Man, I hope that's not the nickname you give me. I'd actually prefer you to call me something related to my clothes."

"How about we try to use real names instead? I'm Gwen."

"Aya Lawson."

"Aya? That's such a cool name! Unusual."

"It's Japanese. My mother wanted me to have a connection to where she's from." She paused. "The fact that my dad then pushed for my middle name be Yorkshire to give a connection to where *he's* from tells you all you need to know about him." She rolled her eyes.

"Yorkshire is your middle name?"

Aya shook her head as she turned onto the M6. "No, it's Jane. Mum never listens to Dad."

Gwen laughed once more. "You're funny. With the risk of sounding rude, I never would've guessed."

"And I never would've guessed you had depression. You seem so upbeat and ordinary, I mean stable, at the café."

Aya bit her tongue. *Ordinary? Stable?* What a shitty thing to say to someone who was ill! She really shouldn't be allowed around people.

Gwen leaned back in her seat. "You'd be surprised at how many people with mental illnesses don't outwardly show symptoms on an average day. Most of us mask it pretty well, until we have a bad day or some sort of episode. Like I did this morning."

"Oh. I see."

Aya kept her eyes on the road, trying to figure out something else to say or do.

Gwen was looking out her window and quietly said, "The worst of it seems to have passed, thank god. The last thing I want now is a week in bed staring at a crack in the ceiling, wondering if there's a point in even eating or going to the bathroom."

Aya had heard every word but was so unsure of what to answer that she blurted out, "Sorry, what was that?"

Gwen shook her head with a sad smile. "Never mind. You focus on driving. That bloke in the Volvo doesn't want to pick a lane, does he? Honestly, there's something about a motorway that makes people drive terribly. The M6 is no exception. Oh, there he goes again."

Grateful to be on more solid ground, Aya nodded. "I know. Arse-brained old git."

Gwen jerked her head back. "Did you just say *arse-brained*?"

"Yeah," Aya mumbled with a shrug.

"That's brilliant!" Gwen chuckled. "I've never heard that. Did you just come up with it?"

"No, I'm pretty sure I heard it down at my gym. The other boxers tend to come up with creative names to call each other. Just trash talk and banter, you know."

"You box?"

"Yep. Used to do it professionally, but I had to quit."

"Why? If you don't mind me asking."

Aya had a moment of phantom pain, an over-whelming throbbing starting at the point where she was hit and filling every part of her skull. Darkness briefly shrouded her eyes, like a hood being pulled over her head. The memory ebbed away, and she cleared her throat, opening her eyes wide to take in the road ahead of her. Nothing had happened. She was okay.

"I took a bad blow to the head in my last match," Aya muttered. "Knocked me out cold."

"Oh. I thought that happened to boxers quite a lot."

"It does. But this time it was bad enough to leave lingering effects and for the doctors to wonder if I'd completely recover. They recommended that I stop boxing." She swallowed and then cleared her throat again. "I decided to listen. Some people said I chickened out. I think of it as that I now had an injury causing a weakness, meaning that the next time there was a TKO in a match I might not wake up again."

"Whoa."

Aya white-knuckled the steering wheel. "Yeah."

"Stopping sounds like a sensible choice to me."

"Sure, but boxing was my life. Now that I can't do it anymore, I'm..." she trailed off, not sure what she was.

"A bit lost?" Gwen suggested.

Aya mulled that over for a moment. "Mm. A bit lost."

"So you thought you'd be less lost if you found yourself in Chester?" Gwen said in a sympathetic tone.

"Maybe. I suppose I... needed to get out of the house for the day. I live with my parents. They keep asking if I've found a job. Or a girlfriend."

Her chest tightened. Why had she said that? Why was she revealing so much?

"Aha!" Gwen exclaimed again. "My gaydar is working, then. You, what's the saying in the US, bat for my team?"

Aya chuckled. "I would've thought that was obvious. And for what it's worth, that saying might be American, but since we use bats for cricket, I think we can use it, too."

"Do you think Mocha does?" Gwen asked.

"What, play cricket?"

"No, bat for our team!"

Aya allowed her gaze to momentarily shift from the road to the horizon. She wasn't sure of how much she wanted to say, how much she wanted to reveal about her feelings and thoughts.

They both had a thing for the woman Gwen

apparently knew as Mocha and she knew as Susannah. It had been a coincidence that Aya was in the same rickety, old café as her gym crush that first morning in Coffee4U. She was going to a job search workshop at the library when it opened and was killing time checking for jobs on her laptop and having a coffee at the closest café. She'd seen Susannah talk to Gwen and realised that this must be a place Susannah came to every day. With that in mind, she'd gone in again yesterday to see her crush and try to talk to her once more. Maybe even make some bloody sense this time.

Had she really thought Susannah was into women? Maybe. Aya hadn't really inspected her thoughts and feelings. She just wanted to be able to talk to a hot woman. Now that she did consider it, yes, she had assumed the striking blonde was flirting, but probably just for fun like straight women sometimes did. In the past she'd had a few brief, casual affairs with older, impressive women. Even if Susannah was sapphic—lesbian or bi or whatever—she was out of Aya's league, at least for something more serious than shagging.

Now, though, with Gwen also being drawn to Susannah and *her* gaydar clearly working well, it might be time to rethink things. Was Susannah only a steamy fantasy? And maybe some sort of symbol of the social interaction Aya was rubbish at? Or could she be more? Could there actually be a *relationship* there?

Aya focused back on the road. This introspection stuff was giving her headache.

"Hello?" Gwen prompted. "Did you hear me?"

"I heard you. The answer is that I don't know if she's gay."

"But I was right in that you're going to Chester to see her?"

"I suppose so," Aya said nonchalantly.

"Right. There isn't really any other option, considering how you gawked at her when you retrieved the napkins for her yesterday." Gwen gave a humming little laugh. "You clearly have as big a crush on her as I do."

"I don't have a crush," Aya protested. "She's just hot, and I've been alone for far too long. Also… ah! I don't know how to describe it."

A beat of silence.

"Do you want to try?" Gwen asked softly. "I wouldn't mock you if you said something weird."

Aya groaned, slapped the steering wheel, and then blurted out, "I guess I feel like if I could be brave enough to talk to her again, and not make an arse of myself this time, it would mean that I'm not as hopeless as I think."

"Oh. Well, for what it's worth, I don't think you're hopeless at talking to women," Gwen said. "You're talking to me right now and making complete sense."

"Yeah, but I'm not attracted to you."

"Wow! Ouch."

"I didn't mean that you're not attractive. You've got that cool hair, an awesome voice and," she looked over at Gwen, "you're pretty."

Gwen held up a hand. "But I'm not mind-blowingly gorgeous like Mocha. I totally get that. Neither are you by the way," she added in a teasing tone of voice.

"Of course not," Aya snapped. "I'm not sure if anyone is. She's in a league of her own."

"Yes," Gwen whispered reverently.

Aya pictured Susannah in her mind. "Her body. Her posture. How the bloody hell does she move like that?"

"I don't know," Gwen said, just as awestruck. "I want to know how she manages to look at people like that. Like they're the most interesting thing in the world? It's spellbinding, makes you feel on top of the world."

"No idea. It's like she breathes out charm like the rest of us do oxygen."

"We *inhale* oxygen," Gwen corrected.

"Yeah, but some of what we exhale contains oxygen, too."

"Sure. But most of it is carbon dioxide."

"Whatever," Aya snapped. "Let's get back to what we were talking about."

Gwen sat back and clasped her hands in her lap. "So. Summing things up here. We're both attracted to this older, daunting woman that we don't know. Neither of us is sure that she is into women. Neither of us seem to think we have a chance with her."

*Not for more than a quick shag if she's lonely, anyway*, Aya thought to herself. Out loud she said, "Right so far."

"And yet we're both taking the day to travel to Chester in the vain hope of seeing her again. Isn't that funny?"

"Funny as in 'funny haha' or as in 'funny strange'?"

"Both?"

Aya thumped her head back against her headrest. "Yeah, both. Bugger me. What are we doing?"

"Sightseeing in a city that's meant to be beautiful and unique?" Gwen said, sounding like she didn't believe it herself.

"That's the nice spin on it." Aya snorted. "Some would say we're stalking a woman we've been lusting after from a distance."

"I prefer *pining from afar*. Besides, we're not going to stalk her. Or at least, I'm not. I'm going to walk around

Chester and be a tourist. If I see Mocha, I'm going to talk to her and see if I can get to know her a bit better. Just so I can keep her in my life, as a friend or whatever she's comfortable with."

"Okay. Same. Although my focus is on getting a damn conversation right with her."

Gwen hummed pensively. "So you're not really interested being around her?"

"I wouldn't say that. I just mean that this possible chat with her is more important to me than flirting or making friends. I'm trying to prove to myself that I can do this. That I can get something right."

"Right, I get it now," Gwen said. She looked out the window for a moment. "I guess I'm just checking up on my competition."

"Oh, no, you bloody don't."

Gwen startled. "What?"

"You are not making this into a weird love triangle or some sort of old-fashioned 'battle for a lady's heart' crap." Gwen just gasped, so Aya continued. "We're better than the cliché of women fighting each other over the same love interest."

Gwen crossed her arms over her chest. "Fine. How would you describe what we're doing?"

"I think of it more as, I don't know, a quest to achieve something."

"A quest? What? Are we playing dungeons and dragons?" Gwen joked.

Aya ground her teeth. "No, hear me out." She grunted. "I find it hard to talk about things so just let me finish."

"Okay," Gwen said softly. "Sure. I'm sorry."

Aya overtook a car, more to give herself time to think

than because she needed to. "What I was trying to say was that for me this is more important than dating. Or friendship. Everything in my life is crap right now so I need something to go right. I need a win. Chatting successfully to this woman, even if it doesn't lead to anything, could be that win."

Gwen was quiet for a long time, and Aya found herself speeding more and more. Despite her every impulse, she slowed; the M6 was the last place you should drive with your emotions in charge.

"Thanks for sharing," Gwen finally said. "I'm sure it wasn't easy. Now that we're being honest and thinking about what this crush is actually about, I guess I should share, too." She pinched the bridge of her nose. "This might sound strange. For me, it's about having something to inspire me and brighten my day. Something that can be a cure for the long bouts of feeling bored, or worse, feeling nothing, that I get."

"What do you mean?"

"I mean that seeing Mocha every morning and wondering if she's going to be flirty or if she's going to reveal something about herself or if I'm going to make her laugh or…" Aya saw her look up at the car roof, as if it held her missing words, before continuing.

"What I'm getting at is that it gives me an adrenaline rush or an injection of joy or, some sort of high maybe. It changes the day from predictable to exciting. It started back when my fiancée left me and I was really down. Seeing Mocha made me feel alive again." Gwen blew out a breath. "I guess I got scared that I'd miss that when she moved. Without that little thrill, I'd be left with my humdrum life and the despondency that comes from depression always looming over me."

Aya kept quiet. What could she say? Time dragged on until she decided on, "This is more than just a crush for either of us, then. That makes this more than some stupid competition for who gets to date this blonde knockout."

"Knockout? Fitting word choice for a former boxer," Gwen said with a chuckle.

For someone with depression, this woman sure did laugh a lot. *There's a lot more to depression than TV shows told me*, Aya mused.

"Do you think I'm right, though?" she asked.

"Yep. I think you are very right," Gwen replied. "More than that, it's nice to talk about this stuff with someone new. That way I don't have to bore my therapist or my best friend."

"I'm sure you're not boring your best friend. I mean, I wouldn't know since I don't have one, but I hear that they're the ones who put up with all of a person's shit."

Gwen snorted out another laugh. "True. Charlotte is very patient with my, as you call it, shit. Still, there's a lot of it, and she's busy with more important things. She's trans and her parents are weird about it, people at work sometimes give her a hard time, and she has these new hormone issues, and... well, I shouldn't bother her with my silliness."

"Don't be daft. It's not silliness."

"Not to you. You have the same obsessive crush. That's why it's nice to talk to you, you get it. Also, I finally have someone I can talk to about how *blooming perfect* that woman is!"

Now it was Aya's turn to laugh. It was the kind of deep belly laugh that she hadn't experienced in months. She wasn't sure why she found it so funny. Maybe it was the relief. After all, she didn't have a best friend or therapist to talk to about this.

"Have you ever noticed that when Mocha talks, every single person in the room goes quiet and listens?" Gwen said.

Aya thought that over. "Yeah. Actually, they stop to watch her, too. It happens all the time in the self-defence class where I met her."

Gwen looked lost in thought. "You know what? I don't think it's only because she's attractive or her powerful businesswoman vibe. I think it's her confidence. She doesn't need to boast or anything like that, she just has this... natural confidence that wafts off her like that expensive perfume of hers."

Aya hummed. "That's sounds about right. You're good at describing things."

"Thanks," Gwen said shyly. "You get used to trying to put things into exact words when you're in therapy. Also, I draw and sell my art online. Usually it's characters from fan fiction or books that I draw for their authors. If you don't learn to communicate precisely, then you get complaints about things you didn't get right. You have to interpret their words as well as put your own thoughts into words."

"You draw for money? You're that good?"

Gwen made a noncommittal noise. "People pay me, so they seem to think so."

A warning light that Aya knew well popped up on the dashboard. She cursed herself, remembering what she was on her way to do when she'd been distracted by Gwen crying on that bench: get petrol.

"Um, this isn't a big problem, but we're almost out of petrol."

Gwen's head snapped towards her. "What do you mean 'almost?' Do we have enough to get Chester?"

"Nope. Not even close."

"Okay, now I'm freaking out a little. I guess we'll have to Google where the nearest station is," Gwen said, getting her phone out of her messenger bag.

"Nah. It'll be okay. We're on the M6. There are services everywhere. I'm sure the petrol will last until we get to one."

Gwen was tapping away at her phone, but paused to say, "That's optimistic of you."

Aya's thoughts halted for a second. It was, wasn't it? Perhaps her sunnier outlook on life was returning?

"I know this old bird." Aya patted the steering wheel. "She makes a big deal of being thirsty but can actually go for miles on fumes."

"All the same, I'd be more comfortable if we didn't risk it. I'm sure you know what you're doing, but considering how my day is going, I wouldn't be surprised if we ran out of petrol any second now."

"It's really not that bad, Gwen. We're fine."

"Better safe than sorry. I'm almost done finding all the nearest petrol stations. We should head to one right away."

"Chill. This sort of negative thinking might be what's making you depressed," Aya joked.

She knew her attempt at banter was a mistake the second she saw Gwen flinch. She'd gotten it wrong as always.

"My depression isn't dependent on me using *positive thinking*," Gwen snarled. "It's a mental illness connected to chemical imbalances in the brain. It's incurable, and I take medication for it. It's not something I can think positively about and be fixed." Rage was now in Gwen's tone as well as in her body language. As much of it as Aya could see from the corner of her eye, at least.

Aya ground her teeth at her clumsiness. This was worse than when she'd used the word *stable*. How long could she keep saying shit like this before Gwen bit her head off?

"I'm really sorry. I know depression isn't something you can just cheer up from. I didn't mean that the way it came out," she pleaded.

Gwen sighed, sounding bone tired. "I know. It's fine. Look, can we just go get petrol? I'm sure it's only me being negative, but I can't take anymore setbacks today."

"Of course," Aya said immediately. "Where did Google Maps say the next services are? Do we need to go off the M6?"

"No, there should be a services in six miles."

Aya checked the dashboard. "That's good. I can promise you, without any doubt, that we will be fine for petrol until then."

"Thank you," Gwen said quietly.

"Don't thank me. It's my old jeep that needs a drink and my fault for not fuelling up earlier." Aya hesitated. Then she blurted out the words that needed to be said, "And there's the fact that I just put my foot in it, and you accepted my apology right away. The least I can do after that is make sure our drive goes without a hitch."

Gwen looked sheepish. "Does that mean this is a good time to mention that I didn't have breakfast and I'd like to pop in for a sandwich and a cup of tea?"

Aya smiled. "Absolutely! We'll fuel up Janet here, and then get some fuel for ourselves, too. After all, if we're going to explore all of Chester we'll need the energy."

"Not all of Chester," Gwen said. "I'm pretty sure Mocha's head office will be in one of the poshest areas."

"True. Imagine us two working-class Stokies skulking around the rich parts of Chester, searching for a swanky bird who probably won't even give us the time of day."

Gwen nodded then stilled. "Hang on. Did you say Janet?"

Aya patted the dashboard. "Yep. This beauty is a 2000 Jeep Wrangler, in the rare fern green I might add, and her name is Janet."

"Gotcha," Gwen said, weirdly uninterested in the Jeep's details. "Well, I'm as thirsty as Janet the Jeep is."

"Don't worry. I'll get you both something to drink very soon."

"Great. I'll pay for half of the petrol, of course."

Aya was about to argue, after all, she was going to Chester anyway. But money was tight right now, maybe she could let Gwen chip in a little.

The warning light flashed again.

*Dammit Janet! Hold it together just a little longer.*

She smiled over at Gwen, hoping she looked more confident than she felt.

## Chapter Nine

# STRAIGHT OUT OF STOKE

Gwen sighed with pleasure as she took another bite of her sandwich. She couldn't remember when she'd last been this hungry.

She could see and hear Aya by the counter, trying to get out of the cashier's small talk. Poor Aya was clearly uncomfortable but answered politely in her thick Stoke accent. Gwen loved that soft but steadfast accent, especially its vowels, and wished she had it herself. She'd grown up in Cilcain, Wales, then lived in several towns on the English-Welsh border, before finally moving here after finishing school to live with her then-girlfriend. All the more reason for her to enjoy hearing a proper Midlands accent, as Aya and the old lady serving called each other "duck" and "shug" in that friendly twang.

Gwen zeroed in on Aya. She was a hard one to read. She was clearly uncomfortable when they spoke of Mocha, although Aya turned quite uncomfortable during most talking.

Gwen sipped her tea and watched Aya stride back to the table with her own order, two takeaway mugs in her hands and a big red and green mottled apple wedged under her arm.

"Sorry for not ordering for you while you filled up the car," she said as Aya sat down. "I didn't know what you'd want."

"No probs. I wasn't sure if I was going to have anything. But this apple called to me and I couldn't resist the irony in buying two of these." She set the mugs down. The smell of coffee and chocolate wafted up.

"Mochas?" Gwen said.

"Yep," Aya said and took a sip.

Gwen followed suit, mainly out of politeness and camaraderie. This was part of their little adventure, right? Part of their quest.

The drink was silky smooth but much too sweet for Gwen's palate.

Aya's gaze moved from her mocha to Gwen's. They both watched her takeaway mug for a beat. Then their gazes locked.

Aya cleared her throat. "Um. Am I the only one who suddenly feels… pathetic?"

"Nope! Right there with you."

They laughed, shattering the tension.

Aya put her mug down. "I just wanted to try it, really. Not my thing."

"No, mochas are far too sugary. Not my cup of tea, pardon the pun."

Gwen didn't mention that their unease was probably because the concept of drinking Mocha's trademark drink together, despite not liking it, felt a bit weird. It would've been fine if they were fangirling over a fictional character or maybe even a celebrity, but behaving like this over a person in their everyday lives felt obsessive. Aya didn't say anything about that either, staying with the much safer, "No, you're a tea lover, and I'm a coffee fiend. Who wants to ruin their coffee by diluting it with hot chocolate, anyway?"

Gwen set her mocha aside and went back to her tea. "Well, I shouldn't complain. First you say I don't have to pay you for the petrol and then I get *two* hot drinks with my lunch. What luxury!" She drank some tea to wash away the taste in her mouth. "Speaking of luxury, did you mean what you said? About how Mocha might think we're beneath her because we're not as posh as she is?"

Aya bit into her apple, shrugged, and muttered, "Who can say? We know that she's always been polite to us."

"That reminds me! You said you'd talked to her once before. Was that in the self-defence class you mentioned?"

"Yep. It's held in the backroom of Muscles & Mitts. I sometimes help the instructor."

"I see. And your chat didn't go to well?"

"Total disaster." Aya swallowed some apple. "Which should make you happy if you do see this as a competition over her attention, or affection or whatever."

"No, you convinced me. This isn't a competition. It's a crush on the surface, but deep down, it symbolises other things for us."

Aya sighed. "I suppose so. The surface crush does feel damn real, though."

"Mm. It's weird that we're pining over the same woman."

"Not really," Aya said. "I bet half of Stoke pines over her."

Gwen couldn't help but make the obvious and not very funny joke. "Just Stoke or the other four towns of Stoke-on-Trent, too?"

Instead of groaning or joking along, Aya surveyed her apple and said, "Wrong. The other five towns. Not four," before taking another mouthful.

Gwen sat back in surprise at her rudeness. "No, Stoke and another four. That makes up the *five* towns of Stoke on Trent."

"Stoke-on-Trent is made up of six towns."

"No, five."

Aya leisurely chewed her apple, nonchalance in every movement. "Six."

Gwen didn't have her normal patience and so had to really school her features before holding up her hand to count down the towns on the fingers. She started with the one that worked as the city centre. "Hanley," she said, folding down her little finger. Then she carried on with, "Burslem, Longton, Tunstall, and Stoke," folding down a finger for each.

Aya swallowed a bite. "You forgot Fenton. Outsiders do that sometimes, especially if they've read *Anna of the Five Towns* by Arnold Bennett. He left out Fenton, and because of that so do others. So, you see, it's *six* towns," she said in a patronising tone.

Gwen sniffed. "Fine."

The food court around them was noisy, but their little table was quiet as the grave. It was the sort of expressive, heavy silence that should be broken as soon as possible.

Nevertheless, there Aya sat, draped over her chair, eating her apple with big, confident bites and taking her time about it. She either didn't care about the tension or was surprisingly clueless to it.

Gwen didn't mind being wrong. She did, however, mind being talked to like that. And then, adding insult to injury, her companion refused to do anything to keep the social machinery running smoothly, instead throwing spanners in the gears every twenty minutes. This woman could be insufferable!

Gwen took another bite of sandwich, contemplating that while they weren't competing, if someone would win Mocha's heart, it had to be her. At least she knew how to be polite, respectful, and friendly.

She hurried up with her tea and sandwich, suddenly eager to get this meal and their journey over with.

# Chapter Ten
## WRONG

Aya watched Gwen drain her mug of tea. She had a deep wrinkle between her nicely curved eyebrows. Was she sulking because she'd been wrong about the six towns of Stoke-on-Trent? Aya wasn't going to apologise for correcting her. She'd apologise for every clumsy thing she had said, but this had been a simple fact. Gwen had been wrong.

Be that as it may, Aya enjoyed this other woman's company. Despite the miscommunications, and Gwen's current mental state, they were getting along well. Aya wasn't even finding her new companion too hard to talk to! It would be brilliant if they could be friends.

She glanced over at Gwen again, who was now checking something in her messenger bag.

*She's still frowning.*

It was impossible for Aya not to feel responsible. Also, if she was being honest, not seeing Gwen upset had quickly become important to her. She punched her fist onto her thigh and thought, *Come on, cheer her up!*

She sifted through her options, discarding them all

before remembering the one thing that cheered most people: someone taking an interest in something that matters to them.

"Um, Gwen, do you have any of your drawings with you? Like, on your phone or something? I'd love to see them."

Gwen put her hand on her chest, subtly tapping it. "I don't know, shouldn't we get going? There's still a bit of a drive to Chester."

"Nah, it's not that far. Besides, I've just finished my apple. I wouldn't want to get going until I've digested it."

That sounded feeble to her own ears. Her system was used to big steaks and mountains of sweet potato, an apple barely touched the sides. She could only hope that Gwen bought it.

Clearly mulling the suggestion over, Gwen watched the food court around them. The hand on her chest climbed higher until it was tapping against her left collarbone. Aya watched as she waited For Gwen's reply. Those long, artistic fingers tapped faster and faster, so close to Aya's favourite part of a woman's body, that beautiful, delicate hollow at her throat. The hollow, and those pronounced collarbones of Gwen's, moved with her rapid breaths. Her skin was pale as moonlight. No, less bluish and cold than the moon. More like, Aya went through every white and beige thing she knew, more like the colour of white roses.

*God, listen to me. Gwen's babbling about particular colours is clearly catching. "Saffron." Bloody bollocks.*

That beautiful hand on that flawless collarbone drew her attention back. Gwen's wrist was so slender, and her hand—unlike Aya's own—was smooth without any visible veins.

Aya looked away, not wanting to stare. She wondered what Gwen's body language meant. Was she angry? Uncomfortable? Depressed? Shy at the thought of showing her drawings? She had seemed fine about it before; humble sure, but not embarrassed about it.

"Fine," she finally said. "I have some I can quickly show you on my phone. Then we should get going again." She put a lot of emphasis on those last words, enough for even Aya to catch on to that she wanted to leave soon.

"Deal!"

Gwen got her phone out, located the drawings, and handed the device to Aya. "Some of them are of women or genderfluid people," she explained, "but my clients mainly want me to draw male characters these days. I don't really get to choose."

Aya quickly noticed the truth of that. The illustrations were of all kinds of humans and imaginary creatures, like elves or whatever they were called, but most of them looked male. A few were slim and delicate, but most of them were big and beefy. Still pretty, though. Clearly, pretty-boys sold well with Gwen's clients.

"These are all amazing," Aya said honestly. "How do you get the faces so lifelike?"

"Thank you," Gwen mumbled. "It's all down to practise."

Aya kept scrolling through the pictures. "The colours are awesome, and the characters all look so different from each other! I have to say," she hesitated but Gwen's 'go ahead' expression made her carry on, "some of the muscles are, well, wrong."

Gwen frowned. "Wrong?"

Crap. Were they about to have another disagreement?

"Yeah. Just a smidge. Like this guy," Aya indicated the screen, "his lateral deltoids are in the wrong place."

Gwen tilted her head to survey the burly bloke with a long ponytail. "Hm, maybe you've got a point. It never did look quite right." She pointed to the shoulder area of the character. "Is this part here what you mean?"

"Yep. The lateral, or middle, deltoid should sit more to the side and a little higher on the shoulder, not almost on top of his biceps like that."

Gwen made an unsure noise and then squinted up at her. "Ignore me if this is weird, but could you pull your top over your shoulder so I can see what you mean?"

"Me?"

"No, the pope," Gwen said, rolling her eyes. "Yes, you. You're muscular. If I check my shoulders in a mirror, all I'll see is some flesh and a lot of bone. It'd be helpful to see exactly where that muscle sits in contrast to the bone structure and the other muscles surrounding it. And not on a screen or an anatomy book, but in the flesh. Pardon the pun."

Aya squirmed. "The material of this top doesn't pull up like that. It would bunch and you wouldn't see the shoulder." Gwen kept looking at her. Wasn't she getting the inference here? "I'd need to take my shirt off," she clarified.

Gwen smiled in a way that Aya could only interpret as cheeky or maybe naughty. "Right. Well, as much as I want to get this right, considering the deadline is this weekend, I don't want to get you arrested for indecent exposure."

"Thanks," Aya muttered. "That's nice of you."

Gwen's smile grew. "I know, right? My generosity knows no bounds."

The ice was broken. They kept chatting about the

drawings. Gwen explained that while most of the characters came from existing TV shows, films, or books, some had been recently created and their authors wanted to see them drawn before they kept writing their stories. There was a whole culture here that Aya had no idea about. It was all new to her but certainly thought-provoking. Anything that expanded her world was valuable to Aya, and if she was honest, Gwen seemed to have a way to make anything interesting.

Aya stopped scrolling. "Hang on. Here's one I finally know. That's Ann Walker from *Gentleman Jack*!"

"Yes, that's poor Ann," Gwen said tenderly. "I relate to her so bloody much. Although, not to those puffy monstrosities." She pointed to the huge sleeves that she'd drawn, exactly as they had looked on the TV show. "Thank goodness women's fashion has changed. If I had to wear sleeves like that, I'd end up filling them with ridiculous stuff, like old sketches, spare change, and sweets. Can you imagine how many chewy toffees you could fit into those things?"

Aya chuckled. "I don't think the sleeves would stay puffy if you filled them with coins and toffees."

"No." Gwen sat back. "Thank goodness I can stick to a regular top and some jeans."

"Yeah, but they don't work as well as holders for toffees."

"I wouldn't say that." Gwen emptied her jeans pockets on the table, displaying a two-pound coin, a pencil stump, and at least eight chewy toffees in golden wrappers.

Aya whistled low. "Impressive."

"I know. Want one?"

"One? I thought you were meant to be generous. At least offer me two."

Gwen pouted theatrically. "Fine. But if I run out before we get to Chester, you'll have to buy me some new ones."

"Deal," Aya said and grabbed two toffees.

They talked for more than half an hour about everything from favourite sweets to Gentleman Jack before Aya's fitness watch buzzed to inform her of how long she'd sat still.

"Ah, damn, time's racing by. We should go."

"Yes," Gwen agreed, packing things back into her pockets and her bag. "The way things are going, it'll be lunch by the time we get to Chester."

"Nah, it won't take that long," Aya said while adjusting her ponytail.

Gwen threw her a glance and muttered, "You really are an optimist, aren't you?"

---

At twelve-thirty, when they'd been sitting in traffic outside of Chester for almost forty minutes, Aya remember those words. She hadn't thought she was being optimistic, and she hadn't been wrong per se. It was just because of a serious traffic accident on the A56 that they were now this late.

Still, it meant three things.

One neutral: Gwen had been right.

One positive: they'd been given more time to chat and get to know each other.

And one negative: Aya's stomach was now growling with hunger, eating itself from the inside.

She switched off the radio and its infuriating jingle. "How can a sixty-minute journey take all bloody morning?"

"Was that a rhetorical question, or do you want me to answer?"

Aya grunted long and hard as a reply.

Gwen covered her mouth, but Aya still heard her half-stifled laugh. "I'll take that as that you want an answer. Well, you had to stop to check on me and pick me up. Then people were driving like tossers on the M6. Then we had to break for petrol and a snack, which turned into a really long chat session with yours truly." She bumped Aya's shoulder with her own. "After that, we made good time until we turned onto this road, where we got stuck in traffic due to what the radio said was a grievous accident. Awful, right? Thank goodness no one was badly hurt."

Aya closed her eyes for a second. "I know all that. I was there. Do you always talk this much?"

"No," Gwen said. "I usually chat a lot more. The only reason I haven't is because I don't know you that well. Although I have gotten to know you quite a lot these past hours. Friendly as I am, it's rare for me to make a such connection in a morning. Especially with some surly, quiet fitness freak."

"Hey! What does my fitness have to do with this?"

Gwen bit her lip around a smile. "That was your only complaint about what I just said?"

Aya shrugged.

"Also, you shrug a lot," Gwen added. "You should use your words instead."

"I'm afraid to. You've spouted out so many that I'm nervous we might use up the entire bloody language."

"Oh! Nice burn," Gwen replied, laughter in her tone.

"Shush. We're moving again. I need to concentrate."

And that was what Aya did. She definitely wasn't

smiling inwardly at the other woman's comments or how Gwen made her laugh. Nor was she marvelling at how easy it was to spend time with this chatty barista with her pretty hands and intense blue eyes.

## Chapter Eleven

# DAY TRIP TO CHESTER

Gwen considered the city as they drove into it. Chester was beautiful with its Roman walls framing black and white buildings, some mock-Tudor and some really from the Tudor era. She remembered that her cousin Dafydd had told her the mock-Tudor ones were built by the Victorians.

Missing him, and the rest of her family who still lived in Wales, unexpectedly jabbed her heart. Considering Chester was so near Wales, this was as close to her homeland as she'd been in years. She shook off the unwanted homesickness. "You know, my cousin studies here. At Chester University."

"Oh, yeah?" Aya said, reading signs to figure out where she was allowed to drive.

"Mm. Dafydd told me all about The Rows last time I talked to him. They're those buildings in the city centre with two floors of picturesque shops in old Tudor houses."

"Okay," Aya replied distractedly.

"Even the big brands have to change their signs to fit

in with the architectural style. It's like traveling back in time. We have to check that out while we're here!"

"Sure. If I can ever find a place to park," Aya muttered.

"Hm. What about over there?"

Aya peered down the side street Gwen indicated. It only had one tiny free space. "No, I'd have to park all crooked."

"Okay, so?"

"So, what if the person who owns the Mercedes next to the space comes back and sees my dusty, old Jeep wedged in like that? They'll think I don't know how to park."

"Does their opinion matter?" Gwen asked it without recrimination, instead sounding like she was truly baffled by the idea.

"Look, I'll park where I'm comfortable parking, okay?"

"Of course." Gwen peered around a corner. "Hm. I wonder where our Mocha is. Where would you be hiding if you were her?"

"I doubt she's hiding. She's not the type to hide."

"That's certainly true. It would be a shame if she did. She's a role model with that confidence, sense of style, those people skills, and, of course, her career. Not to mention, you know…"

"Being easy on the eyes?" Aya said as she turned into a side street.

"'Easy on the eyes?!' More like being an absolute, goddamn delight for every eyeball that ever existed."

"Ha! True. Anyway, where am I heading?"

"I don't know," Gwen said, chewing her lower lip. "She mentioned the name of her company one of the first times I met her. I've been trying to think of the exact name since yesterday, but all I can remember was that it had the word 'growth' in it."

Aya grimaced. "Growth?"

"Yes, as in growing as a person, I assume. Not getting some sort of growth on your body."

"I should bleeding well hope not," Aya muttered.

Gwen picked up her phone. "I'm going to do a search for 'growth' and 'head office Chester.' Carry on driving around and keep your eyes peeled."

"Sure thing, Sherlock Holmes."

Gwen blew a raspberry at her, making Aya grin.

The search brought up two results. "Okay, we have two possibilities," Gwen said. "One of them is a marketing company in the centre of town, and the other is a human resources company pretty close to the train station."

"All right. Well, we're circling the town centre right now. Why don't we start with the marketing company?"

"Agreed," Gwen said, putting her phone back in her bag. "Should we wander around it or actually go in and ask for her in reception? No, wait, we can't do that. We'd have to ask for Mocha and that's clearly not her given name."

"No, it's Susannah."

"What?"

"Susannah," Aya said, gaze still on the road.

"I heard that, you numpty," Gwen said with an incredulous chuckle. "I was inferring that I wondered how you knew that."

"Don't infer stuff. Just say things straight out."

Gwen looked heavenward. "Okay. How the hell do you know her name, and more importantly, why haven't you told me?"

"It didn't come up."

Gwen threw her hands out to the side, smacking her window and pretending it didn't hurt. "Aya, we've talked about her on and off *all morning*!"

"Yeah. I suppose I forgot that you didn't know her name. I mean, it's a pretty basic thing to know about someone, duck."

If Aya thought the term of endearment was going to smooth things over, she was seriously wrong. "Don't sound so smug! I know plenty of other things about her. I've served her and talked to her pretty much every morning for months!"

"But you never asked her name."

Gwen wasn't sure how to counter that. "It, well, it never came up!"

"Exactly my point," Aya said with a smirk that revealed a dimple in her smooth cheek. "Names don't always come up."

"What? That's not the same! That's… argh, never mind." Gwen had to laugh. This woman really was something else. "Okay, I give up. We'll leave it. Where did you learn her name, anyway?"

Aya turned the jeep around as they were heading away from the city centre.

"I asked the instructor of the self-defence class. She told me Susannah's name and said that she was nice, very helpful to the others, and so on."

"Okay," Gwen said shakily. This conversation, and the proximity to the woman of her dreams, was making her uneasy.

"This is pointless. Could you Google where we can park?" Aya muttered.

"Of course. Just a sec." Gwen got her phone out again.

"Hm. Apparently we can park in the shopping centre. Turn here."

Aya did, and after a moment, they saw signs for the car park.

"Here we are. Grosvenor Shopping Centre," Gwen read. "That must be connected to the Grosvenor Hotel. My cousin talked about that, too. Apparently, it's really posh, gorgeous, and old. I mean, by normal standards. Not old like Chester's Roman parts."

"Cool. You can treat me and all your friends to a stay there when you win the lottery, chatterbox," Aya said with a cheeky grin.

They parked, and Gwen's nervousness ramped up. Soon they would check out the first company where Susannah, she had to get used to that name, might work.

Gwen felt for her heartbeat. It drummed fast against her palm. They must be so close to Susannah now. What would she do and say if they did find the goddess? She knew that Aya wanted to have a successful —i.e., normal —chat with her and probably ask her out on a date. But what about herself? To be honest, she wondered if she might not be happy just watching Susannah from afar, maybe sometimes serving her coffee and making her laugh. She only wanted that quick buzz, that elusive spark of colour.

"I haven't thought this through," she mumbled under her breath.

"What was that?" Aya asked.

"I said that I haven't thought this through." Gwen had to improvise. Quickly! "Um, meaning, that if we travel together, we'll waste time. Better to part and cover more ground. But, how are we going to split up to search for

Susannah without me losing my ride home if I can't find you again?"

Aya seemed sceptical of this sudden plan. Gwen couldn't blame her. To distract her, Gwen kept talking. "We should exchange phone numbers. That way we can split up and still find each other when it's time to drive home."

It worked. Aya got her phone out of her jeans pocket and started typing something in. "Okay. I have you down as Gwen the Chatterbox. What's your number?"

Gwen arched an eyebrow and deadpanned, "Oh, whoopsie, you must've misheard my surname. It's Gwen *Davies*." She reeled off her phone number and watched Aya type it all in before ringing Gwen so her own number would be in the call log.

"Hello," Gwen answered the call with fake cheer. "Is this the surly twit who didn't think Mocha's real name might be important in this quest of ours?"

Aya put her phone to her ear. "Oh, hello, chatterbox. I'm so glad to have you on the line. It allows me to do this." She lowered her phone so Gwen could see her tap the screen's hang-up icon demonstratively.

Gwen giggled before getting out of the car. Soon, Aya was next to her, and they were walking to the lifts that would take them into the shopping centre and out into Chester and The Rows. She found herself walking close to Aya, searching for shelter from the storm that brewed in her mind.

"So," Gwen said after a moment, "I'm glad I have your phone number. I have to admit, though," she put her hands in her pockets, trying to hide her embarrassment, "I can be pretty rubbish at replying to texts. And terrible at picking up the phone. Especially when I'm not feeling great."

She was going to add that this was quite common with people with mental health issues but noticed that Aya was busy with something on her phone.

She snapped her fingers for attention. "Hey, can you at least do me the favour of listening to me while I'm admitting my negative traits?"

Aya faced her. "I was listening. Which is why I did this." She showed Gwen her phone. The Facebook app was open and displayed a friend request to Gwen. "If you won't pick up your phone, I'll have to stalk you on Facebook to find out where the hell you are."

Her serious expression slowly melted into a cheeky smile, and Gwen couldn't stop herself from laughing. What Aya had just done was such a light-hearted and sweet way of dealing with her confession, even if she was being a smart arse.

She picked up her own phone and accepted the friend request. "There. Friends on Facebook. Now you're not getting rid of me."

"I wouldn't bet on it," Aya said, the lopsided smirk showing off that deep dimple again.

Gwen's heart skipped a beat. There was no doubt about it, Aya was attractive. And sweet. And despite her many irritating traits, she could be really funny and nice to be around. Still, she was no Mocha. Or rather, no Susannah. Gwen watched Aya as she pushed the lift button and stood back to wait. She was stoically silent and looked bored as she played with her ponytail.

"I like your hair," Gwen tried.

"Thanks," Aya said, not making eye contact.

"Have you always worn it so long?"

"Mm." Aya crossed her arms over her chest.

Gwen gave up. She wanted to distract herself with small talk, but she knew her prattling could annoy people. Aya didn't want to talk; she'd respect that.

*Susannah would have chatted with me, though.*

That wasn't the only difference between the women, of course. Susannah was so much more confident, intellectual, and worldly. Gwen knew from their small talk that she was fascinated by history and culture. She would probably have more in common with Susannah than she did with the sporty, quiet, logical Aya. She was convinced Susannah would understand her mental health issues, her art, and her general way of seeing the world better than Aya did.

Gwen put her hand above her breast again. Her heart beat softer now, so she moved her hand around to feel it better. For a moment she worried that her soothing gesture looked like she was feeling herself up. It didn't matter, though. Aya wasn't watching her. She was too busy on her phone again, checking some game with bright colours and flashing lights.

The slowest lift in the world finally arrived, and Aya motioned for Gwen to get in first. She did so, trying to convince herself that whatever she wanted to say to Susannah would come to her when they were face to face. *If* they were face to face. There was always the chance that this was just going to be a day trip to Chester.

## Chapter Twelve

# FOREIGN CHESTER

Aya leaned against the wall of the lift, inwardly cursing herself. She knew she was being ruder than normal. She ignored Gwen, focusing on a game on her phone because it eased the knot in her stomach. She hadn't seen much of Chester yet, but what she'd seen during the drive hadn't sat well with her. Aya had watched the people of Chester from her jeep. Most of them were dressed like duchesses or professors or something and often deep in lively, important-looking conversation. *This is more Gwen's sort of place*, she thought. She was not quite sure what she'd meant by that, but either way, she wasn't impressed. Sure, this city was clearly unique, but it also gave her a… foreign feel.

Maybe her brain was exaggerating because she was freaking out over seeing Susannah again, or rather, freaking out over having to talk to Susannah. What the hell could Aya say to a perfect creature like that? How would she make sure she didn't mess it up? Should she practice?

Just a few steps out into the high street, Aya could see what must be… what had Gwen called it? The Rows?

Curiosity made her head towards the first set of shops. Uneven, worn stone steps led up to the second floor. She was about to go up when something attacked her nostrils. "Hey, Gwen, what's that stink?"

Gwen came over, sniffing the air. "Perfumes, you heathen. Strong, posh ones by the smell of it."

"Of course," Aya said. She'd known that. What was wrong with her? "I'm not a huge fan of them. You?"

"I like perfume. When I can afford to buy some," Gwen said. She was subconsciously touching her neck, right where you'd spray perfume. "In fact, I think my current one is running out. Come on! Let's find where the smell is coming from."

They walked on slowly, led by their noses. A poster, probably advertising a band, in Welsh caught Aya's attention. Another thing that made this place feel foreign. Great. They weren't even in Wales!

"Do you speak Welsh?" she asked Gwen.

"I learned some when I was little, but we lived pretty close to the English border, so I grew up mainly hearing English. Then I moved, and that was the end of that."

"I see. I always wanted to learn another language, preferably Japanese. My mum refused to teach me, though."

"Why?"

Aya shrugged, the knot in her stomach coming back. "She said that was her past. English was her present. I was never good at learning stuff like that either. She knew it would be hard work."

Aya put her sunglasses on. Then she shoved her hands in her pockets and walked a little faster, trying to move away from the topic. Gwen bridged the distance between them, walking so near that their shoulders almost touched. For some reason, it was nice to have her close. Aya straightened and kept her gaze on the horizon.

"You always look so cool and collected," Gwen said. "How do you do it? Tell me so I can copy you."

Aya just laughed. Partly because she didn't know what to say and partly because it was so absurd that she looked collected. Cool? Well, maybe. Collected? Absolutely not.

The perfume smell got stronger, and they both stopped at once. The storefront said Penhaligon's.

"Oh, I've heard about them. Pretty sure they're supplier to the Queen or something," Gwen said, standing right up against the window.

Aya joined her, seeing bottles all lined up in the shop's muted light. They were on sleek glass and dark wooden shelves. The guy working in there wore the fanciest of three-piece suits. Aya took a step back. Even the air in the shop probably cost a fortune.

She was about to suggest they walk on when Gwen sighed reverently. "They look like jewels when they catch the light."

"What are you on about?"

"The bottles! Or rather the crystal, sapphire, amber, and," she squinted, "rose-quartz liquids in them."

Aya inspected the bottles, too. Sure, they were pretty —all the same shape but with different vintage and classy labels—but they weren't as breathtaking as the pretentious Gwen made them sound. Still, Aya had to admit that she never would've thought that they were pretty if Gwen hadn't pointed it out. Did she always notice stuff like that? Did other people?

She grunted. "Rose quartz?"

"Gemstones that are a pale shade of pink. I was

sticking to my jewel theme," Gwen explained, still gawking into the shop.

"Gotcha," Aya said, feigning polite interest. "And sapphires are green stones, right?"

"They can be, but they're usually blue. The same light shade as the tips of my hair and my eyes," Gwen said, craning her neck to see farther along the shelves.

It was obvious that she wanted to go in, but considering the way she frowned, Aya guessed she was too insecure. Who could blame her? A place like this could make anyone develop an inferiority complex. Even someone like Gwen, who didn't appear very worried about the opinion of others.

"Come on then," Aya said, making an effort to seem casual as she sauntered to the door. "Let's go in and have a gander at these smelly jewels of yours."

She heard Gwen's footsteps behind her and breathed in with pride. It was incredible how much braver she could be when she was doing something for someone else.

*Chapter Thirteen*

# FALLING AND COLLIDING

With nervous steps, Gwen followed the unruffled Aya in. The store was small, but no shelf space was wasted. The air hung heavy with divine smells, each catching her nose in turn as she ventured farther in. In the middle of the room was a circular display of bottles and their testers.

"Hello. May I help you with anything, or are you merely browsing?" said a young man with impeccable clothes and the friendliest smile Gwen had ever seen.

"Just looking, thanks," she replied.

During their conversation, where he promised to leave them to it but encouraged them to ask if they had any questions, Gwen saw Aya from the corner of her eye. She was lifting up a bottle with a Victorian, golden deer head as a stopper and scowling at it.

Gwen hurried over to her and whispered, "Could you look a little less judgy, please?"

"No. I don't think I can. Why the hell is this called The Tragedy of Lord George?"

"That's a cool name."

Aya raised her eyebrows. "If you say so."

Gwen took the bottle and sniffed it. "Ooh, that smells nice. Sort of comforting." She chewed her lip. "It's a cologne, I think. Maybe too masculine for me to wear?"

Aya waved that away. "Wear what you want, shug. Gender roles are made up, right?"

"True," Gwen said, inspecting the cologne.

Aya picked up another bottle and glowered at it. "People often give me crap for being butch, so if anyone complains about you smelling like a bloke, send them to me. I know what to do. I'll sort them out."

Gwen had a sudden urge to hug her. To hold her tight enough to feel Aya's unquestionably strong, steady, and reassuring heartbeat against her own.

*Whoa. Where did that come from?*

She shook the thought off, replacing the bottle on the shelf. She was just about to tell Aya that there was no way she was buying it—the damn thing nearly cost 200 quid —when there was a thump from the counter. In hindsight it was probably the salesperson putting something heavy down, but it scared the daylights out of Gwen, making her quickly turn.

A little too quickly.

Without looking what her bag was close to.

The circle of bottles all clinked as they pushed onto each other like dominoes.

Luckily, they were secure enough not to fall. Sadly, that wasn't the case for the bottle in Aya's hand. It tumbled as Aya, fretting over the bottles in the display all breaking, let go of it to pull Gwen away from the circle.

Gwen, who'd been watching the cologne in Aya's hand and saw it slipping, was more worried about that.

This meant that in a glorious moment in a small shop

in Chester, two lesbians tied themselves into impressive knots trying to protect expensive perfume.

Aya managed to pull Gwen away from the circle of bottles.

Gwen managed to catch the falling bottle of cologne that Aya had been holding.

That was the good news.

The bad news was that they ended up doing awkward acrobatics to achieve it and fell into a puddle of limbs on the small floorspace. Their legs were intertwined, and Gwen was almost in Aya's lap. To make things worse, Gwen was pretty sure that what pressed against her arm were Aya's breasts. She didn't dare look down to check, but instead gradually moved away.

They were both panting from the shock, but otherwise there was a moment of silence as they assessed the situation. When it was clear that nothing was broken, bottles *or* bones, they broke out in relieved giggles.

The salesperson had at some point appeared at their side. "Are you both all right?"

"Yep," Aya said between fits of laughter. "And Gwen here caught the bottle, so don't worry about that."

He knitted his manicured eyebrows. "I was more concerned about the two of you. Are you sure you're okay?"

Gwen paused her giggling long enough to ashamedly hiss, "I want to leave now," in Aya's ear.

Aya stood, pulling Gwen up but still facing the nice salesperson. "Yeah. We're fine. Thanks for asking."

"Sorry," Gwen managed to get out before thrusting the bottle of cologne at his chest and power-walking out with Aya behind her.

Shame made her whole body heat up, and her

continued laughing made her stomach hurt. The whole situation was absurd. What was the one thing you couldn't do in a cramped, aristocratic perfumery? Yes. Exactly what they had done. Thank goodness they hadn't smashed every bottle in the place!

Aya was holding her right hip and saying, "Well, that'll bruise," with a big grin.

Gwen tried to catch her breath and soothe the stitch in her side. "Honestly, Lawson. I can't take you anywhere."

"What?" Aya turned and threw her hands out to her sides. "No way that was my fault. It was you and your bloody bag! You need to learn to control those willowy limbs of yours, not to mention calculating your personal space and staying in it."

Gwen quirked a teasing eyebrow at her and stood straight to show off her *willowy limbs*. "Willowy? Oh, now she gets all eloquent and chatty? So that's what I have to do to get you talking, huh? Nearly smash perfume worth hundreds of pounds and blame it on you?"

Aya shook her head with a reluctant smile. "Shush, trouble."

"Shush me again, and I'll spray loads of perfume on you," Gwen bantered back, bumping Aya's shoulder with her own. "By the way, how can you dislike perfume and have a crush on Susannah? She always wears really strong perfume."

Aya shrugged. "Yeah, but it suits her. It's part of the classy businesswoman package, you know?"

"I suppose it is," Gwen agreed.

Their childish joy and playful banter were gone. The pair were clearly back to thinking about Susannah and their quest to find her.

Gwen noticed a twinge of loss, but she quickly refocused. They didn't come all this way just to have a giggle.

*Chapter Fourteen*

# SUSANNAH

Out of the shop, Aya was more comfortable. Laughing and messing about with Gwen had made this place less intimating. The people of Chester still pushed past without giving her a second look, but now Aya noticed that many of them were students, like back in Stoke-on-Trent, and while the busker next to them sang opera instead of cheesy sixties pop, they were still playing for the same meagre coins. This place wasn't better than her home, just different. Besides, it was tiny in comparison to *her* city.

"Hey, look," Gwen said. "There's one of our options for Moc—I mean, Susannah's—place of work. Gather Growth."

"Where?"

She pointed. "The snazzy-looking place with the neon-green leaves on the sign over there."

Aya surveyed the modern building on a small side street. It certainly didn't fit into the ye-olde-worlde vibe of the rest of Chester. Through Gather Growth's many glass windows she saw bright green walls, big digital screens, and offbeat plastic chairs. Not to mention employees that could be about twelve years old, maybe thirteen, all in fashionable clothing and weird haircuts. Even weirder than Gwen's.

Aya rubbed the back of her neck. *None of them look like Susannah. Although they could be her less sophisticated nephews and nieces.*

"I'm not sure this is the place," she muttered. "Maybe the HR company by the station is the right one?"

"Mm, perhaps," Gwen muttered, sounding uncertain.

Aya inspected Gather Growth again. "You were right before, separating might be sensible."

"Sure. I don't think it's that long of a walk to the station from here. I'll wander down there and keep my eyes open for Susannah as I go. I'll text you if I see her."

Aya tried not to scowl. She'd wanted to go to the other company, and to be honest she walked faster and would get there before Gwen would. Still, she was trying not to be rude, and Gwen had suggested that she go first. "Okay. If neither of us have seen her by dinner time, I say we give up and go back to Stoke."

Gwen put her jacket on. "Agreed. There's a café over there. You could grab some lunch while scoping this place out. You should get a perfect view from there."

*Great idea. And thoughtful, too,* Aya had to admit.

"Thanks," she said. "I'll do that. Good luck."

Gwen turned to leave but stopped. "If I do see her, what do I do after I've texted you? Should I talk to her? Or wait for you so that we can toss a coin over who gets to approach her?"

Aya rubbed the back of her neck again, fingers snagging in her loosening ponytail. "I don't know. I suppose we'll figure that out when we get that far."

Gwen nodded, waved, and then walked off.

Aya was left to head to the café, thinking hard. What *would* they do if they saw Susannah? She realised then that she hadn't truly thought they would find her. She'd been unaware about the word growth being in Susannah's company name, so not known they had that clue. She simply hadn't anticipated Gwen and her search strategies.

Aya adjusted her tangled ponytail and went into the café. She'd thought this trip would be a chance to get out of the house, any sighting of the object of her desire an unexpected bonus. Now here she was, ordering a falafel wrap while staking out a glossy marketing company. Say what you wanted about being around Gwen, but things certainly didn't stay boring.

---

Half an hour later, her phone buzzed with a text. It was from Gwen. In all caps she informed Aya that Susannah was standing at the entrance of the HR company, talking to a bald man.

Why had Gwen wasted time telling her about the bald man? Aya jumped up and began powerwalking towards the station, one eye on the map app on her phone. No way was she going to miss Susannah or let Gwen lose her patience and begin talking to their shared crush. Aya's nerves were all back and threating to make her sweat.

Despite her rush, she only got lost once, nearly stepping into the Roman amphitheatre, too distracted by planning what she'd say to Susannah if she got the chance. Would Susannah remember her? Would she end up saying something embarrassing again? What if she messed it all up even worse than last time?

Emotions overloaded her system, causing tunnel vision and making her push past anyone in her path.

When she finally arrived, she couldn't see Susannah or any men, bald or otherwise. The only one there was Gwen. If Aya thought she looked pale before, now she was whiter than chalk. Her face was frozen in a stricken expression.

Aya touched her arm. "Hey, are you okay?"

"What? Oh, it's you. No. I'm not okay. Susannah… she isn't who we thought she was."

"Huh? What do you mean? Who is she? Kermit the Frog?"

"No," Gwen growled. "He wouldn't say what I just heard her say," she mumbled.

"What the bloody hell are you talking about?"

Gwen rubbed her face. "I… I can't… Can we talk about it in the car? I'd really like to leave."

The blood rushed in Aya's ears. "What the hell! No. It took us all morning to get here, and we finally found her! Against all odds! It's now or never!" She squinted at Gwen. What was wrong with her? "Now you want me to get in the car and drive back without explaining what happened? Why I can't just go talk to Susannah?"

Gwen shot her a nasty look. "You can talk to her, but you shouldn't want to. She's a terrible person."

"Okay, and I'm supposed to take your word for that? Bollocks. Just tell me what she said that was so offensive."

"Later," Gwen mumbled.

"No, I can't wait. I've done too much waiting lately. Come on! Tell me. Right bloody now."

"Was that an order?" Gwen asked shakily.

Aya wasn't so bad at reading people that she couldn't tell Gwen was struggling to speak, but she still had a day full of worry, fear, and desperate anticipation rushing through her bloodstream. Talking to Susannah meant everything right now. Besides, Aya hated not being told all the facts. Why couldn't Gwen sum up what happened? It didn't have to be coherent, just some words to give some sort of explanation as to why they had to give up and go home. How hard could that be?

*Be decent and please tell me!*

But no. Gwen stood there, frozen but for flitting her gaze between Aya, where Susannah worked, and her own shoes.

How bad could it have been? All Gwen had heard was a conversation between Susannah and a possible colleague. Was it workplace banter that the sensitive Gwen had misunderstood? Something she didn't understand out of context?

Gwen still wasn't moving. She began trembling but held her head high. "Fine. If you won't drive me, I'm taking the train." Before Aya could reply, she had stormed into the neighbouring station.

Aya ran a hand over her forehead. *What the hell do I do now?*

She noticed that the door to the stern-looking building where Susannah worked was slightly open. Through it, she swore she could see a flash of mocha brown. Was that Susannah and that coat of hers? Aya's heart began to race. This was her chance.

The chance to heal her broken self-confidence. To erase her humiliation from last time. Aya could do this and get a win. She needed one important win.

She squared her shoulders, swallowed hard, and headed for the door.

*Chapter Fifteen*

# AYA DESERVES TO KNOW

Gwen stabbed the buttons on the ticket machine with frantic fingers. Chester's small train station was busy with chatter and announcements, but all she heard was the tail end of the conversation between Susannah and the bald man, echoing in her head.

Gwen had wanted to hear Susannah's voice, so she'd moved closer to the doorway in which they stood, ducking behind a van to keep out of their line of sight. That was when she had heard her goddess say, "Well, we can't fire him for this. Perhaps we can find some sort of loophole in his contract?"

The bald man had replied, "I hope so. If anyone can fix this, it's you. You've gotten rid of more drains on the company than anyone else." He'd chuckled before adding, "I mean, this young man is quite impossible. His eating disorder isn't a problem in itself, but the amount of sick days he's taken because of it risks a dent in the budget. This stays between us, of course."

"Oh, don't worry. Discretion is my middle name," Susannah had said in that confident voice of hers. "I'll find a way to get rid of him that doesn't risk the company ending up in a lawsuit. You're right, he's an expense and a weak link. We shouldn't have to put up with that sort of nonsense," she sniffed. "After all, employment is for people who actually work, not for those who stay home whinging about problems that are only in their heads."

At that point, she had winked and smirked.

The bald man laughed. "Right as always, Susannah. I knew I could rely on you to help solve this little issue."

"I live to be of service," she said in flirty tones. "Ah, hang on, there's people approaching. We should continue this discussion where we can't be overheard."

"Sure, it's less windy inside anyway!" He replied with a chuckle that suggested that he thought himself very funny.

They went in, leaving Gwen motionless and gobs-macked. Fury crashed over her, robbing her of words and clear thought. It was as if not only the man they were trying to fire had been attacked, but she and everyone else with a mental illness as well. Everyone who fought to get to work but couldn't always make it.

Of course, there were still plenty of people out there who were prejudiced against those with mental health issues. Discrimination still happened every day across the globe. She didn't, however, expect people who worked in a human resources company to hold those views or to behave like that. More importantly, she didn't expect Susannah, who had always seemed respectful and empa-thetic, to be so bigoted.

To make matters worse, the way Susannah had spoken in that cold tone of voice and with that sneer on her face, it made Gwen want to throw up.

*To think I idolised and romanticised that woman.*

Now, Gwen couldn't even find her sexually attractive.

Well, she thought as she punched at the ticket machine, this was one way to cure her sadness over not seeing Susannah every morning.

The method may not have been Edward-approved, but her pining was well and truly over.

The machine finally spat out her train ticket back to Stoke-on-Trent. Gwen took it and put it in her bag, only then remembering that she'd bought an open return when she ordered the ticket for this morning. On top of everything else, she was wasting money, too. Wonderful.

In a daze, she checked the departures board and went to the track where her train was currently rolling in.

She boarded her carriage and picked a seat far away from everyone else. That wasn't hard as it was a worn, old Transport for Wales train. No doubt the commuters would wait for fancier train with plug sockets and an on-board café.

Listlessly, she read the information stickers. First the English translations and then the Welsh, recalling the words and their pronunciations to distract herself. It didn't work.

Her mind stubbornly stayed in the conversation the train was taking her physically, but certainly not mentally, farther away from. Susannah's last words echoed still. "Employment is for people who actually work, not for those who stay home whinging about problems that are only in their head." Gwen wished she'd jumped out from her vantage point and shouted back, "Employment is for everyone, no matter their health. And what's more, sure the problem is in his head. Just like if he broke his ankle, the problem would be in his ankle. What about it, you callous cow!?"

Her thoughts turned to Aya. She wished so hard that

her new friend had left with her. She squeezed her eyes shut in frustration. She should have told Aya exactly what Susannah had said, explained how cold and bigoted their crush was. But she'd been in shock, so upset that she couldn't get the words out.

*Unusual for a seasoned windbag like me. Someone alert the media*, she thought without any mirth.

Aya deserved to know what Susannah had said. Sure, since she was in full mental health she wouldn't take it as personally as Gwen, nor would she be able to relate in the same way. She still needed to know.

Gwen got her phone out to text Aya but paused. Aya also had a thicker skin. Not to mention having the habit of saying the wrong things and upsetting people without meaning to. That might be how she would interpret Susannah's words, a socially clumsy mistake. After all, she hadn't seen Susannah's face and heard her tone of voice.

Yes, Aya was sure to react differently than she had. Nevertheless, she'd seen enough of Aya's kindness and respect for people to believe that she wouldn't stand for that sort of talk without an apology following it. Or for someone being fired for their illness.

Either way, she needed to know who the woman she lusted after was. Gwen wrote the text.

*I'm sorry we argued and for not being able to tell you exactly what she said. I'm still too upset to talk, but I can give you the gist of the conversation I overheard. Basically, they talked about finding a legal loophole to fire a young bloke with an eating disorder who needed to take days off because of it. The bald guy said it could "dent their budget" which I doubt for a big company like that. Anyway, they were really vile about it and particularly Susannah showed no empathy or understanding for someone being what she called "a weak link" and someone who "whinged about problems that are only in their head."*

Gwen sat back and waited for a reply. When it arrived, it wasn't what she had hoped it would be.

*I'm sorry, too, especially for being so harsh with you when you were upset. I guess that made it even harder to talk? Back to what Susannah said. Okay, that's shitty. Are you sure you heard that right, tho? It wasn't just banter or some kind of misguided joke? I don't doubt you, it's just that context is everything.*

Gwen stared at the reply, fury making her body temperature rise. How dare Aya imply that she was overreacting? Or not taking context into account?

She breathed in through her nose and out through her mouth for a few seconds, drawing her mind back to her thoughts from before. Wasn't this what she had expected? That Aya would assume she was being oversensitive and biased?

Gwen put her hand over her chest. Her racing heart was slowing down, fury replaced with sadness. She watched the passing landscape, with its multicoloured autumn leaves falling in droves, as she tried to put herself in Aya Lawson's shoes.

Aya had so much invested in this. Gwen had hero-worshipped and desired Susannah as a tonic and an inspiration, but Aya had made her a symbol for something much bigger. Aya had connected this crush with her own failures in life, with how everything was going wrong. Gwen was pretty sure Susannah was meant to be the thing Aya could control and fix. Something to get her confidence back and help her find her footing again.

She texted back.

*No matter the context, there was no mistaking the intent. I'm sorry, I know you don't want to believe me. So, I guess we'll leave it there. If you have your successful conversation (leading to a successful date) with Susannah, I'm sure you'll see what she's like for yourself. When you do, remember that I warned you and please take care of yourself. She's not a good person and you can do so much better.*

*Bye. xx*

She sent the text and slumped down in her seat, staring forlornly at the screen. She could see why Aya wouldn't believe her. There was so much at stake for her, and Gwen was just a stranger, one who probably annoyed Aya more than anything else.

Yet, after the day they'd shared and how they'd gotten along so well despite their differences and arguments, Gwen had hoped Aya would trust her, at least enough to want more information. Enough to want to talk this through. Enough to listen.

Gwen rubbed her face, again grateful that she wasn't wearing make-up. She wanted to rub this whole day away.

With sadness still coursing through her, she begged with her usual mantra that the sadness wouldn't lead to deeper depression. She didn't want to sink into that dark ocean again, especially not now when she wouldn't have her morning encounters with "Mocha" to give her a bright spark in the darkness. Mocha, the unreachable but oh-so polite, beautiful, and impressive role model. How could she have been the small-minded and cruel *Susannah* all along?! How had Gwen missed that? She threw her phone into her bag with force, stifling a scream of rage. Good, rage was easier to handle than sadness.

The train arrived in Crewe, where she had to get her connection back to Stoke. Gwen got up and marched out of the train and onto the platforms. It was so nice to move. Her shoes stamping hard on the ground reminded her that she was still on her feet and that the rage moving through her could be used as a power source.

She stomped, hands clenched and gaze down, around Crewe station. It wasn't big, Gwen estimated it had between ten and fifteen tracks, but that still made it larger than Stoke's robust, red-bricked Victorian one and Chester's cosy, dark-bricked—but equally Victorian—one. She'd liked Chester station's dark bricks. Not quite black and not quite brown, but sable, like Aya's eyes. Gwen forced her unhelpful mind from Aya back to the stations. Back to clomping her rage out.

Both Chester and Stoke's stations were easy to manoeuvre. Crewe station was not. Not because of its size, but because the train lines were close to each other and some even interlinked. It was like a tightknit spider web of tracks, with stairs and passageways between them. Gwen spent the twenty-minute wait for her next train marching around the small spider web and digesting her thoughts, only pausing to check the board for her track. Her feet moved forward as her mind tried to do the same.

After all, if she could battle depression—with its all-knowing demons created by her own mind—every single day, getting over this part of her life should be easy.

Susannah was in the past.

And Aya… well, she had made her choice. It wasn't as if they were friends or would ever have to meet again. All that had happened today could be left behind, allowing Gwen to focus on her art, her work, and on battling this current downturn in her mental state.

Gwen stopped by her track. Her train consisted of only one carriage and looked like it might fall apart at any minute, but it would take her back to Stoke-on-Trent, away from the pretty Chester, which had promised so much and hurt so much more.

She stepped onto the train, the relief of knowing she'd finally be back in unpretentious Stoke washing over her. Her feet would be on more solid ground. With solid buildings. Solid people.

That brought her thoughts back to Aya and the budding friendship that had become a train wreck before it had even left the station. Oh well. Gwen had other friends. In fact, she had a best friend whom she could always trust. She got her phone out to text Charlotte. Maybe they could grab some takeaway and watch a movie tonight.

## Chapter Sixteen

# TALKING TO SUSANNAH

Aya had nearly been at the door where she'd glimpsed Susannah's coat. Her hand had been raised to knock on it when she was stopped by that text.

Now, she loitered back where Gwen had left her, guilt because of how things stood between them niggling in her chest. She was convinced Gwen was exaggerating, though. As much as Aya trusted Gwen's judgement, she had only known the barista for a day. While she had known the self-defence instructor, who said Susannah was really nice, for months.

*You don't even remember the instructor's name, though,* a small voice in her mind argued. *You know Gwen better.*

Be that as it may, Aya had seen Susannah politely charm everyone in class with her own eyes. Everyone who met her liked her, didn't they? How could Aya let months of observation be brushed aside by a single comment that Gwen heard, out of context and from a distance? No, she had to talk to Susannah for herself. Get to know her. There could be no harm in that.

Aya stood a little taller. Sad as it was that Gwen had left, she could see the silver lining in that her competition was now gone. She knew they hadn't been officially competing, but if Susannah were to pick between them, Gwen was a more interesting person. A more attractive one, too.

*Stop putting yourself down. You're not that bad!*

Aya rolled her shoulders and fixed her gaze on the door where Susannah must be. The bell had been rung, and the match was starting.

Was she brave enough to talk to Susannah? Would she be able to chat her up? To win the incredibly beautiful blonde over? If so, surely that would be an end to her streak of losses in life.

Aya took the first step towards the door. Then another. The blood rushed in her ears. She spotted another glimpse of mocha brown. That was definitely Susannah's trademark coat; she could see it through the gap in the door. The door slid open further. Susannah was pushing it wide and stepping back out, alone. The bald man that Gwen had apparently seen must still be inside.

Susannah adjusted her collar as if she had just put the coat on. She leaned her head back, watching the cloudy sky while she blew out a long breath. She looked exhausted. Or maybe exasperated? No matter. Aya had to move forward with the plan she had figured out on the walk over here.

She shook out her anxious limbs and got on the pavement by the HR company. She made to walk past, stride relaxed and gaze ahead. Then she stopped, as if just catching sight of Susannah.

"Hey," she said in mock surprise. "I know you. Aren't

you in the Muscles & Mitts self-defence class? Um…
Susannah, right?"

Susannah looked at her as if she had dropped in from
outer space.

*Shit. Too weird. Too obviously fake. I messed up.*

The thought hit Aya like a blow to the stomach.

*Even if she believed all that nonsense, why would she
remember me? I'm insignificant, and she's some corporate
goddess.*

Then a smile tugged at her crush's wine-red lips. "Yes,
I'm Susannah. And you're the instructor's assistant, I
believe. The one who asked for my name on the night I
lost my phone."

It wasn't a question. This woman dealt in statements,
not uncertainties.

"Yep, that's me." Aya shoved her hands in her pockets,
trying to think of what to say next. She hadn't planned
this far, and now she was kicking herself for it.

Susannah buttoned the suit jacket she wore under her
open coat. Was she smiling a little? "You know, I did
wonder if you really asked for my name because you
thought I was someone you knew. Or if it was a way to get
to know me."

The sound of blood rushing in her ears grew stronger.
"Um, I—"

Susannah cut her off. "Actually, ignore me, I don't
know why I said that. I'm not usually so blunt. You've
caught me on a bit of a strange day." She rubbed her neck
as if trying to massage tension out of it. "My area manager
was here today. Between you and me, he's a stern brute.
He expects me to behave like him, so I have to put on this
macho, cold-hearted act. Quite frankly it's exhausting."

Aya tried not to ogle the elegant hand massaging the

equally elegant neck. "That *does* sounds like a crap day." She steeled herself and then went for it. "Fancy getting away from it for a while? I could buy you drink. Or I mean, no, it's too early for that. Um. I could buy you a coffee or something. You like mochas, right?"

Susannah stopped rubbing her neck. "Yes. I do, actually. How did you know that?"

Dammit. She couldn't very well say that a barista told her. Not without getting Gwen involved in this.

*Play it cool. Make something up! Hurry!*

Aya kicked a stone on the pavement to buy time and appear nonchalant. "Oh, I happened to be in the same café as you on the day you were moving over here. I overheard your order."

Susannah raised her perfectly plucked eyebrows, now definitely smiling. "Really? As observant as you are fit, then. Tell me, do you always remember women's beverage preferences?"

Now was Aya's time to shine. The mood had changed. This was a flirting game now, not a regular chat. Back when she was boxing and meeting new women in different cities, she'd memorised pickup lines and read online guides on ways to flirt that masked awkwardness and insecurity. Cheesy, sexy, pickup lines she could do. It was normal conversation where she tripped over her own tongue. Now, she needed to dredge that flirting knowledge up. Rusty as she was, she could do this. She had to believe that.

She gave her best roguish smirk and said, "Only when those women are interesting enough to stop time and hot enough to stop traffic."

Susannah laughed. The sound set every nerve ending in Aya's body buzzing with pleasure and confidence.

"Well, why don't I stop traffic long enough for us to cross the street and head to that café over there? Their mochas are a little too chocolatey for me, but with such suave company, I'm sure I shan't mind."

Aya swallowed and tried not to look like a kid at Christmas. "Sure. I've got time and coffee money."

She wanted to slap herself. *Coffee money? What's that? Why the hell did I say that?*

"A woman who both compliments me and buys the drinks. It appears my day is improving," Susannah purred. She winked at Aya and walked towards the café. Aya was too busy trying to calm her heart to remember that she had to follow, meaning she had to do an awkward run to catch up.

When she did, she caught a whiff of Susannah's perfume on the air surrounding her. It was potent, sophisticated, and unique. Just like Susannah herself.

*Play it cool. You can do this, Lawson. Just play it cool.*

"So, how long do I have before you have to get back to work?" Aya asked

"Not long. I have to attend a seminar in about," she checked her minimalist gold watch, "about twenty minutes."

"Damn, that's not long."

"You need longer than that?" Susannah asked, innuendo hinting in her facial expression and voice.

Aya puffed her chest out. "Hell yes. Anything under an hour is far too little. Especially with a woman like you."

They locked eyes. Aya tried to stand tall, casual and suave, certainly not turning into a blob of aroused goo on the ground.

At least now she knew that Susannah was into women. If this was just heterosexual flirting for fun, Susannah was misjudging the volume of her bedroom eyes. And Aya was pretty sure Susannah didn't misjudge social ques.

"Well then," Susannah said casually, shattering the steamy silence. "Sounds like we'll have to find more time. Perhaps go out for drinks. Or dinner?"

"Sure! Either works for me. Tonight?"

Susannah took out a lipstick and started to reapply it with the nonchalance of someone discussing the weather, not a hot date. "No, I have plans. I might be able to do tomorrow."

"Yes, please." Aya checked herself and her enthusiasm. "I mean, yeah, sure. I'm free then. It's a quiet week for me."

"Excellent. We'll try for tomorrow. Right, that only leaves us to get our hot drinks and settle the basic details. Like, for example, your name."

Aya smacked her fist into her thigh. How had she not introduced herself?

"My name's Aya. Aya Lawson. And I didn't give it because I'm more interested in your name. In everything about you, as a matter of fact."

*Nice. Good save. Keep it up!*

"Well, I've never struggled to talk about that particular subject," Susannah said with a chortle, "so we should get along well. Especially if I get my sugar and caffeine hit soon."

"I'll get you the biggest mocha they sell," Aya said with what she hoped was a flirty and gentlemanly tone.

She held the door to the café open for Susannah. As the older woman walked past and inside, she brushed her hip against Aya's crotch. It might've been a mistake. A perfectly placed mistake. One followed by a confident smile from wine-red lips and sparkling white teeth, which left Aya breathless.

No. Not a mistake.

Aya filled her empty lungs and followed Susannah's swaying hips into the café, marvelling at her luck.

*Chapter Seventeen*

# CALL CHARLOTTE

That night Gwen stood by the kitchen window, drinking water and waiting for Charlotte to arrive for their movie night. Small as her flat was, it was hugely quiet.

*Maybe I should get a pet after all,* she mused while watching a man and his dog try to avoid an aggressive cat on the pavement below.

*Guinea pigs are cute. Furry meatloaves with tiny legs.*

She finished her water and chewed an ice cube until there was a knock on the door. Gwen hurried to open it and pulled Charlotte into a hug. "Hey, you!"

"Ooh, now that's a lovely reaction," Charlotte said, wind knocked out of her by the hug. "Much nicer than the sulk I got from the bloke I cancelled on."

Gwen stepped back. "Hang on, you cancelled a date for this?"

Charlotte closed the door. "Yes, but don't worry about it. He was pretty dull, actually. I'd rather be with my best friend. Especially as you sounded upset in your texts earlier."

Gwen ran her fingers through her hair, smoothing

down the blue parts. "Yeah, it wasn't a fun train trip home."

"No, I gathered. I can't believe Mocha—sorry, *Susannah*—said that."

Gwen headed for the living room and collapsed on the sofa. "Me neither."

Charlotte sat next to her. "Nor that this Aya person didn't believe you."

"Like I said in my texts, she has her reasons."

"Still, sounds like you're better off without them," Charlotte enthused.

"I suppose so." Gwen sat up. "Oh, did you want anything to eat or drink?"

"Not right now. We should order pizza in little while, but for now I'd like you to, for once, not change the subject."

*Bollocks. She knows me too well.*

Gwen grabbed a sofa cushion and started playing with its corner. "Sorry. It's all just so sad and frustrating. I don't even know what I'm going to do for my new pick-me-up now that I can't see Susannah every morning. I was actually thinking about getting a guinea pig before you arrived."

"That's a cool idea. However, you do have to clean their cage a lot. I remember from my little sister's one that they poo loads."

"Yuck."

Charlotte scooted closer, looking nervous all of a sudden. "Hey, fancy having someone around who is house trained?"

"Huh?"

Charlotte took the pillow from Gwen and hugged it. "You know how my parents feel about me being trans."

"Yes," Gwen griped through gritted teeth.

"I appreciate the support but don't take that tone, shug. They could be worse. I know of parents who've beaten their children, thrown them out, and even refused to let them transition into their right bodies at all."

"Well, they can't bloody well do that with you. You're twenty-six."

"They wouldn't do that no matter what age I was. They're trying to understand and accept. They need time, that's all." She brushed the cupid's bow over her upper lip, making sure her lip gloss hadn't smudged. "It's just, now that I'm staying with them while my apartment building is being renovated, their discomfort is showing. They keep giving me strange looks and acting tense. It's driving me bonkers, and I wondered—"

Gwen interrupted by putting her hand on Charlotte's shoulder. "Say no more. You're coming to stay with me here. I don't have a lot of room, but this sofa pulls out to a bed, and I'd love to have you around. Who knows? Maybe your company will be my new pick-me-up thingy."

"I think," Charlotte said, "that having your best friend around might be a comfort and distraction, but I doubt it'll be the buzz of exhilaration that Susannah's presence used to offer."

Gwen clicked her tongue. "You may have a point."

"I'm afraid so. Anyway, I'm massively grateful for the offer and would love to move in here whenever works for you. I'll only stay for a couple of weeks until the renovations are done."

"Move in whenever you fancy and stay until you get tired of the small flat. Or you get tired of me."

"Sweetie, I can't get tired of you," Charlotte said with

warmth. "Even if you do leave books and mugs of tea everywhere."

"You say that now, mate, but as I've told you, I've been spiralling down for a while now. You know what it's like to be around a severely depressed person. They can be a sink-hole of despair, dragging you down with them. Especially if you have to put up with it 24/7. Remember how it got too much for Sarah?"

Charlotte flapped her hand in dismissal. "Don't talk to me about Sarah. She told you she could handle it and that she wanted to marry you, then one day just walked out while whinging that it was too hard."

"It wasn't her fault," Gwen mumbled. "Not everyone can handle being with a depressed person."

"Look, it can be hard being around you when you're in a rough patch, yes. But it's always worth it. You're a wonderful person and my best friend. Also, being honest," Charlotte said with a twinkle in her eye, "I'll handle it better than a guinea pig would. They get rashes and fevers and, um, tinnitus around depressing sinkholes, I hear."

Gwen laughed. "Is that so? Well then, that settles it. I'm picking you over a furry meatloaf pet. Speaking of meat, less chatting and more ordering pepperoni pizzas!"

## Chapter Eighteen

# CHARMING SUSANNAH MCVEY

The night of the date had arrived. Aya felt like she had ahead of big matches: every heartbeat rushing adrenaline through her system, her body humming with readiness. She wore a black, fitted shirt with white pinstripes and black skinny jeans. She wanted to show Susannah what she could get if she wanted it. She pulled at the shirt front; it was getting a little tight over her breasts. Had she gained weight or just worked her pecs a little extra?

She stood by the door to the bar in Chester that Susannah had picked. It was clearly posh. Hopefully it wouldn't be too grand; Aya needed to be comfortable tonight.

Like a bolt out of the blue, Susannah McVey—Aya had found out her full name during their coffee date—appeared. Aya hadn't even heard her high heels against the pavement. Maybe she'd been right when she thought this woman was a goddess; maybe she got here through some divine magic trick.

*Or maybe it wasn't magic. Maybe you missed her because*

*you were distracted tugging your shirt over your tits*, she chided herself.

"Good evening. My, you scrub up well," Susannah said as she stopped by Aya's side.

"S-same," Aya stuttered.

It was the understatement of the century. Susannah wore her usual suede coat, which looked pristine despite Britain's frequent rains.

*Yet another magic trick.*

The coat was open, and under it, Aya could see a dark green, velvet dress which ended high up a pair of very shapely legs in black stockings and stiletto heels. Susannah's make-up was heavy but tasteful, and as always, she moved like a panther, all coolness and sleek femininity.

Textbook femme fatale.

Aya had suddenly developed a breathing problem again, not to mention a slight drenching of the knickers.

Susannah gave a wide grin. "Let me guess, you like my new eyeliner?"

"Yeah," Aya croaked before clearing her throat. "Yes. I was admiring the eyeliner. Exactly. You'll have to give me the recipe. Or, I mean the store. Where you bought it, I mean."

Susannah sniggered. "I got it. And before you tack on another sentence, I know you were joking. You don't strike me as the make-up type."

"Nope, not my thing."

"Good," Susannah said, touching her curled, blonde locks. "I prefer my women butch."

"I prefer my women… you," Aya breathed, raking her gaze up and down Susannah again.

"And I prefer to be inside bars," Susannah said, unaffected. "Not standing out here like we're the bouncer."

"What? Oh, yeah. Let's go in."

———

Two drinks later, cognacs for Susannah and beers for Aya, the conversation had covered Susannah's past and how Aya stayed so fit. In short, Aya had let her date choose the topics. Not that she minded those topics; in fact, she was happy for the lack of pressure on her to open up.

Susannah put her glass down on the bar and said, "Penny for your thoughts?"

"Huh?"

"You were miles away."

"Oh." Aya scrambled. "I was thinking about what you told me about your university days." She remembered an old pick-up line that fit and went for it with waggling eyebrows and tongue in cheek. "You know, I'm very sorry about not being part of your past. Maybe I can make it up to you by being part of your future?"

Susannah placed a hand on Aya's arm and gave a smooth laugh. "That was terrible. Luckily for you," she leaned in, giving Aya a view down her cleavage and whispered, "I liked it."

Aya swallowed, noticing that her earlier breathing problem had returned with a vengeance. Susannah sat back and sipped what she had said was a Cognac Croizet, whatever the hell that was.

Charm and glamour shimmered off this woman like her intoxicating perfume. Aya couldn't get enough of it. It was as addictive as it was intimidating.

To give herself something to do, Aya undid her ponytail and started gathering her hair to put it up again. Before she'd finished, Susannah grabbed the hair tie.

"Keep it down for a second. I want to see." She surveyed Aya with dark red lips slightly parted. Heat prickled wherever Susannah's gaze travelled. "I like it. It changes your whole face. Still, best to put your hair up. You'll need it out of your face later."

Every sapphic woman knew that statement meant giving oral sex, and even Aya in her arousal-drunk state began to mentally prepare and celebrate. Suddenly drinks seemed like a slow, unnecessary idea. Couldn't they skip to the part where her hair needed to be up?

"Actually," Susannah revised, taking another sip of the expensive cognac, "I don't think there'll be any of that tonight. I have an early morning budget meeting."

"Right, sure," Aya said, reeling in her libido.

"Naturally, that means we'll need another date. One where you'll certainly need to keep your hair up."

*Yes! Yes! Another date!*

"Okay. Sounds good to me, shug," Aya said, guzzling from her beer to hide her enthusiasm.

She watched Susannah, heart pounding in time with the lifting and lowering of Susannah's enticing chest as she breathed.

Aya caught herself and marvelled at how inappropriate she was being. Something about Susannah brought out the animal in her. She looked away. If Susannah had noticed, she made no reference to it. Instead, she stood up and said, "I need to powder my nose. Be back soon."

As soon as she'd left, Aya picked up her phone. She needed the distraction. She checked her email, then Twitter, and finally Facebook. Struck by a thought, she searched for Susannah McVey and soon found her. She hesitated a second before hitting the friend request button. Then she sat back and drank deep from her beer. Her phone screen updated, displaying that Susannah had accepted the request.

"Looks like we were online at the same time," Susannah said, walking up behind her. "I stopped on the way back from the bathroom to check my phone. I wouldn't want to be on my mobile when talking to a delicious bit of crumpet like you."

While Susannah sauntered to her barstool and sat down, Aya fell for the temptation. How could she not tell the world, or at least everyone who was on Facebook, that she was on a date with such a catch? She checked in to the bar and tagged Susannah before typing in the words, "on a date with the most beautiful woman in Britain." She had been about to write "sexiest woman in Britain," but this sounded more respectful.

She saw Susannah glance at her screen and freaked out. Maybe she wasn't out of the closet? Or perhaps she wouldn't want her friends, family, and colleagues to know she was dating a younger woman.

Susannah gave a wry chuckle. "I have to admit, I like dating someone, be they man or woman, who boasts. Especially if it's a woman, actually. Humility was foisted on us by the patriarchy. I won't stand for anything that's *expected* of me." She paused to lean close to Aya again before adding, "I'll also admit that my favourite brand of boasting is when a sexy, young thing brags about being in my company."

Aya gave a sigh of relief and tucked her phone back into her jeans pocket. She quite liked the fact that women tended to be humbler, feeling that men could learn from that, but she wouldn't say that. She was in Susannah's good books now, and that could mean a good night kiss later. She'd do just about anything for that.

## Chapter Nineteen

# SLEEPLESS IN STOKE

It was 2 a.m. and Gwen couldn't sleep. She'd considered getting up to watch TV but didn't want to wake Charlotte. Then she'd tried to read a book but couldn't focus; the words just blurred together. Now she doodled in the notebook she kept on her bedside table. She usually created her final artwork with her Wacom Cintiq and Photoshop, but liked to sketch out ideas with old-fashioned pen and paper. She carried on for quite a while before realising what she was drawing: Janet the Jeep.

*Dammit. You're not even meant to be drawing for your own benefit. You need to work on your commissions!*

She stared at the jeep. Was she subconsciously missing Aya? She reached for her phone. She wanted to look at Aya's Facebook profile, just to check if she was okay. There was no harm in seeing what she was up to.

The first thing she saw was that Aya had checked in at a bar in Chester and tagged one Susannah McVey.

*That must be Mocha's full name*, she realised.

She read the words, "on a date with the most beautiful woman in Britain," and sighed. She was over Susannah, but it made her sad to think about Aya in a relationship with someone so fake and cold. Aya could, and should, do so much better.

Gwen put the phone down and picked up her notepad. She'd start sketching out her next commission. Drawing sapphic mermaids kissing would surely cheer her up, or at least the effort would make her tired enough to be able to sleep.

———

Much later Gwen woke up, or tried to wake up, and found everything fuzzy and somehow… weird. Why was she so uncomfortable? She blinked a few times against the light and the incorrect shapes of her surroundings. This wasn't her bedroom. No. This was the kitchen. Why was she slumped on the kitchen floor? And why did her hand hurt?

She checked it. It glistened with something yellowish and seemed a bit pink by the fleshy part where her hand met the thumb.

She heard someone clearing their throat. "Good morning. Or rather, good *4:37 a.m.*, love."

Gwen blinked again, taking in Charlotte perfectly now. Her roommate was standing over her, hands on hips and an amused expression on her face.

Gwen sat up properly. "Sorry. I… Why am I here? What's wrong with my hand?"

"Answer to first question: you sleepwalked. Second question: when I came in here, you were finishing up slathering butter on it. Then you bit into it."

"I WHAT?!"

Charlotte pressed her lips together, probably stifling a

giggle. "I can't think of any other way to explain the scenario, duck. I woke up because you were making a racket out here. I came to check you were okay, assuming you couldn't sleep and got up for a glass of water." She paused to offer Gwen a hand up. "When I got in here, you weren't answering my questions and you acted like a zombie. Also, you were buttering up your hand and then tried to chew it."

Gwen groaned. "Bloody hell. Sometimes when my depression really kicks in, I sleep a lot in the day. Then at night, I either can't sleep at all or I have restless nights with nightmares and sleepwalking."

She surveyed the kitchen in amusement. The tub of disappointing butter-impersonating spread was right on the floor where she'd been slumped. Next to it was a knife and, for some reason, three spoons. It was frightening to think that she was doing things in the kitchen while asleep. What if one night she thought she was cutting carrots and ended up chopping her fingers off? She needed those to draw, not to mention lovemaking. Oh, and the small issue of being able to make latte art on customers' posh coffees!

She put her hand over her eyes and laughed at the absurdity of it all. Only then did she realise that it was the buttered hand. She now had spread on her eyebrows, making her laugh all the more.

Charlotte joined in before gently steering her friend to the kitchen sink and pointing at the soap. "Unless you're going to eat that hand, I suggest you wash it, shug."

"I will. My eyebrows, too! Tomorrow I think we should talk about locking up any knives and sharp utensils," Gwen said with a tired giggle.

*Better to laugh than cry, right?*

"Sure, I can hide them. Or we'll get a drawer that locks. Either way, it'll be fine, I promise." Charlotte smiled kindly. "For now, I hope you've finished with your sleep-walking. You need your rest, and I have to be cooking greasy sausages in a few hours and would like a little bit more sleep."

Charlotte worked in a local pub, known for its cheap Full English in the morning and its extensive array of ales and beers throughout the rest of the day.

"Of course. You head to bed, mate. I'll clean up in here. Sorry I woke you."

Charlotte patted her shoulder. "It's perfectly fine. Just try and get some sleep."

Gwen gave her a nod and watched her leave the kitchen. Charlotte kept throwing surreptitious glances back at her. She was worried. That made sense; you would worry if your best friend was buttering their limbs at night. Or, as the case was here, if you thought they were about to lapse further into their chronic illness and wondering if this was the time they wouldn't be able to get back up.

Gwen cleaned up the kitchen, then washed her hands and eyebrows with warm water and the kitchen's lavender soap before heading back to bed. She didn't believe in god, but she found herself praying for more sleep and less fear of that big, black ocean of nothingness. Also, for less buttering of body parts. After all, she needed that spread for sandwiches.

## Chapter Twenty

# THE COUGAR AND HER WILD THING

Aya stretched out in Susannah's big bed. Her hand brushed the warmth Susannah had left on the expensive sheets. The owner of the sheets was in the bathroom now. Aya heard water running. She closed her eyes and exhaled blissfully, enjoying the soft bedding and the scent of Susannah, which enveloped the room.

When she opened her eyes again, Susannah was returning to bed. She was even more gorgeous without clothes on. Every scar, bit of cellulite, and mark on that feline, hourglass-shaped body paraded her life experience and the confidence with which she showed it off. She slid back into bed and laid herself on top of Aya in one lithe, precise move. Her head rested on Aya's chest, right on top of the smoke creature tattooed between her breasts.

Aya started playing with Susannah's silky hair, glad that the older woman couldn't see her. She knew she was smiling like a teenager after a first kiss and wanted to appear a little more worldly than that.

"I'm glad you came back to my place tonight," Susannah said. "I move between cities often, and it can be tricky to find new lovers right away, especially one as wild as you. Shame I didn't find you back when I lived in Stoke-on-Trent. We could have enjoyed many more nights together by now."

"Agreed. Still, I don't mind the drive here from Stoke. I'd travel the whole damn country for a taste of you."

Susannah craned her neck up to connect their gazes but stayed resting on her. Susannah's warm weight, with every curve so very noticeable against Aya's currently hypersensitive skin, felt too good to be true.

Aya tried to read her expression. Susannah looked pleased with her reply, showing a self-assured smirk and twinkling eyes.

"Keep saying such sweet things, and I'll let you taste me again right away."

"I'm ready if you are," Aya said, leaning up on her elbows.

Susannah's smirk grew. "Whoa. Slow down, wild one. We're not in a hurry."

Aya fell back onto the pillow, hoping she didn't look embarrassed. "Right. No, of course not. Just proving my point."

Susannah leaned down and planted a row of kisses on the tattoo along the alley between Aya's breasts. Aya tried to relax her eager body, reminding herself that she wasn't a seventeen-year-old virgin but an experienced woman.

She startled when Susannah's mouth moved on to the flesh of her breasts and the scraping of teeth entered the kisses. Susannah only hummed in an amused manner at Aya's jolting but did, eventually, stop the sharp kisses.

"I suppose I *could* come to you next time," Susannah said, looking back up. The intense eye contact made Aya's mouth go dry. Susannah, however, merely gave slow blinks of her blackened, long eyelashes. "Did you hear me, hot stuff? I offered to come to Stoke when we next have sex."

Aya couldn't imagine having such confidence. Susannah didn't for a second consider that there might not be a next time. Or pause to ask. A voice in the back of her mind wondered where the line between confidence and conceitedness was. That voice sounded a lot like Gwen's, she realised. She dismissed the thought as petty and buried it deep.

"Sure," Aya replied, breaking eye contact before Susannah could see her vulnerability. "But, if we're going to end up in bed together, um, we'll have to be here again."

"Suits me, but I do have to ask why? I trust you're not ashamed of me," she said with a fake pout.

Aya snorted. "I'm about as ashamed of you as I'd be of boxing for Britain in the Olympics. No, it's just that I…"

"What?" Susannah asked, trailing a finger around one of Aya's breasts, starting at the base and making smaller circles until the fingertip landed right on Aya's nipple.

She tried not to moan at the touch. This was hard enough to talk about without that sort of stuff distracting her. "Because I still live with my parents."

Susannah retracted her fingers. "Really? How old are you?"

"I'm twenty-seven."

"Blimey, for a moment there you had me worried you were much younger than you look. I thought I might be some cougar robbing the cradle."

"Nope, not at all. There's only, what, ten years between us?"

Susannah gave her a meaning smile. "That's very kind of you, honey, but it's more like fifteen. And a few more if we go by the age on my passport and not the one I give when asked."

"There's nothing hotter than an older woman."

"Thank you, wild thing." Susannah patted Aya's abs almost patronizingly, then began running her fingers over the hills and dips of them. "So, you still live at home, hm? Well, I suppose that is more common these days with the housing market being so challenging."

"When I used to box, I was on the road a lot," Aya said, looking up at the ceiling to feel less watched as she explained. "Spending most of my time in the gym meant I didn't need my own place. It was more convenient to have a home base that someone already cleaned and stocked with food. I pay rent, of course."

"As in a monthly bill or as in you let your mummy keep your weekly allowance to cover the detergent she uses to do your laundry?" Susannah joked.

It was banter. Aya worked out with testosterone-filled, manual-labour blokes all the time. She'd heard much worse insults than that and always batted them off with a roll of the eye and a foulmouthed comeback. This was different. She didn't want Susannah to use that tone with her. Especially not when she was naked underneath her, in her stylish bed and in this posh town. She couldn't stand Susannah thinking of her like that. Her cheeks grew hot, and she clenched her free hand.

"No. I pay properly." She retracted the hand that had rested on Susannah's shoulder. "It's not like it's weird. You were right about the UK housing market, only it's not 'challenging,' it's complete rubbish! Younger people can't get a bloody mortgage, can we?!" She heard her voice get louder and her Stoke accent more pronounced with every word, and yet she couldn't stop herself.

Susannah didn't laugh, but she carried on smiling in a way that spoke of holding a chuckle back with great effort. "Calm down. It was only a joke. My, you can get touchy, can't you?"

Aya wasn't sure what to say. She felt as much rage as she did unexpected shame. She still wanted to impress Susannah. To seduce her. Feelings warred within her, her heart thudded like a jackhammer, and her mind gave no answers. Luckily, Susannah answered for her.

"However, that shows passion. I like that in my lovers." She paused to place a nibbling kiss on the side of Aya's breast. "Besides, 'touchy' can mean so many things. And you're certainly very 'touchy-feely' in bed. I can't remember being so wildly and thoroughly pawed in my life."

Aya gave a small chuckle, the worst of the negative feelings beginning to ebb.

"Would you like to paw me again right now, wild thing?" Susannah asked in a tone of voice erotic enough to count as porn.

Aya's emotions shut off like light bulbs burning out, one by one, leaving her only with physical sensations, and her body... it knew what it wanted. She grabbed Susannah by the shoulders and hoisted her lover the small distance up her chest until their mouths could connect. Then she put every bit of effort she could muster into kissing Susannah's breath away.

*Chapter Twenty-One*

# DOWN

Gwen frowned at her reflection in the hallway mirror. Her hair was so flat today, and she couldn't get it to behave, despite having tried three different sorts of hair products. It hung there, limp and taunting. She was trying to dredge up the energy to find a solution. Or to truly care.

"Hurry, pleeease," Charlotte whinged. "It's a Sunday. If we don't hit the shops early, all of Hanley, no, wait… all of bloody Stoke-on-Trent will be there."

Gwen let her frown sag into the empty stare that had proceeded it. "Sure. Let's go."

She grabbed her bag and followed Charlotte to her car.

When they were seated and belted in, Charlotte surveyed her. "Shug, are you all right?"

"I'll be fine. I just need to get out and do something."

"Okay, well, let me know if you change your mind and want to go home and rest."

"Will do."

They parked in the Potteries Shopping Centre, and Gwen trailed after Charlotte, who was desperately hunting for an autumn coat. They were in their third shop when

Gwen froze by a rack of shirts. A couple of metres away, stood Aya. She was browsing the shirts with her usual focus and force, so Gwen had time to duck away before she looked up and spotted her.

Gwen couldn't face her. She slunk out and stood outside the shops' doors, waiting until she could motion for Charlotte to join her.

When Charlotte finally did, her worry lines signalled what she was about to say. "Gwen? You all right?"

"Yeah, I'm fine."

Charlotte watched her with big eyes full of concern. "No, you're not. You're really pale. Why are you hiding out here?"

"Aya was in there."

"Okay, so? I mean, I get that you didn't leave it at the best of places, but there's no reason for you to avoid her, is there? You could've just smiled or nodded at her and then gone about your business."

Gwen closed her eyes and leaned her head against the wall. "I can't face her right now. Not when I look like this. Not when I feel like this."

Charlotte rubbed her arm, bringing some heat to Gwen's cold extremities. "Okay, shug. We'll go to another shop."

"Thank you."

As they walked away, Charlotte kept casting glances at her, those worry lines still in place under the trendy, contoured make-up.

"What, Charlotte? Spit it out."

"I was just wondering. Do you think this deeper depression phase was set off by missing Mocha's visits at the café as a pick-me-up?" She paused before adding, "Or maybe by losing Aya? You know, before you'd even started this promising friendship properly?"

Gwen wrapped her arms around herself as she walked. She was constantly cold these days, no matter the temperature or how many layers she put on. "Come on, you know I was diving down this rabbit hole before Susannah moved and I met Aya."

"True, you were showing all the signs before, but—"

"No," Gwen interrupted. "This isn't normal sadness or world-weariness. It's a chronic mental illness; it comes with ups and downs. This is a standard down period. That's all."

Charlotte gave a quick nod, but those frown lines didn't smooth. Gwen could read them. They said that the situation with Aya and Susannah might've made things worse. Sadness worsened depression, and there were usually triggers to down periods. Gwen shivered. They walked on in heavy silence.

---

The next day, Gwen woke up just before 4:00 a.m. She tried to go back to sleep, knowing her alarm would go off in two hours, but no luck. She sat up, sighed, and switched the lamp on before getting her sketching implements out.

She brought the pencil down to touch the notebook's page. She'd finished her latest set of commissions, so now she had time to draw for fun. She usually didn't feel confident enough to put time into her own designs. She used her drawing skills for extra income and to make people happy, and her own art was usually on the backburner. Here was the moment, though.

She stared at the pencil tip resting on the expanse of white paper. It would normally have started moving by now. She would've drawn something, started a line, begun a shape. Even if it was something silly or bad, she would have started.

The pencil was frozen in place.

Her mind was a smooth, dark surface of water. There was nothing coming from it.

She thought about the last commission she'd done, the kissing mermaids. Maybe she could try drawing that again? Then she wouldn't have to think up a motif. She set out to sketch the outline of the first mermaid, but it was as if somewhere between the will to draw and the action of it, something in her had decided it was pointless. Not because she couldn't sell the illustration, the author who commissioned the last one would be happy for a slight variation of her mermaids, but because *everything* was pointless. Every part of her mind was blank and rigid.

For the first time in a long while, the fear of her mind and life force collapsing crawled into her like a cold, diseased snake.

She threw the pencil and pad down on the floor and stared at them as if they'd bitten her.

Her world narrowed, and she hugged her knees to her chest. Not being able to draw. That was how it had started all those years ago. Then it had been darkness, sadness, and emptiness for more than a year, leading to the point where she didn't think she could go on any longer. She would forever love Charlotte for stopping her that night and for getting her to an emergency room.

Gwen wasn't sure how long she sat staring at the pencil and paper, but after a while she knew she had to do something. She used a huge amount of willpower to get herself out of bed and out into the kitchen. Hoping she wouldn't wake Charlotte, she drank a tall glass of cold water and then stared at the empty glass. There was no putting it off anymore, she had to call in sick and get an appointment to see her therapist as soon as possible.

She forced herself to eat some yoghurt, take her medication, and get her shaky breathing under control. As soon as it was a decent time to do so, she called the couple who ran Coffee4U.

The husband, Alan, answered. "Gwen?"

"Yes, hello, sorry for the early hour."

"That's fine. I need to get to the café soon anyway, so I was up. Is everything all right?"

"No. I'm having… a depression day. I'm so sorry, but I can't come in today."

There was a beat of silence, only a beat.

"All right. I'll take your shift myself. Let me know how you're getting on, so I know if I need to find someone to take your other shifts this week."

Gwen wanted to cry. Partly out of gratitude, partly out of shame for cancelling on such short notice, but mainly because she hated not being able to do her job. Still, no tears came. Only a dense, gnawing ache in her heart and lungs.

"I will. I'm hoping it'll be better tomorrow, but as you know, it doesn't usually pass that fast."

"It's okay, Gwen. Take your time. I know you'll make it up to me later with extra shifts and your go-getter spirit, you always do. Just… try to heal best you can, duck."

"Yes. Thank you," Gwen croaked.

They said goodbye, and as soon as the call was over, Gwen dialled the number to Edward, the therapist with the sock issue.

Chapter Twenty-Two

# CONFIDENCE

Aya stood by Susannah's shiny, new kitchen table, checking her phone for the hundredth time. Susannah was late. More than two hours late.

About an hour ago she'd texted Aya to tell her that she was stuck at work and to have dinner without her. That had happened a lot during the two weeks they'd dated. Susannah would invite her over and then be extremely late. This time, however, it really bothered Aya.

There was a biographical movie about a female boxer on at a small, artsy cinema close by, and it was only showing for one night. She'd been dying to see it, and when Susannah heard that, she decided they should go together, make a date of it with a steak dinner before the movie, and hours of incredible sex after.

That was tonight, and the movie was starting in twenty-eight minutes. If they hurried, they could still make it, missing only the trailers. If Susannah came home in the next five minutes. And if traffic was light.

Luck was on Aya's side. There was the sound of a key in the door, and in the next moment Susannah came in, dropping her designer bag on the floor and unbuttoning her mocha coat.

Aya watched her in confusion. Why had she taken her makeup off at work? She only did that when she was working late and wanted to go straight to bed when she got home.

"Hi, gorgeous," Aya said. "No need to take your coat off; we'll have to rush to the cinema right away."

Susannah's supermodel features twisted into a scowl as she hung up her coat. "No. I'm in for the night. Sex and sleep are all I have energy for. I hope you've eaten as I told you to. I had a salad at work."

"B-but we said we'd go see this movie? You know how much I've been looking forward to it." Aya paused to clear the whinge out of her voice. "I was going to go on my own, remember? But you said I should book tickets for us both."

She looked from Susannah to the door. Should she go on her own? She could still make it. No, it was more important to have this discussion with Susannah. They had to settle this. She was done constantly being disrespected.

Susannah slipped off her high heels with movements calculated to draw Aya's gaze to her shapely, bare legs. Annoyingly, it worked. "I know you don't have a job, honey. If you did you would know how tired you get after long day." Susannah sighed. "Especially in my case, as I have to pretend to like, and even want to flirt, with the idiots I work with. They all want to tell me about their boring, little lives and their families. Or worse, drool over me and think I don't notice."

Aya crossed her arms over her chest, trying to not look as hurt as she felt. "Hey, I might not have a job now, but when I boxed professionally I'd spend almost all day in the gym and sometimes whole evenings in the ring." She stopped to catch Susannah's eye to ensure she was listening. "I still made time to go out with my girl-friends. Especially if there was an event that meant a lot to them."

"Girlfriends? Oh dear, do you think I'm your little girlfriend?" Susannah said with a smirk. She smoothed down her thin designer dress, drawing attention to how it hugged her hourglass figure. She bit her lip seductively before adding, "That's not why I keep a sexy ex-boxer around, wild thing. I want your quiet mouth and that hot body. Not to mention your stamina." She walked into the kitchen, taking her earrings off while adding, "Not that you'll need much of that tonight. I doubt I'll last very long."

Aya felt herself bare her teeth and closed her mouth. Two instincts fought in her, not fight or flight, but fight or fuck. She didn't want a quarrel, especially as she knew Susannah would talk in circles until she won the argu-ment. Until Aya felt silly and like she was overreacting. They'd tried that out a few nights ago. Not tonight.

She prowled over to Susannah and pulled her into a rough kiss. Susannah dropped the earrings and responded with enthusiasm. As annoyed as Aya was with her, the way this woman kissed… it took her breath away. Susannah's hands moved over her body, grabbing and stroking greed-ily. Aya's body replied in kind, pressing closer and closer to Susannah's inviting curves.

Aya pulled away from the kiss, breathless. "Don't think the fact that I want to shag now means we won't talk more about your comments later."

"Talk? Oh my gorgeous wild thing, didn't you hear me

when I mentioned your quiet mouth? I picked you as flavour of the month because you so rarely talk."

Aya ground her teeth at those words.

*Quiet mouth. Flavour of the month. Wild thing.*

She had loved that nickname at first. Loved being wild for Susannah. But now, all she heard was the "thing" part. As if she was a belonging. Or an animal that Susannah got as a pet. Well, Aya Lawson was no one's pet.

"Stop trying to piss me off. I know what you're doing. You're trying to rile me up to have wilder sex."

"Is that what I'm doing," Susannah purred. "Or am I just too tired to pretend to be nice tonight?"

"Keep bloody talking like this, and things might not go your way."

Susannah gave her an incredulous look. "Oh? What are you going to do? *Spank* me?" Her voice dripped with condescension and mockery.

"Yeah." Why not, Aya figured. Maybe it could make her feel better. "Yes, that's exactly what I'm going to do."

"Ha. By all means, little darling. Be my guest," Susannah said, turning around to hike her dress up and her lacy knickers down before bending over the kitchen table in slow, deliberate movements.

The sight was mouth-watering, and for a moment Aya forgot about the fight. Hell, she forgot her own name. Then she saw Susannah craning her neck to glance back at her and give her an arrogant smirk. Then she remembered.

Aya gave the rounded, soft arse a smack. Then another one on the other cheek. Then a third, harder this time. Susannah didn't make any sign that it stung or that it was making her think twice about her behaviour. In fact, her happy laughs and theatrical moans made it clear that she was still very much in charge and that this was what she had wanted all along.

Aya gave up. Spanking had been a silly idea anyway. Her whole body still pulsated with its need for Susannah. Her brain faintly registered that it wished her body would shut the hell up. Nevertheless, it wanted the woman in front of her. Needed her. Needed to be in control, even if it was only for a few hours.

"Go to the bedroom. Then get on your back," Aya growled, trying to quell the emotional quiver in her voice.

"Certainly," Susannah said, standing up straight before slipping out of the lace underwear around her ankles. As she sauntered to the bedroom she called, "Does that mean we're done with your little temper tantrum and are getting down to what matters? Because I've had a very long day and want some stress relief."

Aya didn't reply. She simply set her jaw and watched Susannah take her dress and bra off with efficient speed before draping herself on her satin-sheeted bed.

With harsh movements, Aya got on the bed and parted Susannah's thighs. Aya drank in the heady scent of Susannah and how she looked right now, splayed out and eager. Nothing else between them worked, but this... this was just what Aya had wanted. What she had daydreamed about. Aya got comfortable and moved in with careful fingers to pull up the clitoral hood and place a few nibbling kisses on the swollen nub. There was no doubt that Susannah had enjoyed the spanking. Aya stopped teasing and got down to devouring every inch of pink in front of her. Tonight, she'd make Susannah tremble.

She shifted between quick circles with the tip of her tongue, long strokes, and deep kisses, darting back up to the clit in the pattern she knew Susannah liked. She tongued forth louder and louder moans from Susannah, wanting to drive her wild, to make her weak with pleasure. To make Susannah yield to her in some small way.

It didn't work.

As her mouth took Susannah, Aya found herself frequently looking up to get reassurance from her lover. Strange, she knew she was doing this right. She could hear that. Feel that. Besides, she'd always been good at this, mainly because she enjoyed it. Nevertheless, something about Susannah always made her doubt herself. She wondered if that doubt was something Susannah had wanted all along, something she had implanted during their every interaction.

Susannah moved against her mouth now, undulating her pelvis to get the pressure where she wanted it and to add friction. They got into a rhythm, and for a few moments, everything in the world narrowed down to simple sensations. Warm, wet, soft, pulsating. It all made sense for a little while, and Aya didn't have to think, only do.

Now she made Susannah tremble, just as she had wanted. Susannah gushed against her mouth with a possessive growl, holding Aya's face in place as she rode out her orgasm.

When she was done, she pulled Aya up to give her a quick kiss and mumble, "Mm, brilliant as always." Another kiss, then Susannah stretched and said, "Wow. I'm too spent to even brush my teeth. We'll have to call it a night, wild thing. Sleep well." She moved aside and appeared to pass out more than fall asleep. She always did that, slept like a drunk person or a baby, only the blink of an eye separating being awake and being deeply asleep.

Aya envied that. Envy wasn't all she was experiencing,

though. The unsatisfied throbbing between her legs and the unease in her heart fought over which would make her feel worse. She wiped slickness off her chin while thoughts crowded her mind. This wasn't the first time Susannah had left her feeling small, disregarded, and unsatisfied before bed. It hadn't bothered her this much before; she'd been busy with her adrenaline rush and the confidence boost of being this woman's pick of all the lovers in the world.

Tonight, though, something had shifted, both in Susannah's behaviour and in her own reaction to it. Aya watched the sleeping blonde. She was as strikingly beautiful as she'd always been. What had changed was how Aya saw that beauty. It no longer made her heart soar; instead it made her draw back.

*It's like one of those toxic plants or venomous animals*, she realised. *All beautiful colours that pull you in but are actually meant to warn you of the danger underneath.*

Aya's arousal drained away. How had she ended up here?

She ground her teeth. *No, no cop-outs. You know how you ended up here.*

She'd made Susannah a symbol of her own failures. Winning Susannah's affection had been the ultimate victory and proof of her own worth. Keeping her, date after date, had only solidified it. Now, she was disgusted by her own choices. How had her need to prove herself become more important than caring for her own well-being and having a partner she could be proud of? A partner who wasn't disrespectful or had an ugly heart under her charming and pretty veneer? Even the lovemaking, if Aya was honest, had always been the way it was tonight: amazing at first, but disappointing in the end. Even when Susannah reciprocated or they came together, she showed in a million ways that she was more interested in taking than giving.

Aya slowly stood up. The thought that had been planted at some point during these two weeks was now in full bloom: she deserved more. Aya could no longer allow herself to be in a relationship with someone as cold and fake as the woman sleeping there. Couldn't ignore the way Susannah behaved.

Gwen had been right. Susannah wasn't who they'd assumed she was. Who they had dreamed she was.

Aya tilted her head as she watched Susannah sleep. Perhaps Gwen hadn't been exaggerating the awfulness of what Susannah had said that day. Aya hadn't believed it then, mainly because she didn't want to. It was easier to assume her crush had only said unpleasant things because she was impressing her boss. But now Aya knew that Susannah never said anything she didn't want to say. She found ways to twist situations so that she only had to do what she wanted deep down.

Susannah slept on, that cold beauty of hers showing in the smug smile tugging at her lips. Aya wished she'd listened to Gwen. Believed Gwen.

Guilt spread through her, like an infection in the blood.

She pushed that aside. She needed to deal with what was happening here and now: she and Susannah in whatever this relationship was.

She quietly gathered the things she'd brought over for what she thought was going to be a romantic evening and a sleepover. She wrote a quick note for Susannah and left it on her kitchen counter:

*This "wild thing" won't be caged, especially not by you.*

*I'd wake you to say goodbye,*
*but why bother when you only picked me because I don't talk.*
*Don't contact me.*

Aya laced the boots—which Susannah had complained were too old and scuffed— tighter and strode out, filled with the confidence of knowing she'd made the right choice. Confidence? Yes, she decided. This gave her more confidence than winning Susannah ever had.

## Chapter Twenty-Three

# ELEVEN CENTIMETRES OF FURRY ANTIDEPRESSANT

Gwen sat in Edward's office, staring at that ridiculous poster of the bridge. Its quote was surely mocking her. "Be not wishing and pining but thankfully content. For it is a short bridge between wanting and regret."

She'd pined and wished, then met the real woman behind the daydream, leaving her with plenty of regret.

Edward sniffed. "I haven't seen you in a while, Gwen. You've cancelled two weeks' worth of appointments, and your excuses have been less than convincing."

Like she didn't know that.

She stalled, sipping the cup of tea he'd given her, then put it down so she could place her hand over her heart. It was beating rapidly, but not fast enough to be in panic attack mode. "Sorry about cancelling. I've been having a rough time."

"That's when you should have more therapy, not less."

"I know. I'm sorry."

"Don't apologise to me, Gwen. It's you who suffers. You should come to these appointments for your sake, not for mine."

"Yes. I know that," Gwen snapped.

Silence sank into the room, filling every corner. He was looking at her, but she avoided his gaze.

After a moment, he spoke. "So, last time we met, you'd come home from Chester and your infatuation with this 'Mocha' had been dashed."

"Yes."

He consulted his notes. "The things she said, they must've affected you. Hit a nerve, so to speak?"

"You mean because she invalidated and mocked people with mental health issues? Yeah, that didn't feel great."

"Do you think that worsened your depression peak?"

Gwen wanted to punch something, preferably the poster with that damn bridge on it.

"Why does everyone keep asking me that? I don't know." She grabbed onto her chair's armrests. "Maybe I spiralled faster and further down because I used to have a fun diversion to brighten my mornings, and now I don't. Maybe I subconsciously had Susannah as a replacement for a real love interest, and now I'm lonely. I DON'T KNOW!"

"Okay, okay," Edward held his hand out in a calming gesture. "That's fine. This is probably a natural depression peak, brought on by hormonal changes or lack of sleep. Maybe even part of the usual cycle of your clinical depression; I haven't treated you long enough to be sure."

"Which is why you want me to keep a journal, so I can measure when my highs and lows come, I know," Gwen muttered. "I will start that. One day."

He cleared his throat. "Yes. Well. Anyway. This whole Mocha, or Susannah, debacle could've worsened your depression, or perhaps you would have ended up here without any triggers. We don't know."

Triggers. Gwen's thoughts went to Aya. She hadn't spoken to Edward about her, had she? Maybe she should tell him how she missed the friendship that never was? Or about the pain of Aya taking Susannah's side over hers, about that Aya didn't believe her. Maybe even tell him about how Aya's Facebook updates about her dates with Susannah made her queasy. No. She couldn't make herself voice all of that. Not yet.

Edward carried on. "Whatever triggered it, we might need to discuss increasing your dose of antidepressants. And schedule in more frequent appointments."

Gwen took her time considering that. More appointments made sense. More medication? In her experience, that *could* help. Or it could leave her numb, bloated, and tired, making her sleep her days away. She didn't want to go through that again. Not unless it was absolutely necessary.

She chewed the inside of her cheek. "To be honest, it's not that bad right now. I'll come in for more frequent appointments, but I think we should save upping the medication for if it gets terrible. This time, I think I caught it before it got completely out of hand."

"You do?"

"Yes. The proof is that I'm here now," Gwen said honestly. She picked up her mug and gazed into it as she thought out loud. "I think you're right. This low period *did* hit harder because of Susannah, but more because I used Susannah's visits to the café as something to look forward to each day. An extra antidepressant, you know? Now that I don't have that, it's harder to keep my head above water." She took a sip. "I think I just need a distraction. Something to focus on each day. Something on the horizon to set my gaze on while I battle through this crap."

He tugged on an earlobe. "I see. Why haven't you tried that in these past two weeks?"

"I don't know. I guess…" Gwen stared back into the comforting russet brown of her tea as her thoughts settled into their rightful slots. "I saw no point. I didn't think I was worth that effort, so I didn't motivate myself to really try. But now that I can't draw or work, I'll *have to* motivate myself."

"That is an easy thing to say but a harder thing to do, especially if you have clinical depression," Edward warned.

"I know," Gwen said. She fixed his gaze with her own, showing that she was serious and had the power in her to manage it this time.

After a moment he reluctantly nodded. "Try that out. Maybe ask your friend—Charlotte isn't it?—to help you and keep you accountable. Then, if this new thing to focus on each day doesn't help, we will discuss further medication and therapy. Shall we give it a week? Or two?"

"Say two. If my depression gets worse before then, I promise to let you know."

He nodded again. He didn't look convinced, still tugging on that earlobe and watching her. Gwen didn't care. She had thought a new daily pick-me-up would work from the start; now was the time to put that into action and prove she was right.

———

A couple of days later, Gwen was in bed talking to her mum on the phone, hearing all about every relative and acquaintance spread throughout Wales. They were only a few hours travel away from her, and yet her family might as well have been in another universe.

"Did I tell you that Carys had a baby?"

"No?" Gwen said, desperately trying to remember who Carys was. A distant cousin? A neighbour? A stray cat?

"She did! Both mum and baby are happy and healthy." A pause. "Have you thought anymore about having children one day?"

"Mum. I've told you. I don't plan on having kids."

"I know, I know. You can't blame me for asking. I only want to be a gran. Oh, and to make sure you aren't lonely, of course."

"Mm," Gwen said, trying to stay patient.

There was the clinking sound of cutlery being put away before her mum asked, "So, is sweet, little Carl doing all right?"

Gwen jumped, knocking a pillow off the bed. "Mum!"

"Oh, sorry! It's Charlotte these days. Of course! Silly, silly me. Why do I always forget? I'm so sorry! Please don't tell her."

Gwen picked up the pillow. "Relax. I won't. And Charlotte is doing fine, busy working and dating the most sought-after bachelors in Stoke."

"That's good. She'll probably get married before you do, then."

*Nice one, Mum, you managed to work in my lack of both children and a wife in about two minutes.*

There was a long, low grumble in the background that Gwen recognised as her dad talking.

"Oh my, yes!" her mum squealed. "Look at the time! I'll have to ring off, Gwen love. Your dad and I are going over to Carys' house to see the little nipper."

"Great. Give her my regards and kiss the baby's head from me."

There was more grumbling as her dad spoke in the background. "What was that, love?" her mum said distractedly. Gwen wasn't sure if she spoke to her or to him.

"Never mind. Have a nice time and hug Dad for me," Gwen said.

"Will do. Speak soon, love."

"Bye, Mum."

As she hung up with a sigh, she heard Charlotte open the front door and shout hello.

"Hey, sensible person!" she shouted back. "I'm in the bedroom."

Charlotte walked in with her hands behind her back. "Hiya, duck. I'm not interrupting an afternoon nap, am I?"

"No. To be honest, I *have* slept most of the day, but just now I was on the phone with mum to ask about the homeless shelter she volunteers at. Although we wound up talking about who had a baby and who had hernia surgery." Gwen blew out a breath. "Anyway, I'm not sure a homeless shelter would be a useful distraction considering my depression. Too sad. Maybe if I volunteer at a library instead?"

Charlotte took a step forward. "About that. You know how your therapist wanted me to help you with your daily 'bright spark' or whatever you want to call it?"

"Yes?"

"Well, I brought something for you."

Now Gwen noticed why Charlotte had her hands behind her back; they held something.

"What is it?"

As if answering the question, a small, keening squeak rang out.

Gwen knew that sound from TV and from her childhood dreams. Her mouth fell open. "A guinea pig!?"

Charlotte beamed and nodded. From behind her back, she produced a small pet carrier. She put it on the bed and opened it to reveal a long-haired, rust-brown creature bounding around inside. Charlotte used a finger to pet its head. "I bought her from a local, trusted breeder. The same one who provided my sister's guinea pig back in the day, actually."

Gwen whirred with joy and affection as she watched the little fluff ball sit still to be petted. The emotions were so needed, so rare these days. "Her?"

"Yep, it's a girl," Charlotte confirmed. "She's ten weeks old and in perfect health. She was the cuddliest and bounciest of all her siblings, so I thought she'd be a good fit for a pick-me-up."

"She's perfect," Gwen breathed with worship.

Charlotte smiled. "You can pet her, you know? She's your pet. You don't have to just sit there staring at her like she's a miracle."

Gwen took in the critter with her cylindrical body and giant head. "But she is! She's so cute and excellent and... and... small!"

"I'll have you know she's big for her age, eleven centimetres!"

Charlotte picked up the eleven-centimetre miracle and handed her to Gwen. With careful hands, she accepted the furry baby. It sat in one of her palms and stared at her with inquisitive, albeit not very clever-looking, eyes.

"Hello, little one," Gwen whispered. "You're going to live with me from now on. I'm sorry if I'm rubbish at looking after you. I've never had a guinea pig. The only pet I ever had was a huge dog when I grew up."

"Don't worry about that. I know what to do, and I got you a guide, too," Charlotte pointed to the book that was on top of the pet carrier's lid. "It has all kinds of information on how to clean their cages, maintain their health, and what they eat."

"A cage! I need to go buy her a cage right now!"

Charlotte laughed. "You mean you didn't hear the racket when I came in? I bought you a cage, shug, and everything that goes in it, including a water bottle. It's all out in the hallway. It's going to be huge for her, but she'll soon grow into it."

Gwen watched the creature, who was now wiggling her nose as if it itched. "How big will she get?"

"The breeder said anywhere between twenty and forty centimetres. Considering she's already eleven centimetres, I bet she's going to be big lady."

Gwen felt her smile go from ear to ear. "Whatever size she gets, she'll be brilliant."

"Phew." Charlotte pretended to wipe her brow. "I know you shouldn't buy pets as a surprise for someone, but I was pretty sure I knew what you'd want. You have talked about guinea pigs a lot."

"You were absolutely right. How much do I owe you? For her and for all her stuff."

"Nothing. Think of it as my rent for staying here for weeks."

Gwen said nothing. The fact that Charlotte's apartment building was finished and she should've moved out days ago was something they didn't talk about. They both knew Gwen needed her at the moment.

"Charlotte," Gwen said, gaze locked on the guinea pig

as she prepared to ask something this difficult, "if I… get worse and can't care for her, will you do it?"

"Of course," Charlotte answered softly. "But it won't come to that, I'm sure."

The guinea pig squeaked, and it sounded like a question. Gwen interpreted it as her wanting to get down. As soon as her tiny legs touched the pet carrier, she began running around, sniffing everything.

"We should get her cage set up so she can eat, drink, and have toys and more room to play," Charlotte said.

"Sure," Gwen agreed, forcing her reluctant body out of bed. After all, her pet needed something. That was more important than her heavy limbs and foggy mind.

They headed for the cage. "What are you going to name her?" Charlotte asked.

"Hm. Something quirky, like Baroness Brush or Lady Lovely Locks."

Charlotte giggled. "If you want something like that, you could name her after that perfume you liked so much in Chester, the Tragedy of Lord Something?"

"No," Gwen snapped. "I don't want any reminders of Susannah or Aya or anything from that horrible trip."

"Okay," Charlotte said cautiously. "It was only horrible at the end, though? The bit in the perfume shop was good, wasn't it?"

"I'm not naming her anything to do with Chester!"

"Okey-dokey. How about something connected to Stoke-on-Trent, then? One of our famous potteries?"

Gwen glared at her. "I'm not bloody well naming her something like Royal Doulton or Wedgwood."

"Fine. I'll stop suggesting things."

"Probably best," Gwen said with a playful grimace.

She placed the gingery-brown creature in the large

cage. "Look at her! I love that big head, the barrel body, and those teeny-tiny legs. She really does look like a little meatlo… hang on, that's it. I'm naming her Meatloaf."

Charlotte scrunched her nose. "Like the singer?"

"Sure, but in her case, she would do anything for cucumber, not for love."

Charlotte rolled her eyes at the reference. "All right then. Meatloaf it is."

## Chapter Twenty-Four

# SORRY

Aya was in the gym, wrapping up her hands. She had a match in a few minutes. Well, no, not really a match; she'd agreed to be the sparring partner for a rising star, a girl of about nineteen who was tall enough to make Aya feel tiny. At least they were the same weight class, and they had agreed to be wary of punches to Aya's head, to keep her old injury safe.

Bill came moseying over and poked Aya in the ribs. "How are you getting on, kid?"

"Pretty rubbish. Relationships suck."

"I meant more along the lines of if you were ready for the sparring match, but hey, we have a few minutes. Tell your old coach what's up," he said, leaning against the scratched wall.

"You know how I told you about dumping Susannah?"

"Yep. About time, too."

"I know, don't rub it in. Anyway, remember Gwen?"

He scratched his broad, wrinkled chin. "The Welsh chick who warned you off Susannah?"

"Yeah. I want to apologise to her. For not believing her warnings. And for not staying in touch."

"You know what I always say, kid."

"Flowers and spill your guts," Aya dutifully repeated.

"That's the one. Whatever happened between you and a lady, buy her the best flowers you can find and tell her everything." He pointed a crooked finger at her. "Keep nothin' back from a woman you care about. I learned that the hard way. Total openness, kid, even if it's hard."

Aya finished wrapping her hands. Bill kept his tall frame plastered to the wall. He knew her well enough to give her lots of time to get what she needed to say out.

"Do you... think that'll be enough?" she finally mumbled.

"Sure. If you're honest enough and apologise enough, why not?"

Aya flexed her hands. They were strong and sure. Sadly, the rest of her wasn't. "Gwen did read my thoughts and actions very well. She probably knew I'd have to give Susannah a try. And why I did it."

Bill inclined his head as some sort of noncommittal agreement.

Aya blew out a breath. "Okay, I'll give it a go." She bumped her wrapped fists together. "But first, let's go whip this nineteen-year-old into shape."

---

That night Aya stood outside the door to Gwen's flat. She shifted her weight from foot to foot. Her palms were beginning to dampen around the huge bouquet of white roses she'd bought.

*Get a hold of yourself, Lawson.*

She rang the doorbell. After a while, Gwen opened the door with a surprised expression. She was wearing scruffy jeans and an oversized, washed-out sweater.

They watched each other in weighted silence.

"Hi," Aya managed to blurt out. "Sorry for showing up here like this. I'm not stalking you, the guy at the café where you work said you lived here."

"Why are you always assuring me you're not stalking me? It's starting to sound suspicious. Wait, someone gave a stranger my home address? I bet that was *Dave*," Gwen said with disgust.

"I'm so sorry," Aya blurted out.

"About Dave being a thoughtless wanker?"

"No, about—"

A smile tugged at Gwen's pallid lips. "I know, I was messing with you. Let me help you out, you were apologising for ignoring what I said about Susannah and dating her anyway?"

"Yes," Aya said in an uncharacteristically small voice.

"No need. I get it. Want to come in?"

Aya nodded and stepped inside.

They watched each other silently again.

"Do you want to give me those, or are they just a prop?" Gwen said, pointing to the roses.

Aya thrust them forward, nearly hitting Gwen in the chest.

She expected to hear Gwen's beautifully raspy laugh at that, but all she got was a tired smile. Everything about Gwen looked tired, now that she thought about it. The limp hair, the ashy skin, and the listless eyes.

"Are you okay?"

Gwen waved the hand not holding roses dismissively.

"I'm fine. Just my depression getting worse. I get these low periods sometimes."

"Oh." Aya chewed her thumbnail.

"I seem to be doing better than you anyway," Gwen said kindly. "You look like you've come to your own execution."

"Yeah, I bet I do." Aya dropped her hand from her mouth. "I, um, won back some of my confidence when I dated Susannah, but clearly that's not helping me tonight."

Gwen surveyed her with what was probably pity. "Are you sure that had to do with Susannah? It wasn't that you dared to step up and achieve something which you'd failed at before that did it?"

"Maybe," Aya mumbled.

Gwen caught her eye. "That's a good thing. It means you might get a confidence boost if this interaction goes well, too."

"I guess. Thanks for being nice."

"Thank *you* for the flowers. I love cream roses." Gwen sniffed them. "They smell nice, too."

*Cream, not white. I should've guessed,* Aya thought with amused fondness. "Glad to hear it."

"Do you want to take off your jacket and stay for a while? Or do you need to run away?"

*She really does get me.*

"No. I'd like to run off, but I'm not done. I owe you an explanation. And…" She hesitated. "I want to see you. I mean, talk to you. Or both, I guess."

"I'd like that. I'm going to go put these in water." She held up the roses. "Charlotte is staying with me, but she's out on a date with some heroic fireman, so it'll just be you and me."

Aya hung up her waxed canvas jacket, self-conscious

over how scruffy it looked compared to the coats on the hooks.

In the kitchen she watched her hostess cut the stems of the roses. Her movements were slow, sure, and calm, but never lazy. She had her own sort of confidence, Aya realised, the kind that doesn't need to boast or steal attention.

She pushed herself to ask the question that had been bothering her. "Do you really think my boosted confidence had nothing to do with Susannah?"

Gwen, concentrating on putting the roses in a vase, hummed. "I think there were a lot of your own actions that increased your confidence. Helping me that day, for one. You're clearly not comfortable with strangers, especially ones that are complicated, like I was. Still, you picked me up and you helped me through the day, even though it unsettled you." She stood back and surveyed the roses. "After that, you dared make your own decision about Susannah. Then, from what I've seen on Facebook, you not only managed to talk to Susannah, but to charm her."

"Turns out that it wasn't so much me charming her as that I didn't talk much and I had low self-esteem, which let her treat me anyway she wanted," Aya said bitterly.

Gwen's focus snapped from the roses to Aya. "What? I'm sorry to hear that." There was no 'I told you so' or smugness in Gwen's voice or demeanour; only empathy.

Aya stared down at her boots. "It's what I deserved for not listening to you."

"No! No one should be treated like that, especially not for wanting to believe the best about their crush and needing that person's validation." Gwen stepped closer. "I should've been clearer earlier when I said that you didn't need to apologise because I got it. What I meant was that, on that day, I assumed you were going to think I was exaggerating. And I understood why you wanted to believe I was, so you could pursue Susannah and prove to yourself that you could win."

Aya gaped. "How the hell do you understand me so much better than I do?"

"I guess therapy teaches you to analyse thoughts and behaviours. Besides, you told me what Susannah symbolised for you, remember? Drawing the conclusions after that wasn't rocket science."

"Aha. I thought it was because we were somehow compatible or something," Aya mumbled.

"Maybe that, too. Or maybe I just overanalyse everything. Look, all I know is that if you're here and talking about Susannah like this, then you did the right thing for yourself and broke up with her. Also, the fact that you haven't posted about her on Facebook in ages proves that conclusion."

"Hey, how about that? Now you're the one stalking me."

Gwen smiled a little, but it didn't sit right with Aya. That was definitely a point where Gwen would usually laugh. Aya's heart twinged at the change in her.

*I wish there was something I could do to help.*

"And you're changing the subject," Gwen admonished her. "I know that tactic."

"Fine, yeah, I had enough of the way Susannah treated me. One night about a week ago, I got my stuff, left her a note, and walked out."

"Good for you. That takes some confidence. And self-respect."

"I guess it does. Sorry for not coming here earlier." Aya

heard how quiet her voice was and made herself raise it to be heard. "I guess I've been too afraid to say the wrong thing if I saw you. It was easier to just bury my head in the sand."

"Don't worry about it. I could've contacted you as well. I'm just glad that you're out of that woman's claws. And, as much as it pains me to admit, I'm a little bit relieved that I was right and not blowing her bad behaviour out of proportion."

"Hell no! I absolutely believe she said those things, in that tone of voice, and with that body language. What's worse, I'm sure she meant them. She was probably pulling her punches actually, considering the low opinion she has of other people. I'm ashamed to have dated someone like that."

"There you go again, getting all talkative when you're not overthinking every word," Gwen said with an expression that looked almost proud.

Aya laughed. "Not always. I'm never going to be a natural chatterbox. But you do make me more relaxed, so I worry less about saying awkward stuff."

"Good. And for what it's worth, when you do say 'awkward stuff,' I like it. Not in a condescending way or anything, I just enjoy that you think and speak differently to most people. You're never boring."

Aya watched Gwen toy with one of the cut-offs from the roses. Something occurred to her. "You get bored easily, don't you? I bet that was one the reasons you liked Susannah's visits to the café; they made your days less predictable."

Gwen contemplated the bit of rose stem in her hand. "I guess so. Less predictable and less mundane. I suppose

I've always wanted that little bit of… I was going to say magic, but that sounds so pretentious and childish."

Aya thought hard. "Do you mean those moments when something kinda wakes you up? Like, little things that give you a buzz and make you feel alive?"

"Yes. Something to take you out of your everyday life."

"I think I get it, then. Getting in a flawless swing in a match used to do that for me."

"That makes sense. Seeing Susannah might not be a big thing, but it was something to look forward to. Something that was different every time it happened and snapped me out of my routine, in a good way. A little treat, I guess."

"And now you don't have that, it made this, what did you call it? Low period? It made that worse?"

"Charlotte and my therapist both seem to think it aggravated my low period, yes. That it was some sort of trigger."

Aya slowly squeezed her hands into the tight pockets of jeans. "Do you agree with them?"

"Yes. Although, I think Edward, my therapist, feels that what Susannah said subconsciously triggered me. Charlotte, on the other hand, constantly hints that it might have been…" Gwen trailed off.

"What?"

"Losing you as a potential friend and losing your trust in me. Which is silly, because we didn't even know each other that well."

Aya smoothed her ponytail as she considered that. "I don't agree. We didn't know each other for that long, but somehow, we got to know each other really well. And I've sort of missed you, I guess. Or wanted to have you in my life, or something. Does that make sense?"

Gwen's cheeks darkened to rosy pink. "Yes. And I feel the same."

It was good to see some colour on her face. She was so deathly pale.

*Has she lost weight, too? I thought people comfort-ate when they were depressed?*

"Gwen? Um, I know I keep saying that I'm sorry for stuff, but if my actions that day had anything to do with your depression getting worse, I'm sorrier than I can ever say."

"Oh, no! I didn't mean to blame you for any of this!" Gwen reached out to touch her arm, her hand cold but reassuring. "As I say, this was just Charlotte's theory. It doesn't actually take a certain trigger for someone with clinical depression to get more depressed. We have peaks and troughs in life."

"Yeah?"

"Yes. Please don't blame yourself."

"Well, whatever, I just… really wish there was something I could do to help you."

"There is. You can be my friend. You can distract me when it gets bad and be patient with me when I have to cancel on you. Notice that I said when, not if." She gave a smile that was clearly forced. "You can try to understand when I'm locked into a loop of negative thoughts and this dark void my brain creates and you can't reach me. Charlotte will tell you, it gets frustrating and scary. I mean, I don't want to chase you off before our friendship has even started, but as I'm really struggling at the moment, you might as well know what you'd be signing up for."

The misery in Gwen's eyes was heart-breaking. Aya had to step closer to her. She didn't know what to say, but she wanted to make it obvious that what Gwen was telling her wasn't chasing her away.

It was a serious moment, one that deserved full attention and sombreness. With that in mind, it was a shame that it was broken by a loud, long, high-pitched squeal followed by a serious of shorter ones.

"What the hell was that?" Aya exclaimed.

"Meatloaf."

Aya moved even closer to hear her better. "It was *what?*"

"Meatloaf."

"Um, they don't usually make noise. Unless you count the squish when you bite into a slice. Or hang on, do you mean the rock star? Man, his voice has not aged well."

"No. Meatloaf, the new love of my life."

With that, Gwen walked off and returned with an orangey-brown ball of fur in her cupped palms. It made a chirruping noise, and Gwen held out her hands with the squeaking thing for Aya to see.

Aya scratched her neck. "Um. It's a… hamster?"

"No, baby hamsters are like a third of this size. This is more the size of a rabbit. So, guess again."

"Not a rabbit, then. Hm. Mouse? Rat? Gremlin?"

Gwen quirked an amused eyebrow. "I think you mean gerbil. And no, those are all smaller, too. She's a guinea pig. Just a little baby for now, but soon she'll be a—what do you call it in boxing? Heavyweight?"

"Yep. She looks pretty fat, though. Heavyweights have more muscle."

"She's not fat. She's cylindrical and fluffy. Also, you try to grow muscle on a diet of leaves and cucumber."

Aya bent down to squint at the silly-looking thing in Gwen's hands. "Hey there, shug. I've got a protein bar in my jacket pocket. You can have a bite, and then we can do some squats. You need to work on those tiny legs."

"You are not my guinea pig's personal trainer," Gwen protested. "Besides, she's not meant to be shaped like a boxer. She's meant to be shaped like a meatloaf, hence the name."

The guinea pig stared Aya right in the eye, yawned, and then turned its back to her and began washing.

"I like her. She's got attitude," Aya said.

There was the sound of a key in the door and then someone coming in and calling, "Hi, duck, I'm back early."

"I can tell," Gwen replied. "I have company."

"Oh?" A slim woman, as tall as the nineteen-year-old Aya had sparred with earlier, came in and smiled at her. She took off her high heels while saying, "Hi, I'm Charlotte. I'm the poor wretch who has to live with Gwen and the ridiculous new love of her life." She pointed to Meatloaf. Aya couldn't help but laugh at how both Meatloaf and Gwen glowered at her in response.

"This is Aya," Gwen said. Aya and Charlotte shook hands while Gwen added, "Your date didn't last long."

Charlotte scoffed. "No, he wasn't for me. He wouldn't stop talking about his two favourite subjects: rugby and himself."

"Having just dated someone really self-absorbed, I feel your pain," Aya muttered.

"She's referring to Susannah," Gwen clarified quietly.

"Yes, I guessed," Charlotte replied. "I'm sorry to hear that, but I'm glad you two," she nodded at Aya and Gwen, "are friends again. You are friends again, right?"

Aya looked down. "That depends on, well, if Gwen's okay with what I did and is willing to start over."

"Oh, I'm sure she is." Charlotte put an arm around her best friend. "You've never been one to carry a grudge, have you?"

"Nope," Gwen said, leaning in. "And I could really use more friendship right now. As I said, I might not be the easiest or best friend in my low periods, but I always try to make up for it when I'm feeling better."

Charlotte made a disagreeing noise, but Aya replied before she got a chance to speak.

"Please don't think about it like that," she said. "There's not some contract of mutual friendship actions that you have to fulfil. I just want to be part of your life."

"Well said! So, sounds like its settled, then," Charlotte said. "That's good. Now you can show her those drawings."

For once, Gwen said nothing, so Aya had to ask. "What drawings?"

Charlotte gave Gwen a peck on the top of her head and went to hang up her jacket. She called over her shoulder, "After the two of you lost contact, Gwen kept drawing your car and once even sketched you."

"Argh! Why did you tell her that?" Gwen muttered.

Charlotte came back and gave her a maternal smile. "Because the two of you have lost so much time and it seems to me as if you need a bit of help. I know how awkward things can get when two people get close very fast and then something negative tears them apart."

"I suppose," Gwen grumbled, bumping her head, lovingly but irritably, on Charlotte's shoulder when she was close enough.

Charlotte petted the guinea pig in Gwen's hands. "I figured I'd be the one to break the ice and push things along. Like you've done for me in the past."

"True. You never would've patched things up with Matt if I hadn't stuck my nose in."

"Exactly! I got a good three-year relationship out of that!" Charlotte smiled. "I also know that you're not in your best place to communicate right now, so I wanted to help speed things up. Was that okay?"

"Yes," Gwen muttered with some reluctance. "It was helpful. Embarrassing but helpful."

"Sorry about that, duck," Charlotte said. "I should've been more subtle."

This was a like a masterclass on opening up and having a sappy heart-to-heart. Aya wondered if she should be taking notes. Maybe she should've left the best friends to their discussion, but she had to ask the burning question.

"I still don't know what you two were talking about before. Did you actually draw Janet the Jeep?"

Gwen hooked her lower lip with her teeth. "Yes. Twice."

"And you sketched me?"

"Yes. Not very well, though. I was sort of frustrated with you at the time, so I might not have drawn you as flatteringly as I should've."

Aya crossed her arms over her chest. "You mean you made me ugly?"

"I don't think it's possible for you to be ugly," Gwen said. "However, I might've given you horns, huge caterpillar eyebrows, and a massive overbite."

Aya couldn't help but laugh, and Charlotte joined in.

"Go sit in the living room," Gwen said. "I'll give you Meatloaf so you can put her back in her cage in there, Charlotte. I'll join you when I've rustled up some drinks and snacks."

"And the drawings?" Aya dared to ask.

Gwen handed Meatloaf over to Charlotte and then winced at Aya. "Well, the ones of Janet, at least. Charlotte can go get them in my bedroom."

"Sure," Charlotte said. "I'll lock up Meatloaf. Then go get the drawings and leave Aya to peruse them. I have to get out of this tight dress and into some comfy clothes." She walked out of the kitchen, signalling for Aya to come along.

When they were in the living room and Meatloaf was safely in her cage, Charlotte whispered, "Give Gwen a moment to digest everything. She's having a really rough time and needs longer than usual to adapt."

"I bet. She looks like she's been heated up on the wrong setting in a microwave." Aya punched herself on the leg. "No, that came out all wrong. She still looks as attractive as always, just not very healthy. She's clearly been through the wringer."

"She has," Charlotte said grimly. "Which means that if you're not nice to her or if you upset her in any way, I *will* scratch your eyes out. No offence."

"None taken. I'm glad she has such a good friend."

"And I'm glad she's making a new one in you," Charlotte replied. "I'll be right back with the drawings."

Aya smiled to herself as she sat down. Gwen had been right. This interaction going well had given her confidence another boost. This time, a healthy one.

## Chapter Twenty-Five

# BUTCH BEARING

Gwen stood in the kitchen, listening to Aya and Charlotte whisper in the other room. It sounded like leaves rustling in the wind.

She didn't mind that they were talking about her; she knew Charlotte was paving the way for their friendship. That meant she could focus on taking a few deep breaths and watching the beautiful roses.

*They're huge, and there's a dozen of them. They must have cost a fortune, especially for someone on benefits.*

She was happy about the roses, but much happier about seeing Aya again. That truculent demeanour, the awkward speech, that big heart, those graceful features. Not to mention that butch bearing... she had missed it all. And yes, her apology had healed some wounds that she hadn't even acknowledged before.

She made some popcorn and got three cans of different fizzy drinks out of the fridge. While she put it all on a tray, she considered quickly brushing her hair and getting changed but decided against it. If Aya was going to be her friend, she'd see her like this sometimes. She filled her lungs again, enjoying the scent of the roses one last time before leaving the kitchen.

When she walked in, Aya and Charlotte were next to each other on the sofa, checking out Gwen's two drawings of Janet. Gwen could barely remember when she'd drawn them.

Aya looked up, her usually sable-coloured eyes gleaming like black ink in the lamplight. "These are amazing!"

Gwen tried to not fixate on her guest's eyes. Instead she put the tray on the table. "I'm glad you like them. It'd make me happy if you kept them."

"What? Really?"

Gwen handed the popcorn bowl to Charlotte. She never ate much on dates, so she was probably peckish. "Sure, what am I going to do with pictures of your jeep?"

"She's got you there," Charlotte said, taking the bowl.

Aya ran her fingers over the nearest drawing, then rubbed the back of her neck. She was adorable when she was touched and not sure how to respond. "Thank you, Gwen. I-I'd like to return the favour."

Gwen picked up a can of cola but didn't open it. "By drawing a picture of my bicycle? Sure, it's green, still in my parents' garage, and has a puncture," she joked. While her heart wasn't in it, she wanted Aya and Charlotte to have fun.

"No," Aya replied. "I was thinking of something more in my wheelhouse."

"Okay." Gwen sat down next to Charlotte. "Like what?"

"I remember you telling me that endorphins from working out can sometimes help depressed people?"

Gwen put the can back on the table, recalling her babbling on the drive to Chester. "Mm, that's right."

"Then why don't I teach you how to box? It's a great workout and you'll learn some self-defence at the same time. That's always a good idea, especially in a city like ours."

Gwen slumped on the sofa. The depression fatigue that started deep in her marrow and spread throughout her body had hit her like a sledgehammer. Today she'd barely managed to shower, eat, and get dressed. Now Aya expected her to learn to box? Would she have to go to the gym to do it? Buy boxing gear? Would she have the energy to box for more than a minute before she fell in a heap?

She wanted to say no, but she also wanted to spend more time with Aya. More importantly, she didn't want to hurt her feelings by saying no to the kind offer.

Charlotte must've picked up on her unease. "Cool idea! Maybe start smaller and then build up to full-on boxing lessons, though? At the moment, Gwen has limited energy. Don't you, love?"

Relief washed over her. "Yeah! I'm afraid so."

"Sure," Aya said right away. "We can start with practicing the ready position; that means proper stance and posture. We can do that right in this room."

"Okay," Gwen said, her uncertainty slipping through the faked enthusiasm in her voice. "Fair warning: it can be hard to take in new information when you're depressed."

Aya leaned past Charlotte and put her hand on Gwen's. "Hey, it won't be a big deal. Just some fun and movement. If you forget what I teach you or if you get bored and want to stop, that's fine. It doesn't matter."

Aya's hand was rough but warm. Gwen had to stop herself from turning her hand to hold it tight. "All right, if you promise to be patient and not take it personally if I don't understand things or if I run out of energy."

"I swear. We'll just have some fun, duck. No pressure." She turned to Charlotte. "You can join us if you'd like."

"No, that's all right. Not my thing," Charlotte said kindly, adjusting her delicate silk pyjamas. "I think you two should try it, though. What do you think, Gwen?"

Still not sure what she thought, Gwen rubbed an eyebrow and said, "Why not?"

## Chapter Twenty-Six

# BRIGHT SPARK

Aya stood back to check on Gwen. Was she having fun? Was she getting too tired? No, she seemed okay.

They were in Gwen's flat, practising posture and the toe-heel alignment. The different swings would have to come later. Aya had mentioned a hook before, and Gwen had thought she was talking about something to hang her coat on. They had a long way to go.

Still, Gwen was up and about, even appearing a little less listless than the night before.

Aya returned to her position next to Gwen. "Always protect your body, especially your face. Keep your hands up and your chin down. Feet shoulder-width apart, with your right foot in front of the left."

"Like this?"

"Yep, loads better."

Aya suggested a few more corrections to her toe-heel alignment until Gwen stood perfectly balanced.

"So, how is the job search going?" Gwen asked out of the blue.

"Not great so far. I do have another interview tomorrow, though."

Gwen smiled, but it didn't reach her eyes. "Great. What's it for?"

It killed Aya to see how hard Gwen was fighting to seem positive and engaged. "It's an admin job for a company called Explore. They make and publish magazines about hiking, mountaineering, angling, and outdoorsy stuff like that."

"Interesting," Gwen said.

Aya scratched the back of her neck, looking down. "Well, I mean I'd be up to my neck in spreadsheets and paperwork, not dealing with the actual magazines. But yeah, it'd be a job. The pay's not bad, actually."

"That's good. Best of luck! If you want to practise your answers or do any other sort of job interview prep, let me know."

Aya gave Gwen a grateful smile. "Thanks. I will."

"You're welcome. So, um, are we doing anything else today?"

The usual light in Gwen's blue eyes had faded, and her pallid face looked drawn and tired. Even though they'd only been practising stances for about fifteen minutes, Aya made a judgement call.

"Maybe we should call it a day?"

Gwen flopped back into her normal posture. "Probably best. Sorry."

"Hey, don't ever apologise about something like that. You have to work twice as hard to do things now. Of course you'll be knackered. We'll try some more tomorrow."

"Sounds good. Thank you for being patient."

Aya shrugged. "You're always patient with me; the very least I can do is return the favour."

"Especially if I make you tea, right?" Gwen said with another polite smile.

"You don't happen to have any coffee?"

"No. Devil beans don't enter this house! I get enough of them at work."

Aya laughed but took a step back at the venom in Gwen's tone. She held her hands up as if to defend herself. "Wow… Right… so… water's fine."

A smile twitched on Gwen's wan lips. It wasn't the expected laugh, but it looked more genuine than the fake smiles Gwen had been giving today.

That little twitch hit Aya square in the chest. It was an achievement with Gwen feeling like this, and to Aya's surprise, it made her deeply proud to have caused it.

---

The next day's boxing lesson got cancelled. A text came in at 6 a.m. saying:

*Hi Aya. I'm terribly sorry to have to change our plans but I'm in a rubbish state today. I'm just going to sleep. Maybe call my therapist later. So sorry again. Good luck with your interview today, I'm sure you'll rock it!*

Aya thought about Gwen all morning, then on her way to the interview, partially during the job interview—which seemed to go well— and then after it, too. While driving home, she wondered what it must be like being stuck in the meanest, darkest parts of your mind. She knew she couldn't fix Gwen's depression. That wasn't how it worked. However, there had been that twitch of a smile yesterday. Maybe she could cause that again? Let a bit of light into the darkness? Just to let Gwen know that she wasn't alone.

As she wandered into her empty house, Gwen's words about the 'bright spark' came back to her, those moments that gave you something to look forward to and interrupted the grey of everyday life. If Susannah could do that by just breezing in and flirting a little, surely Aya could accomplish it, too? Sure, she couldn't flick champagne-blonde hair and smirk with a sophisticated air, but she could come up with something else. Something real. Something with actual feelings behind it.

She did the dishes her dad had left in the sink, wondering how to show Gwen how much beauty and magic there was in life. Not actual magic, of course, like wizards and crap, just something with a hint of wonder. Something cool, something new, something special. A little boost.

She went upstairs and sat down on her bed, still unsure of what to do. This wasn't really her thing. Boxing was her thing. So was driving, mending stuff, and taking charge. Hell, even shagging could be seen as 'her thing'. But this stuff, the emotional, gentle, and flowery? That would take some thinking.

She undid the top buttons of the white shirt she always wore to interviews, then leaned back and looked around her bedroom as she pondered. Her gaze stuck to a small object on her dresser. *That* was what she should bring Gwen! It would take some explaining, though. She could do that, right? Yeah. She could. It wouldn't be easy, spilling her guts like Bill had taught her, or being sappy and open like Charlotte and Gwen the night before, but she could do it. She chuckled. The first piece of everyday magic she wanted to bring Gwen had been right under her nose.

## Chapter Twenty-Seven

# FIRST DAY OF BOOSTS

Gwen pulled on a robe and dragged herself to the front door. "Okay, stop knocking. I hear you!"

She opened it. There was Aya, in formal trousers and her saffron hoodie, with a sheepish look on her face.

"Aya? Hello." Gwen rubbed her sleep-gritty eyes. "Didn't I text you? I'm in too bad of a shape to box today. Or to socialise in general."

"You did. And I respect that. I'll leave you alone soon. I just have something to drop off."

"Drop off?" Gwen queried, standing aside to let her in.

Aya stopped in the hallway, probably to mark that she wasn't staying long. "So, you know how you wanted a daily, um…" Aya waved in the air as if hoping to waft forth the right words. "I think you've called them pick-me-ups, bright sparks, or tonics?"

"Yes?"

"Well, I'm going to call them boosts, and I'm on a mission to bring you some."

Gwen must've looked sceptical because Aya cringed and clarified. "I mean, I know Charlotte got you a guinea pig, and I think having Meatloaf will help in the long run. In the short run, though, you need something easier and flashier."

"Easier? Flashier?"

"Yeah," Aya said with one of her signature shrugs. "You know, something more fun and low maintenance. Right now, you're struggling to care for yourself, so caring for Meatloaf isn't helping you. Even though her furry face would normally make you smile. Right?"

"Very perceptive," Gwen said, genuinely impressed.

"So, I got you something. Hopefully it'll be a boost."

Gwen leaned against the wall, nearly stabbing her back on a coat hook. "That's *very* sweet, and I'll be happy for whatever you brought me, but Aya, I have to repeat this: my depression can't be cured. Not by anyone or anything."

"I'm not trying to cure it," Aya said vehemently. "I want to give you something to look forward to as you battle through each day. Besides, I would've given this to you anyway."

Gwen couldn't remember ever seeing the cool Aya this enthusiastic. Or was she anxious and covering it up? Whatever it was, it was heartwarming.

"Okay. Thank you for thinking about me. So, what's the thing?"

Aya retrieved something from the big pocket of her hoodie and cupped it in her palm, looking so vulnerable. She held her closed fist up to Gwen, looked her right in the eye, and whispered, "Here."

Her hand opened hesitantly and revealed a smooth, oval stone. It was grey with a band of pale, rosy red going through it.

"That's cute," Gwen said, hiding her bewilderment. How was this pebble a boost?

"I know it's not big or grand, but small things can be important." She took a step closer to Gwen. "It's from Shirahama Beach, close to where my mum grew up. I've never been there, but Mum says it's beautiful. She picked up that stone on the morning of the day she emigrated to Britain." She held it out closer to Gwen, who took it. The pebble still held Aya's body warmth.

They both regarded the stone, and Aya continued her story. "I guess it symbolized a new beginning for Mum. She gave it to me when I quit boxing and was starting my new life."

Gratitude made Gwen choke up. "Wow! Then you can't give it to me, kind as you are. You have to keep it."

"Nah, I never much liked it. I didn't think it brought me any luck. You know, no job, no new purpose, no friends, disaster of a love life. But..." She hesitated. "When I was thinking about a boost for you, I saw it and thought it might bring you better luck. That was the *first* meaning of it."

Aya swallowed so hard that Gwen saw the bobbing of her throat column between the sculpted neck muscles.

"I also... realised that you've been more of a 'new beginning symbol' for me than this pebble has. You've become my first new friend in years, Gwen. You pushed me to dare pursue Susannah, then your sensible side guided me to end it when it was clear she was toxic. You make me want to try new things."

She closed her mouth with a snap, as if wanting to stop it from spilling words. Then she put her hands in her pockets and, again looking sheepish, shrugged.

Gratitude and affection tugged at Gwen. For the first time today, she actually felt something that wasn't a dull hint of disappointment or fear.

"I don't know what to say," she said gently. "This is a wonderful gift. Would your mum be okay with you giving it away?"

"Mum doesn't much care what I do these days. Giving me that stone was the last time we talked about something important. Now, I'm as much a disappointment and puzzle to her as I am to myself, I guess."

"I think you might be projecting. I'm sure she's proud of you."

"Maybe. I don't really know much about what she thinks and feels. Both she and Dad live their lives from day to day, never stopping to remember things, analyse stuff, or talk stuff through. They just happily plough on with everyday life." Aya's gaze went to the stone in Gwen's palm again. "Mum never has much time to spend with me."

"Is that why she never took you to where she grew up?"

"Yeah. That and the fact that she and Dad rarely travel. They work, shop, eat, watch telly, and sleep. That's it." Aya peered down at her boots. "When I ask about going to Japan, Mum says that the flight is too long. I wonder if it's just that she doesn't want to go back."

"Maybe she has bad memories there?"

Aya tilted her head from side to side, weighing the alternatives. "Mm. Maybe. Or more likely in her case, she doesn't see the point in dwelling on her past. Or she doesn't like being with me. Neither of us knows how to spend time with the other; we're too different. Anyway..." She trailed off, scuffing one boot against the other. "Maybe... no, never mind."

"Please tell me?"

Aya looked up from her boots. "The *second* reason that

stone is a boost gift for you is that I figured I'd attach an exciting promise to it."

"An exciting promise?" Gwen prompted, trying to make her voice as comforting as she could.

"I thought I could save up to bring you to Shirahama one day," Aya blurted. "We would walk down the beach so you could find it a pebble friend. Then we could go see the hot springs. At night we could have an adventure in town, try out some proper Japanese food." Aya dipped her chin, avoiding eye contact. "Now that sounds silly, though. Like it would be a gift for me, not you. I don't know what I was thinking. Forget it."

"No! I'd love that! All of that. Japan... wow. I've never been farther from home than Greece."

There was another hint of emotion in Gwen now. Was that a faint throb of hope? Probably not; it was more likely Aya's passion being contagious.

Aya perked up. "Then, when I have a job again and have saved up the money for a few years, I'll buy us a trip. We'll go to Shirahama together?"

Gwen closed her fingers around the smooth stone. "Yes. That sounds amazing."

*If I ever get back above the surface. It's been weeks of this now. Maybe Edward is right. Maybe I do need a higher dose. That way I can be a little more normal for Aya.*

Unaware of her thoughts, Aya gave a shy smile and said, "Anyway. I'll let you get back to recovering. If it's okay, I'd like to come back tomorrow afternoon and bring you another boost?"

"Aya, I'd love that, but you don't need to," Gwen stated kindly but clearly. "You have your own life, and this is so much effort."

*Which I'm not worth.*

"Rubbish," Aya dismissed. "I'll help you get through this, duck. Both because I want to and because giving you a bit of fun, something interesting to add to your day, will be the win I've been searching for."

Gwen couldn't supress her scepticism. "Okay. As long as you get something out of it, too."

"It's not about that for me. Not really. I just want to be there for you. It feels important."

"Thank you," Gwen said, self-loathing jangling her nerves. "I don't deserve such good friends as you and Charlotte. You're both saints."

"Nah, we just found a great person and want to help her feel better. Call me if you need anything."

Aya opened the door, waved goodbye, and left in a hurry.

Clearly, she still struggled with emotional chats. Gwen opened her fingers again and surveyed the stone. That sliver of rosy red running though the grey stone, it was a perfect symbol of Aya's visit on this truly shitty day.

Fatigue flooded her again. Had she eaten today? Not since that small glass of coconut milk to swallow down her antidepressants this morning. Maybe she should make some tea with lots of honey? The tiredness made her ache and decided for her.

*Charlotte will make dinner when she gets home from work. That'll have to be enough.*

Gwen hauled herself back to her bed. The bedroom was stuffy and dark. She should open a window. She should dust the room. She should shower. She should get dressed. She should eat.

All of that was impossible right now. That black, void-like ocean pulled her down, sucking the energy and will to fight right out of her. She fell into bed and closed her eyes.

Something hurt under her hip. She ignored it. She deserved the pain. Then, the pain got too distracting and she removed the cause. It was Aya's pebble. It must have fallen out of her hand and landed on the bed before she did.

She held it in her palm and thought of Aya, the brave woman who wanted to stand by her through this mess. The woman who was broken, too, but in a different way.

Aya's words lingered in a corner of her mind. "Something small can be important."

She peered at her bedside table, remembering that Charlotte had left a packet of those chocolate-covered almonds Gwen loved on there. When was that? Two days ago? Three? Days blurred when she felt like this.

She made herself grab the packet and open it. She popped a few almonds into her mouth. Chewing took so much effort, but if she ate these, she would've done something small that would be important. She swallowed them and drank half of the contents of her water glass. It was lukewarm, but she didn't care. She'd eaten something and drunk something. It was small, but it was a start. She wrapped her arms around herself and let herself fall back into that deep ocean. Mercifully, sleep caught her instead.

## Chapter Twenty-Eight

# SECOND AND THIRD BOOSTS

Aya sat on the stairs to lace up her boots. With her parents at work, the house was so quiet that she could hear the afternoon rain against the windowpanes as clearly as if it was in the room with her.

By her side lay the next boost she wanted to bring Gwen, a beginner's guide to boxing. If Gwen couldn't leave the house or socialise, but still wanted to learn, maybe this could be a good solution. Especially since Gwen liked to read.

She pulled her jacket on and flipped the hood up to ward off the worst of the rain, then ran for the jeep. While driving she noted that the muscles in her shoulders and arms were tight. She wasn't sure if that was down to her weightlifting session this morning or last evening's sparring match with Bill's nineteen-year-old prodigy.

*Jenny. Her name is Jenny. I have to think of her as that, not as some random kid who's taking my place and having a shot at the future I left behind.*

She rolled her shoulders and turned into Gwen's street.

As she parked, she squinted through the rain up at the building and towards Gwen's window. No movement up there. There was a chance that Gwen was asleep. Quite a big chance; Gwen slept most days away at the moment.

Aya had gone online to read up on depression, as well as antidepressant medication and its side effects. Not that it did her much good. All depressed people seemed to have different experiences. Sleeping a lot was a common symptom, though.

She texted Gwen to let her know that she was downstairs and asked if it was okay for her to come up. No reply; she was probably asleep then.

Aya took the stairs instead of the lift, partly because she wanted the extra exercise, partly to shake off some rain, but mainly because she needed more time to think about what to say and do. She wanted to be helpful and sensitive. Almost as much as she wanted any excuse to see Gwen again.

She knocked and waited. The book was heavier in her hand now, awkward somehow. Maybe Gwen wouldn't like it. Maybe it would make her feel pressured into learning how to box when she should be focusing on getting back on her feet.

After what felt like an eternity, the door opened. Gwen was wearing that fluffy robe again. Her hair didn't fall limp and listless like it had lately. Instead, it stood on end on one side. That and the quick blinking and yawning that Gwen was doing made her look like an overgrown toddler after a long nap. In short, she was adorable.

"Hey, sleepy," Aya said. "Sorry to bother you, but I wanted to drop off the next boost." She used her sleeve to wipe the worst of the rain off the cover and then handed over the book.

Gwen took it as if it were a fragile, priceless object.

"Aya. I… It's…" Gwen shook her head as if in disbelief. "You really don't have to do that. I mean, I know I said this before, but I have to repeat that while I'm so very grateful, you don't have to do this every day."

"And if I want to?"

Gwen leaned her head against the doorframe. "I certainly won't stop you. I've, well, I've been thinking about you every waking moment today." She put a hand over her eyes. "Look at me babbling at you while making you stand out there in the stairwell. You must be soaked from the downpour. Come on in."

Aya entered and hung up her jacket. Rain pearled on its waxed canvas and then dripped down on Gwen's floor. "Ah! Sorry, duck. I'm making a puddle."

"That's okay. Charlotte will happily clean up later; she says cleaning is her therapy. She's the dream housemate."

"I'd say so. Can you send her over to our house later, so I don't have to do so much of the cleaning?"

"*Our* house?"

"Yes, I live with my parents. Pretty sure I told you that?" Her heart began to pound. She could hear Susannah's remarks and mocking tone when she'd told her that she lived with her parents.

Gwen put her hand over her eyes. Was the light bothering her? Aya had read that antidepressants could make you light sensitive.

"Yes, I think you did," Gwen mumbled. "Everything is a confusing haze right now. I can barely remember my name."

"Don't worry about it." Aya saw that water was pouring off her boots and took them off before she went farther into the flat. "I plan to rent somewhere as soon as I get a job. If I can ever afford the deposit."

"I know. The housing market is murder for anyone under forty-five, even here in Stoke," Gwen muttered.

Aya followed her hostess into the kitchen. Meatloaf's cage was in there now. With slow movements, Gwen got a cucumber out of the fridge and began cutting off tiny pieces.

"Sorry for doing this while you're here, but I have to make the most of my awake time. Charlotte is being a hero and cleaning the cage and feeding Meatloaf when I'm too ill to do it, but I still want to treat the gluttonous piglet with extra cucumber so she'll… I don't know… like me, I suppose."

"No worries," Aya said, sitting down. "I just wanted to drop off the book and chat to you. I can do that while you're dicing. In fact, chop off a piece for me."

"Sure. Here you go."

Aya munched while Gwen filled Meatloaf's bowl and put it in the cage.

"She will, you know. Like you, I mean." Aya pointed to the chomping guinea pig.

"I hope so. I don't have much energy or affection to spend on her right now. She deserves a better owner than me."

"That's the depression talking. You'll get over the worst of it, and then you can shower her with affection. Besides, she's not a child; she's a pet. As long as she's fed, safe, and has a clean home, she'll be fine.'

"I'm pretty sure she also needs company," Gwen mumbled while squatting on her haunches to watch Meatloaf eat.

"And even when you're this ill, you are still giving her that." Gwen looked over at her with confusion, so Aya clarified. "Look at you. Most people, if they were in such a bad state that they could barely take care of themselves, wouldn't spend precious time and energy worrying about a guinea pig that's clearly getting its basic needs met."

Gwen scrunched her face up. "You don't think so?"

"Nope, most people are more selfish than you." She chewed her last bite of cucumber. "Not to mention being less aware of the creatures around them than you are."

"Really?"

"Absolutely. No one has ever seen or understood me the way you do. And I know you're like that with everyone. I've witnessed it with these bad boys," Aya said, pointing at her eyes.

Gwen didn't laugh, but Aya could have sworn that the twitch of a smile returned for just a millisecond.

"What's it like?" Aya said before she could stop herself. "Being depressed?"

Gwen's shoulders curled in, and she sat down fully. "Where to start? Well. Hm. It differs for everyone. Some describe it as a dark room in your mind that you can't get out of. For me, it's a deep, black ocean."

"An ocean? Is it pretty?"

*Of course not. It's her illness, stupid!*

"No, not like a real ocean is. It's just scary. In my case, this huge, void-like ocean has layers." She held up a hand, palm down. "First there's usually sadness and loss of energy, sometimes with annoyance at everyone and everything. Almost like when you're grieving." She lowered the hand a step. "Then there's negative thoughts, usually self-loathing ones, like 'you're just a burden to everyone' or 'you don't deserve food or happiness.' Also, the classic 'you'll never feel okay again.' That's what I think of when people talk about the demons in your mind."

Aya tugged her shirt collar. She wasn't equipped for this conversation. Why had she asked? "Okay. Um. So, what's the bottom layer, the worst one?"

"Emptiness." Gwen shivered, staring into space. "You lose your emotions and any form of caring about things. Once, I stabbed a fruit knife into my hand, just to see if I'd feel something more than the easily ignorable physical pain. You know, regret over having done it, fear that I might've severed a nerve, disgust at the blood pooling around my hand and dripping off the table." She looked down at the back of her hand. "I didn't. I just sat and watched it bleed for ages until my dad walked in and took me to hospital. It was like it didn't matter, somehow. Nothing did. That was when I was diagnosed with depression."

Aya saw a scar on Gwen's left hand. A white, raised line on the bit between her thumb and forefinger.

Gwen put her other hand on her chest and was taking long, shaky breaths.

"I shouldn't have asked," Aya whispered. "Now you feel worse."

"I'm glad that you did," Gwen said, her voice breaking. "If you can understand what's happening in my head, my actions might make sense. And I'll feel like I have to apologise less."

Aya cleared her throat to get rid of the lump that had formed there. "You never have to apologise." Her brain worked frantically to think of something to lighten the lead-heavy mood. "Not unless you put artichoke on pizza."

Gwen rolled her eyes. "In that case, I owe you an apology. I love artichoke."

"What? Artichoke is an insult to vegetables and shouldn't go on anything, especially not on the marvel that is pizza! And don't get me started on pineapple!"

"Fine, fine." Gwen held up her hands in surrender. "We'll leave the pizza debate." She stood and fetched the boxing guide Aya had brought her, then leafed through it. "This looks interesting. Not too technical or tedious."

"No, it's good. I decided to buy you a copy because it was so helpful to me when I started boxing. There are pictures showing the ready position and all the main punches. You already have the stance sorted."

Gwen closed the book. "That's kind of you to say, but I'm pretty sure I've forgotten all about it."

"Good, I get to show you again and feel important for being a teacher."

Finally, Gwen smiled, though Aya could tell it was fake. She let it slip, not wanting to ruin the lighter mood they were cultivating.

Gwen snapped her fingers as if she'd just remembered something important. "I never asked how your job interview went!"

"Pretty good, I think. It's mainly blokes who work there, and they're the kind of rugged, quiet guys that I'm used to from the gym, so I seemed to fit in. Hopefully I gave them the answers they wanted."

"Did they tell you when they'd let you know?"

Aya clicked her tongue. "That's the annoying thing. They want me to talk to their boss, who's on holiday right now, so basically, I'll have another interview before they decide. They did say that I was one of the three people who passed this first interview, so there's that at least."

"I think you'll get it," Gwen said with an earnest expression. "I don't know why, but I have a feeling this is the job for you."

"I hope so." Aya's stomach clenched. Time for a subject change. "The real question today is if that boxing handbook was a proper boost?"

Gwen hugged the book to her chest. "Absolutely."

"You sure? I know this is more in my line of interest than yours, so maybe it's not a real boost for you. I just think boxing could be a fun way of getting your serotonin levels up and *that* would become a boost." It sounded feeble even to Aya's own ears.

"I get what you were thinking, and I'm sure boxing will be a boost for me one day. Right now, it's a boost in different way."

"Yeah? How?"

Gwen held the book closer against her fluffy robe and the bare, pale chest underneath it. "Because you thought about me enough to search this book out for me. And then you came through that hideous rain to bring it to me."

They shared a long look, and by the end of it, that faint tug at the corners of Gwen's mouth was back.

Outside, the rain picked up, knocking against the window as if it wanted to come in. Aya didn't care; nothing could distract her from her suddenly sunny mood.

---

The next day, the afternoon sun had overcome Stoke's usual rain. Aya had just been let into Gwen's flat and managed to trip over a pair of dainty shoes.

Gwen caught her by the arm. "Whoops."

Aya steadied herself. "Shit. There's my huge, clomping boots getting in the way *as always*."

"They're not huge or clomping. I always thought they were cool with that worn-leather look. Anyway, that wasn't their fault. Or yours. Charlotte came in late last night after a date and must've just kicked off her slingbacks. I don't know why she didn't put them away this morning. She must've been in a hurry."

Gwen picked up the high-heeled shoes and placed them on the shoe rack. Aya quickly averted her gaze when it became clear that bending forward made Gwen's robe open at the chest.

"Um, how are you today?" Aya croaked.

"About the same as yesterday. Maybe a little bit better, it's hard to gauge. How are you?"

"Less drenched than yesterday. Thank goodness the weather picked up."

"Yes! The last thing anyone needs is the weather being as depressing as my brain."

Aya chuckled. "It amazes me that you still make jokes even though you can't see the funny in anything."

"It's a coping mechanism. And a fundamental part of my personality, I guess. Come into the kitchen. Do you want something to drink?"

She walked off, and Aya followed her. "Water would be great. It's not just the weather that's different from yesterday, you know."

Gwen ran the tap, feeling the water before filling a glass. "No? What else?"

"Today's boost isn't something I bought for you."

Gwen handed over the glass. "No? Are you telling me that you stole something for me?"

Aya swallowed a mouthful of water and grimaced at Gwen. "No, I'm telling you that the boosts won't all be objects. I'm not that much of a capitalist."

"Ah, I see. Well that sounds less criminal."

Aya rolled her eyes, put the glass on the table, and got her phone out. "Some of the stuff I have planned are outings. But you can't leave the flat right now, I get that, so I made you something."

"Is it cake? If so, it's got to be bloody small to be wedged in the pockets of those tight jeans."

"It's not cake." Aya pointed to her phone. "It's something in here."

"Okay?"

Embarrassment burned in Aya's face and neck. Would this be awkward? "Do you, um, remember when we were kids and we all burned CDs for our friends with our favourite songs?"

Gwen scrunched her face up for a brief moment. "Aha, you made me a playlist?"

"Exactly," Aya said, incredibly relieved she didn't have to explain further. "I assumed you had a Spotify account, so I created a playlist and made it public. I named it 'Boosts for Gwen.' It's all songs that rev me up when I'm feeling sad or tired."

"Aw, that's so sweet of you! Thank you so much."

"You're welcome," Aya mumbled.

Gwen came to stand next to her and peered at the screen. "Hey, I know some of these," she said. She used her forefinger to scroll down. "I've never heard most of them, though."

"Go get your mobile and download it. I want to make sure it works."

Gwen poked a finger into her ribs. "Fine, bossy boots!"

She walked off to get her phone, leaving Aya to drink her water and wait for her return. That was when Aya realised that there wasn't a thing in the world she wouldn't do for this woman. And just how happy that made her.

*Chapter Twenty-Nine*

# FOURTH AND FIFTH BOOST

Gwen had pushed herself that day, managing both a shower and getting dressed. She knew from the last four days that somewhere between 1 and 3 p.m., Aya would text that she was downstairs and ask if she could come up with her boost gift and her steadfast wish to help. Today Gwen had spent her daily ration of energy on getting ready for that. She lay on the sofa now, trying to stay awake, trying to keep the hateful thoughts at bay.

They'd rolled through her mind like thunder all day, reminding her of how little use there was in her cleaning herself up. How Aya would soon hate her. How the planet was dying around them. How she'd probably get a terrible disease and die herself, and how utterly she'd deserve that.

She watched Meatloaf run in and out of the small tunnel Charlotte had bought for her cage.

*Well, I found it online, ordered it, and paid for it, Charlotte just did the legwork by going to the shop to pick it up.*

"I'm not completely useless, am I, Meatloaf?"

Her pet stopped and stared at her as if she'd said something offensive.

"Calm down, I was only making conversation," Gwen said with a shake of the head.

A staccato rhythm of far too many knocks rang out. "That'll be Aya, Meatloaf. Go open the door, would you?" Gwen sat up. "No, of course not. You stay there and be cute, piggy. We all have our jobs in life."

After the door had been opened and Aya was coming in, Gwen got a serious head rush and had to lean against the wall.

Aya held out her hands to steady her. "Gwen! Whoa. Are you okay?"

"Yeah. I might've overdone things today. I'm not used to being this active anymore."

"Have you eaten anything?"

Shame made her look away. For a moment she couldn't remember, but deep down she knew the answer. "Only tea and some coconut milk to swallow my pills with this morning."

"Well, I bet that has something to do with it," Aya said in a, for her, unusually incriminating tone. "Is there anything I can make for you? Something I can go get that you think you might eat?"

Gwen's head swam. "I-I don't know. Something sugary and filling, maybe? I think I have some chocolate digestives in the kitchen."

Aya placed an arm around her waist. "Here, let me steady you, and we'll go find those biscuits."

She was so warm and smooth in the compression shirt she wore. It was as tight as a second skin and soft against Gwen's cheek. Aya was so solid, but still gentle in her movements. It was perfect to just lean on her and be towed along. She smelled good, too. Gwen halted. That wasn't Aya's normal scent.

"Why do you smell like... dried flowers or something?"

"Ah. Yeah. I might've spent way too long in that shop on the way over here."

"What shop?" Gwen asked as Aya led her to a kitchen chair and made her sit down.

Aya gave her shy, lopsided smile, and the sight of that dimple made Gwen even dizzier for some reason. "A tea shop."

"Tea shop?"

"Yep. You know, they sell teas."

"I know that, Aya." She shook her head. "I was trying to prompt you for more info on why you were in one."

"Oh, right. Your daily boost. You love tea, so I thought that cool, unusual teas might be good. I don't know." Aya scratched the back of her neck in a self-conscious way. "Maybe I don't know you well enough to tell what might be a boost for you? Especially not when it has to be objects and not stuff we can go out and do. I'm much better at activities."

"No! Flavoured teas are great." Gwen tried to fill her words with all the enthusiasm that her wonky brain no longer produced. "Thank you so much. I'm normally a regular tea kind of woman, but I'm willing to experiment."

"I'll let the single ladies know," Aya said with waggling eyebrows.

"Stop it, you perv. You know what sort of experimenting I meant."

That reminded her of her lost sex drive. Yet another way she knew when things were bad. She enjoyed sex in all its forms, but when the depression crept in, sex crept out. She chased the thought away. "Anyway, can I see the tea? I hope you didn't spend too much money on it. Your wallet must be pretty lean these days."

"It wasn't that pricy. Hang on, I left it in my jacket pocket."

She went out to the coatrack in the hallway. Gwen watched her go. It was bizarre how the kitchen shrunk and darkened when Aya left it. She had such a presence. She didn't usually say a lot, but just by being in a room, she could change it.

*How does she do that?*

Aya walked back in with those proud strides that belied her short stature. In her hand was a cardboard box of tea.

Gwen accepted it and read the contents out loud. "Stoke-on-Trent blend: A fragrant tea with local flavours." She looked up at Aya who stood over her. "Local flavours? What, like oatcakes?"

"Oi! We have other flavours than oatcakes around here. We're a very tasty city!"

"Fine, fine! I wasn't putting Stoke-on-Trent down, just asking. What does it actually taste of then?"

Aya shrugged. "Put kettle on, duck, and we'll find out together," she said in an even broader Stokie accent than normal.

Gwen went to get up, but Aya put a gentle but firm hand on her shoulder. "No wait! You were dizzy. Stay there. I'll make us tea and find those chocolate digestives."

"Okay. Thank you. They're in the cabinet over the microwave, I think."

She watched Aya fill the kettle. Her movements were so efficient, not an ounce of energy wasted. The muscles in her arm and shoulder jostled as she lifted the full kettle and put it into place.

Gwen leaned her head in her hands and regarded her guest, realising she could watch Aya for hours. She only wished she could draw again. If she could, she knew exactly who all her drawings would be of.

––––––––––

The next morning was a Saturday. Gwen knew this the second she woke because it was late enough to be light out and Charlotte was still home, making breakfast and talking to Meatloaf in the kitchen. The scent of toast, butter, and that fragrant tea Aya had bought wafted into Gwen's bedroom. It made her nauseous.

She groaned at herself. If she felt better, she'd get up and greet Charlotte, take over the breakfast duties, and play caterer to her hard-working best friend. She'd apologise for Charlotte being forced to do all the cleaning and cooking and make silly jokes that she knew Charlotte liked.

If she felt better, she could be a better friend to Aya, thank her for everything she'd done and find ways to return the favour.

If she were better, she could work. She could draw. She could maintain her appearance. She could have fun. She could be of some goddamn use to the world and herself.

The self-loathing made her more nauseous than the food smells had.

Her eyes snapped open. The self-loathing. She felt it more strongly than she had in a long time. She'd thought she was on her way down to that deepest level of her depression ocean – the cold, nothingness. Now, while this wasn't a good feeling, she was feeling something.

She forced herself to push the covers off. Then to sit

up. Was she improving? She tried to check and found only painful thoughts and that tiredness leeching deep into her bones. No. Not improving. It was never that fast or easy to improve. But she had truly felt something, without the dampening filter depression could cover emotions in. More importantly, she had a quiet thrumming in her veins saying that something had to change. Was there a thin thread of ability to fight running through her now?

Gwen blinked. She had no idea how, but something had to give. Upping the medication or whatever it took, she wanted to protect that weak thread of wanting to fight. She needed to be better, before everything that she was sunk to the bottom of that ocean for good. Not just for Charlotte or Aya, but for herself, she could cling to that frail thread. But how?

*Wait. You pay someone to figure that out.*

"Charlotte! Could you come in here?"

Charlotte came rushing in with a piece of half-eaten toast in one hand. "What's wrong, duck?"

"Nothing. I just think I need to see Edward right away. Could you please drive me? I don't think I have the energy to walk."

Charlotte's posture slumped. "Oh, love, you know I normally would, but I'm incredibly hungover. I don't think I can drive."

"Oh. Okay. Well, I'll just call an Uber or a taxi."

"I'll do that. You just take your medication and get dressed. Then you—" She stopped. "No, wait, why don't we call Aya? She's been dying to help you in some way. She'd love to take you."

"I've already bothered her enough," Gwen mumbled.

Charlotte took a quick bite of toast. "Nonsense. Call her or I will."

Gwen found herself coming back from disassociating. How long had she been staring into space, disconnected from the situation and her own body and mind?

The answer was long enough for her friend to sit down by her side with a worried expression. The toast was gone, too. It must've been long enough for Charlotte to eat it. Disassociating was a bad symptom; it belonged at the bottom level of the ocean.

"I'm calling Aya, and then you're going to see Edward," Charlotte stated. "Something's shifting, right?"

"Yes."

"Are you getting better or worse?"

"I don't know. And that scares me."

Charlotte combed her fingers through her unwashed hair. She must be really hungover to not have her beloved chestnut tresses cleaned and styled. "Are you feeling something?"

"Yes," Gwen croaked.

"That's good, right?"

"I think so."

Charlotte gave her a quick hug. "That's a start. Try to get up and have your medicine and something to eat. Or at least the tea I started making for you. I'll call Aya."

She left, presumably to get her phone, and Gwen watched her leave with the knowledge that she didn't deserve such incredible friends.

---

About thirty minutes later, Gwen sat next to Aya in Janet the Jeep. She'd drunk two cups of tea, brimming with honey, in addition to a full glass of coconut milk with her antidepressants. That, and the miracle of wash cloths and dry shampoo, made her look and feel almost human again.

"Thanks for the lift," she said, shame roiling in her sloshing stomach.

Aya didn't take her eyes off the road. "Please don't thank me, shug. You know I want to help you."

"I should thank you, you've been amazing. You've spoiled me with attention, support, and those lovely presents."

"Ah! That reminds me, I brought your next boost. It's in the glove compartment."

"Aya. You didn't—"

"Stop telling me I don't have to do that. Just accept the gift and make me happy."

Gwen hesitated. "All right. Thank you. Again." She opened the glove compartment. "Is that another book?"

"Yep. Not on boxing, though."

Gwen took out the dog-eared, worn book and read the cover. "*Welsh for Beginners*?"

Aya nodded, gaze still on the road. "The second-hand bookshop didn't have a 'Welsh for those who learned some as kids but can't remember all of it,' so I thought you could use this one. Also, since I bought it in a charity shop, we're both doing a good deed."

Gwen skimmed through the book, trying to focus on the words even though her mind was in flux. "It's perfect. Wow. I didn't even know Stoke-on-Trent had a charity bookshop."

"Our city has a lot of great things," Aya said as she stopped to let an old man cross the road. "You shouldn't write Stoke off just because it's had a tough time."

Gwen watched Aya's focused face as she checked that

the man had crossed safely and then carefully drove past him.

"Yes. Best of all is its people," Gwen said, brushing away a lock of hair that had fallen onto Aya's slim nose.

Aya threw her a quick glance, an amused but maybe a little embarrassed expression lighting up her graceful features. "Don't get all soppy on me. Now, is your therapist on this road up ahead? To the left?"

"Yes. That's his office on the second floor of that grey building."

"Great. I'll wait in the car while you're in there."

"No, Aya. I can't ask you to do that. You'll get bored!"

"I won't. I have snacks and a game on my phone to play. Not to mention your Welsh book. I should pick up some phrases for our future trip."

"Our future trip?"

"Sure, if flying to Japan is on our list of boost things to do when you feel better, obviously going to Wales should be, too. We'll tour the cosy villages you have family in so you can chat to all your cousins about singing, mining, and Tom Jones."

Gwen cocked her head with incredulity. "Wow. That was a lot of kindness muddled with a lot of annoying stereotypes!"

"I give and I take. Now, go see your therapist." Aya grabbed the book. "I need to look up what 'can I have three beers and a packet of crisps' is in Welsh."

Gwen got out of the car. "You know, you really are the sweetest person I've ever met."

"Shh. I'm a tough boxer from Stoke. I can't have you ruining my rep like that."

Gwen stared right into those compassionate, dark eyes. "Your secret's safe with me."

Aya was still for a moment before quietly saying, "And you're safe with me, Gwen. You've shown me what true courage is by fighting this shitty illness you've got." She looked at her hands, which fidgeted on the wheel. "You've also showed me the truth about myself. And about Susannah, too. For that… I guess I really want to help you and keep you safe and happy."

"Likewise. You've got a friend for life, tough boxer. You're not getting rid of me now."

"Well, I will for a while because I'll be damned if I let you miss your appointment. Hurry on up to your head shrinker!"

Gwen almost laughed. It was there, bubbling up in her brain. Before it could reach her lips, though, it was dragged down into that unfathomable ocean in her mind. Instead, she blew Aya a kiss and closed the car door.

She headed up to Edward's office, her steps a little lighter.

## Chapter Thirty

# GETTING BACK UP AGAIN

Aya did one last bicep curl before putting the barbell down on the gym's scuffed floor. She should've done a few more reps, but she was too excited. It was only ten minutes since she'd got a call from her possible future boss.

The managing director of Explore was back from his holiday and wanted to interview her and the other two candidates for the job. The way the conversation had gone, she thought he was leaning towards hiring her. That was not just her 'glass half full' mentality having returned; she was pretty convinced that he wanted her for the job.

*I can't wait to tell Gwen.*

Aya gulped down a protein shake and headed for the showers. She quickly washed off, got dressed, and put her wet hair up in a ponytail, not wasting time drying it. She almost forgot her deodorant in her rush. She had to tell Gwen her good news.

On the way out, she gave Bill a resounding clap on the back and said, "I'm off. Take care, you old sod!"

"You're in a good mood, kid." He guffawed. "That girl of yours getting some more flowers?"

She stuck her tongue out at him, then laughed along and left. Only when she started the jeep and drove off did she realise that he'd called Gwen "her girl." She sniggered. She'd have to explain to Bill that they were just friends.

To be fair, she *had* bought something for Gwen. Not flowers, but a package of light blue hair dye. She'd given this particular gift a lot of thought. Some of her presents had been nice but, in hindsight, not great as boosts. However, she knew that Gwen got a boost from the blue streaks in her hair. Now that her hair was all faded, even the blue seemed less vibrant. This gift would fix that.

She parked Janet the Jeep and hurried up to Gwen's flat, taking the stairs two steps at a time.

When she got there, she stopped dead. The front door was ajar. Why the hell would that be open? She couldn't think of any natural, safe reason. Especially not in a big, overcrowded apartment building in quite a rough part of Stoke. She scanned the surroundings but there was no one around.

Not on this side of the door, at least.

Fear tingling her skin and making the little hairs on her arms rise, she pushed it all the way open. Gwen was sitting in the hallway, unscathed.

Aya's relief made her weak in the knees. Her mind had painted pictures of burglaries, abductions, self-harm. She took a closer look. Gwen was safe and intact, but was she okay?

Aya crouched down next to her. "Shug, orate?" When Gwen didn't answer, she made her question less Stokie so Gwen would understand. "Are you all right, shug? What's happened? Why is the door open?"

Gwen sat curled in on herself, arms around her knees. She wasn't rocking back and forth, but she looked like she might at any moment. Dark rings were under her wide eyes and tears streamed down her cheeks, but she wasn't sobbing or making any noise. It was almost creepy, but Aya pulled herself together and repeated her questions.

"Breakdown," Gwen slurred, as if in a trance. "I knew you were coming, so I opened the door in case I couldn't do it later, and then everything just fell apart."

"Fell apart?" Aya croaked.

"I had a panic attack, convinced my heart was giving out and that I'd die, and then everything… drained away. I think I dissociated. I don't know how long I've sat here. I don't know how I'm meant to get up. I don't know anything anymore," Gwen said in that dead voice, staring into space.

Aya was lost for words and actions. She tried to tug her hair, but it was slicked down in that wet ponytail. She couldn't even do that. Panic rose in her. Part of her wanted to shake Gwen, to make her less weird and vacant; another part wanted to hold her close until everything was okay again.

Aya wiped her damp palms on her jeans. "Okay. Um. I'm just going to close the door. U-unless you want me to drive you to the hospital? Or to your therapist?" She brushed tears away from Gwen's cheeks. Her face was cold to the touch; only the tears felt hot.

"No." Gwen looked at her as if she'd just realised Aya was there. "No, there's no need. I know this must look bad, I suppose it is, but it's not dangerous."

"Are you sure?" Aya said with a shaky voice, closing the door. "It looks bloody dangerous! I'm worried."

"Don't be, I've gone through this plenty of times. I'm sorry for scaring you and for looking this terrible."

"You could never look terrible." Aya realised that she

meant it. Gwen was both scary and paler than death, but she was still beautiful to her. Despite, or maybe because of, how her eyes looked now. Gwen's eyes were pretty and normal when they met; during the depressive phase they'd been dull and listless; now they shone with a supernatural intensity, like they were lit from within. Her skin, while still pale, was less matte and had a slight blossom of rosiness at the cheekbones.

"I can't tell for certain if I'm worsening or improving," Gwen slowly said. "Yesterday, when I talked to Edward, he said these phases often get worse before they get better."

"So, this is things being worse? Or improving?" Aya whined in bewilderment. "I don't… I don't know what to do." She sank to the floor with a thud. "Gwen, you're crying soundlessly and helplessly on the floor in the hallway with the *bloody front door open*, and you might've done that for hours as far as we know." For some reason, she paused to tap her fitness watch, as if seeing what time it was would answer how long Gwen had sat there. "Shit. I don't even know what this dissociating is, but it doesn't sound bloody good, shug! How can any of that be a sign of that you're improving?"

Gwen puffed out a shallow breath. When had she last taken a deep breath? "I know this is hard to understand, but I can promise you that I've been through worse. I've spent days on the floor, or in my bed, just staring into nothing. No tears coming, no forethought to open the door so that someone could check up on me. I know this sounds crazy, but this could be a step forward."

"Okay, I trust you and you know best, but… I'm so sorry, I just don't get it."

They locked eyes for a while before Gwen reached up to cup her cheek and rub a thumb along it. "Aya, it's never going to make sense. My useless brain is just completely, bloody broken," she said with a hollow laugh.

Something in Aya tore open at the dejection in Gwen's face and voice. She put her hand over Gwen's on her cheek. "It's not broken, duck. It's different and has to work harder. Sometimes that means it gets knocked down. It always gets back up again, though, right?"

Gwen watched her for a moment. Then she sniffed and in a quiet, small voice said, "Like a boxer?"

Aya's heart thumped with affection. "Yeah, shug. Just like a boxer."

"Then I should get up," Gwen said, her voice still small but now with more life in it. "Only, I'm ashamed to say it, but I don't know if I can. Aya... can you help me off the floor?"

"Of course."

She knew Gwen was probably thinking that she'd give her a hand up, but that wasn't enough in Aya's opinion. Gwen had fought enough today without having to fight to stand, too.

Aya planted her feet. "Shug, I'm going to lift you. Don't worry, I've got you. But make sure to let me know if you want me to stop, okay?"

Gwen's eye went wide. "What? Lift me? Aren't I too heavy? I'm taller than you?"

"Yeah, but you weigh about as much as a cup of coffee," Aya said while crouching to put one arm under Gwen's knees and the other around her back.

She lifted her in a bridal pose. Gwen didn't ask her to stop or second-guess the action. Instead she leaned into Aya's embrace, wrapping her arms around her neck and lying there in surprising serenity.

"I'll carry you to the sofa."

"Thank you," Gwen murmured, her breath tickling Aya's neck. "Then let me sleep."

"Are you sure? Isn't that dangerous?"

"Sure, if you have a concussion. Not if you have depression."

"Oh, right." Aya cringed. "So, sleeping is a good idea?"

"Yes, I'll sleep and maybe I can eat or drink something and see how I feel."

"Okay. I'll put you down on the sofa. After that I'll get you some biscuits and leave them on the coffee table for when you wake up."

"No, stay with me," Gwen said, her voice suddenly urgent.

Aya was by the sofa now, still with her arms full of Gwen. She scanned the room for places to sit. "Um, sure. I'll go get a chair from the kitchen."

"No, I meant stay with me on the sofa. Your hair is wet and you smell of that pine soap from your gym, so you've worked out and you're probably tired. Rest with me?"

"Okay, Sherlock Holmes," Aya joked.

She gently laid Gwen on the sofa and tried to settle in next to her. There wasn't much room, but her hostess budged over so they could stretch out close to each other without Aya falling off the sofa.

Gwen's body now radiated feverish warmth. It was a striking contrast to how cold she'd been lately.

Aya propped her arm under her head as a pillow. All was silent for a moment.

"You know," Gwen said, so quiet that Aya had to strain to hear her, "no one has ever done this."

"Done what?"

"Not tried to fix it, like my friends tend to do. Or

shied away, like my parents. No one has just… stayed with me. No one has seemed this comfortable, this… secure, despite me being like *this*."

The statement, as well as Gwen's vulnerable voice, made Aya's heart crack into a thousand shards.

"I'm not scared. And I don't need to cure you. I'll stay right here with you for as long as it takes. Hell, I'll stay until the stars go out. You just rest, shug," Aya replied.

"Thank you. For staying."

"Thank you for needing my company. People don't usually need me around. I'm glad you do."

Their bodies lay puzzle-piece tight against each other, their hips and arms pressed together and everything else brushing close. They could feel every movement and fidgeting of the other. The heat where their bodies touched was so palpable that for a moment it distracted Aya from everything else. She engaged her muscles to keep her frame from encroaching on Gwen's space, not wanting to disturb her or distract them both by touching too much.

Aya watched the faded ceiling but was very aware of Gwen's breaths slowing and deepening. Her own breaths were calming, too, as her worry over Gwen—and any possibly distracting touching—quieted. Her usual positivity took its place. Gwen knew her mind and body; if she said this change was improvement, it was. Aya only had to trust her and keep asking how she could help.

*I can do that.*

She relaxed into the sofa and against the warm woman next to her. All was quiet but for the ticking of Gwen's wristwatch and Meatloaf snuffling about in her cage.

"Have I scared you off yet?" Gwen mumbled, half asleep.

Aya considered that for a while. "No. You've given me

a purpose. I'm meant to be by your side. I get to have your back while you're fighting. I like that."

"I like it, too. I'm so glad to have someone who just rides out the storm with me."

Something occurred to Aya. "What did you mean before, by that your friends try to fix it?"

"Most people, even Charlotte at times, get scared and want to do something to make me better again, to make me normal," Gwen said, her voice muffled by drowsiness. "They freak out when they can't find a solution. It's a kind sentiment, but not what I need."

"This was scary," Aya admitted, "but I'm learning how to handle it."

"Just wait until you've seen me have a real panic attack. Charlotte called an ambulance the first two times."

"Then I'll ask her what she does now instead."

Gwen hummed her agreement.

Silence fell again.

"Are you sure you don't want to leave?" Gwen whispered.

"Leave what? The sofa?"

Gwen shuffled a little, making their fingers brush. "No, this friendship."

"I'm sure. It's where I belong."

"Where you belong?"

Aya kept watching the ceiling. It was easier to admit to things now, when they were sleepy and quiet and there only seemed to be the two of them in the whole wide world. "Yeah. This is a terrible thing to say when you are fighting for control of your life and mind, but things are falling into place for me."

"They are?"

"Mm-hm. I know what gives me pride and confidence

now, and it wasn't what I thought it would be. I figured it was something like being a famous boxer and dating someone like Susannah. I know better now."

Gwen shuffled about again. "Okay. What is it then?"

"I think I'm about to be employed again, and that'll give me a sense of pride; I'm sparring with a young boxer, helping her fulfil her dreams." She turned her head to face the sleepy blonde next to her. "And most of all, it feels like a win whenever I can help you. And whenever someone as smart, funny, kind, and good as you wants to be with me... and, I don't know, *approves* of me..." Aya groaned. "Not that I just want to be with someone I can help. Or someone who approves of me."

"I don't approve of you. I admire you," Gwen answered without hesitation.

"Oh, give over!"

"No, I mean it." Those blue eyes shone with sincerity. "Your life fell apart, and you had to rebuild it. Most people would've rebuilt it like their old life and their old dreams. You dared to start over, to go where life led you."

"It led me to you," Aya said with a shrug.

"Yes, but you decided to take the steps towards me. To not run from the mess that comes with staying with me. And you decided to help that young boxer. And to get a job that wasn't all excitement or fun. What does that make this new Aya?"

"An adult?"

Gwen stifled a yawn. "Sure, but also selfless and responsible. That's something to admire. That's something for you to be proud and confident over."

"That's what I was trying to say! I just didn't have all your insightful words for it. How do you do that, clever clogs?"

Gwen tapped her skull. "Side effect of a broken brain."

"Nah, I think you have a gift for understanding people and our complexities. You should use that in your art."

"Well, I might have lots of time for that," Gwen said, frowning. "Coffee4U can't keep letting me take sick leave. They can't stay this short-staffed, and they can't afford to pay both me and someone else to take my shifts. They can't fire me, but they could nicely ask me to leave."

"Then do it, shug. Focus on your art full time. Sell more drawings online. Or get a job as an illustrator. You're brilliant; we'll see if we can't find a way to make it work."

Gwen yawned. "Thank you. Maybe. Let's not talk about that now. I need sleep. Then food. After that, I can examine how my mind is doing. Thinking about what to do for a living will have to wait."

"Of course, beautiful. Just sleep. We can solve everything else later."

"Okay." Gwen moved her head to rest the tip of her chin on Aya's shoulder and then closed her eyes. Their faces were so close that Aya felt her every breath.

She watched Gwen fall asleep, worried brow smoothing and a slight smile forming on those lips that had been so tense earlier.

It was like seeing a miracle.

## Chapter Thirty-One

# THOUGHTS

That night, Gwen was on her own. After they'd woken and eaten some sandwiches, Aya had left to spar with... what was the girl's name again, Jenny? She'd been buzzing; clearly the sparring meant a lot to Aya.

Now Gwen was alone, but not lonely. She had Meatloaf in her arms, and soon Charlotte would be home. Charlotte. Gwen would have to tell her about today's breakdown.

She stood by the window, patting Meatloaf and looking out at the view. On one side was Stoke, and in the other direction was Hanley. She tried to figure out in what direction Muscles & Mitts lay. Where was Aya's gym, and where inside the building was Aya? Was she sparring in the ring? Working out in the main area? Chatting to Bill somewhere? Showering that frustratingly perfect body?

Where was Aya, the woman with the strong arms to hold you with and the sensitive heart to appreciate you with? She remembered the warmth of Aya against her on the sofa, recalled the safety and the comfort.

*I owe her so much.*

She wanted to help Aya. In a more direct way, not just by steering her away from Susannah and then acting as a life coach. It wasn't only because she wanted to repay her kindness, but because Aya deserved so much more. She was capable of so much more.

Gwen's thoughts shifted from one friend to another when she heard Charlotte come through the door.

"Ay up, duck," Charlotte called. "I hope you can eat something tonight because I brought dinner!"

"Great."

Charlotte stopped, put the bag of food on the floor, and squinted at her. "Hm. Your mouth says 'great', but your eyes say 'disaster.' Spill!"

So Gwen did. Every part of the story, from Edward's words about things worsening before they got better coming true, to how everything had turned from hollowness into a cocktail of sadness, rage, panic, and grief this morning until she collapsed by the door for hours, and finally finishing with how Aya had been so sweet and napped with her on the sofa before sharing egg and cress sandwiches with her.

Charlotte picked up her bag of food and put it on the counter. "First of all, great that something's changed. Secondly, Edward is probably right: most of your depressive phases have had a meltdown at the end. That and an eating binge, so that's probably next."

"I hope not," Gwen grumbled. "It takes ages to lose all of that weight again. I think I still carry some of the last breakdown on my hips."

"Don't interrupt," Charlotte said. "I was going to say, thirdly, what really caught my attention was the part about Aya."

"Really? Not my breakdown? Not the fact that I sat

semi-unconscious with an open door in a city not known to be the safest in the world?"

"That is scary, but familiar. What's new here is the Aya factor. Interesting, isn't it? That she's dropping everything to nap with you and share sandwiches? Showers you with gifts and jumps at the chance to be your saviour?"

"Not my saviour, my company. What, are you implying that she has a saviour complex?"

"I don't think her motives are that simple."

Gwen buried her nose in Meatloaf's hay-scented fur as she deliberated. "She said that looking after me gave her a purpose and a source of pride."

"Aya doesn't look *after* you. She looks up to you. She looks at you as if you hung the stars and probably constructed the moon while you were at it."

Gwen lowered Meatloaf. "What are you saying?"

"Just that she clearly adores you, and at some point, you'll have to figure out what that means."

"Adores? Are you making this about romance?"

Charlotte took Meatloaf and kissed her little head before putting her back in her cage. "Forgive me for wanting you to be loved the way you deserve to be."

"Oh, drop it. I'm focusing on getting better, that's it."

"You're right, dropping it." Charlotte mimicked letting something fall out of her hand. "You *do* seem to be getting better."

"Mm. That's just it… I seem to be. What if I'm not, though? Or I am, but I ruin it?"

"That's your wonky brain chemistry talking."

"Yeah." Gwen sighed. "Did you say you brought food? I need all the food."

"You're changing the subject."

"Yes. I know. Let me, please?"

Charlotte held up her hands in a defeated gesture. "Fine. It's only random leftovers I snuck back from the pub. Chips, salad, guacamole, and a burger patty."

Gwen quavered her lower lip and put on the biggest puppy eyes. "Can I please have all of it? And the ice cream you left in the freezer? Aya says protein will help get my strength back fast."

"Gwen. Sweetie. There's enough food for both of us, we'll share. But you can obviously have my ice cream. I'm thrilled you're eating again, duck."

Gwen leaned against the wall, suddenly exhausted. "Me too. Let's see if I can keep it to normal eating or if it's time for depression binging."

"You can't binge until I've gone grocery shopping," Charlotte said. "Unless you're about to scoff all of Meatloaf's cucumber?"

She gathered enough social energy for one last joke. "Hm. Maybe if I dip it in the guacamole?"

Charlotte tut-tutted and began microwaving their dinner.

Gwen set the table, trying to focus on how to get better so she could pull her weight in their little household, *not* daydreaming about a warm, strong body gently pressed against hers on the sofa.

---

Next morning the sun broke through thick clouds to peek one sunbeam at Gwen's window, straight into her newly opened eyes. Still, she wouldn't complain about the sunlight; its brightness would help her maintain the little energy she'd woken with. She'd use it while she had it! Charlotte had been right; she couldn't let her wonky brain overthink and tell her that there was no point in doing anything because of the fear of ruining her progress.

She took her antidepressants and cleaned up a little in the kitchen. She knew that Charlotte wouldn't expect, or want, her to do that, but it made her feel better.

It was when she put some clean bowls away and grabbed one for her breakfast that she spotted Aya's boxing guide.

*Perfect.*

She read it during her breakfast of tea and yoghurt with dried fruit, and the digesting period that followed. Hopefully her stomach would soon remember how to handle normal-sized meals again.

Finished with breakfast, she placed the book on the coffee table and herself in the proper stance on the living room floor, hearing Aya's guidance in her head. With one eye on the pictures in the book and the other in a mirror to check she was copying them right, she practised some punches and feints. She looked ridiculous, this pasty, awkward beanstalk in her knickers and t-shirt flailing around and playing at being a boxer. It almost made her laugh, and that was a good thing in herself. She was eager to be able to really laugh again, even if it was at her own expense.

She lasted for about an hour before all energy sapped out of her and she crawled back into bed. Still, she returned to bed with a sense of pride.

---

Hours later she woke to the rumble of her stomach. Her burst of energy was gone, but she still obeyed her body and dragged herself up. In the kitchen she weighed her options. Chocolate biscuits? Crisps? Jelly babies? She stopped the hand reaching for the bag of sweets. No. If she was going to improve, she'd need more nutrition for lunch. She wasn't able to cook a whole meal, but she could fry an egg. That would be protein, right? Aya had said that might give her some strength back.

When she got the egg out, she saw the bag of spinach that Charlotte used for those disgusting smoothies she swore by. She grabbed it. She'd have an egg for Aya and some vegetables for Charlotte. She might not be ready to look after herself for her, but she could do it for them. At least a little. She'd still have that bag of sweets afterwards; she would've earned it.

As she whisked the egg and spinach together, she found herself thinking about Aya and wondering if she'd visit soon.

She texted her and quickly got a reply. After a few texts back and forth they'd established that Aya had her final job interview at the magazine company in an hour and that Gwen was still convinced she was going to get it. While her lunch fried, they'd discussed Gwen's burst of energy; Aya had said how thrilled she was about that, almost as thrilled as she was about the idea of soon earning a pay cheque again. When Aya had to stop texting, Gwen wished her good luck and they said goodbye.

She dished up her lunch and ate it with her biggest mug of tea. She kept re-reading their texts, especially the part where Aya mentioned that the job, while giving her a pay cheque, was only part-time. Aya had shown how badly being on benefits and not providing for herself sat with her personality type.

Gwen put her fork down. Perhaps this was an area where she could finally help?

She sat back and considered what extra job would make Aya feel accomplished, what would interest her. What was Aya passionate about? Boxing. That was why she kept training and why she sparred with Jenny. Shame that sparring didn't pay.

Gwen picked up her fork again but paused with it held in the air. Something had occurred to her. However, it would all come down to what Aya's old coach said. She had to talk to Bill.

*Chapter Thirty-Two*

# SUPPORT AND PRIDE

When Aya came home, she was drunk on excitement. The interview had gone so well that she'd all but been promised the job. Only the formality of the other two competitors' interviews stood between her and a start date.

She listened to the empty house. Her parents were working as always, ignoring that they were nearing retirement age and should slow down. How many vacation days had they let go to waste throughout the years? They didn't even like their jobs. Maybe they only worked so much because it was the one place they didn't have to see her?

She shook the thought from her mind; Aya didn't want to see them anyway. She wanted Gwen. She wasn't as clear about how she wanted to celebrate as she was in who she wanted to celebrate with, but it didn't matter. Even if she only lay on a sofa watching Gwen sleep, or drove her to therapy. Anything was exciting or interesting if Gwen was there.

She got her phone out and used her recent calls log to get Gwen's number.

After three rings, Gwen answered. "Hey, tough boxer."

Aya shifted her weight from foot to foot, unable to stay still. "Hey, soft barista! Guess what?"

"Is it that you're a knobhead for nicknaming me 'soft barista'?"

"Sure, that, too, but what I was calling about was that I'm back from the interview."

"Cool! And…?"

Aya fist-pumped the air. "And the bloke pretty much promised me the job!"

"Ha! I knew it. This job was meant for you," Gwen said adamantly.

"Look at you with all the answers," Aya bantered, too happy to stay serious.

"Well, I am older than you. Of course I have the answers."

Aya stopped moving. "I never thought of that. How much older are you?"

"Guess."

Aya groaned. "Don't make me do this, duck. You know I say the wrong things even in harmless topics. This one's dangerous."

"It's fine. Go ahead. I like getting older; I won't be offended if you get it wrong."

"Okay, thirty-nine."

Gwen coughed. "Sorry, I was drinking water, and it went down the wrong way. I'm a little surprised you think I'm more than ten years older than you," she said, sounding amused.

Aya squeezed her eyes shut and braced herself. "Thirty-seven?"

"Wrong. Try again."

"Just bloody tell me, Gwen!"

"Okay, okay, calm down. I'm thirty-three, love."

"Really? Wow. I thought it was much more."

"Uh. Okay?" Gwen said, now half amused and half offended if Aya was reading that tone of voice right.

"I meant because you're so mature and in sync with your thoughts and feelings." She mentally added that she preferred the company of older women so had assumed Gwen was older.

*That's borderline flirty, though, isn't it? I can't say that.*

Maybe she should tell Gwen about Bill's theory that often people who spend their teens being pro athletes and not regular teens, never grew up. It might explain why she sometimes seemed younger and less experienced than she was.

The moment to say something passed, though, as Gwen was already replying. "No need to defend yourself. As I said, I have no problem with getting older. We should all be so lucky. There were times in my life when I doubted I'd get even this far."

Aya's heart sank as she realised what that meant. "Oh. Sorry."

"No, no, don't be. Ah, bollocks, I'm ruining the mood here. This is a great day and should be celebrated!"

"Agreed," Aya said on an exhale. "So, how do we celebrate?"

"Any way you'd like! However we do it, though, it'll have to be tonight. I have some errands to run right now."

"Yeah? Anything you need help with? I'll tag along for whatever."

There was a pregnant pause.

"Aya, you're not my carer," Gwen said softly. "Maybe take the afternoon off from being with me?"

Aya tapped her forehead against the wall. "Of course, yeah, we should have some time apart. We're not teenagers having to hang out every day of the week." She had tried to sound nonchalant but wasn't sure it worked. Why was she so clingy?

"As I said, I just have something I need to do."

She bumped her forehead again. "Sure! I don't know what I was thinking offering to tag along. Saying the wrong thing again, huh?"

"No, you didn't. I want to spend time with you, too. On that note, fancy coming over at about six tonight instead?"

Aya froze mid-forehead-thumping. "Yeah! I can pick up some food for all of us from that Mexican place in Hanley that Charlotte loves?"

"Perfect. Now, treat yourself this afternoon! No more worrying, especially not about saying the wrong thing. You must've really wowed that bloke at the interview and said all the *right* things."

"Um, I guess. Thanks," Aya replied, unsure of how to proceed in the face of all this unconditional support.

Luckily, Gwen filled in the silence. "I'm proud of you, love. See you tonight!"

"Thanks," Aya said again, just as feebly as the first time. "I'm proud of you, too. See you then."

She hung up and stared at the screen. Why had she said that she was proud of Gwen? Sure, she was, but that wasn't a normal thing to say in that conversation, was it? Clearly Gwen was wrong about her saying the right thing.

She fidgeted for a second, unsure of what to do. She completely understood Gwen's point and knew they'd see each other tonight. Still, she wanted to see Gwen right away. She wanted to celebrate with her in this very moment.

She smacked herself on the arm. Co-dependency

wasn't an Aya Lawson trait. Neither was attaching her happiness to someone else. The last remnant of that had been killed when she walked out on Susannah.

*You're an independent woman. And you like being alone, remember? Working out, watching movies, going for long drives.*

Long drives! Yes, perfect. But where to? She thought about her last long drive and immediately knew where to go and what to do. Or rather, what to buy. It was extravagant, yes, but what a way to celebrate! She picked up her jacket and car keys before heading out to Janet.

*Chapter Thirty-Three*

## MUSCLES & MITTS

A cold pit of unease sat in Gwen's stomach as she gathered up the energy to leave her flat. Aya had sounded so upset over that they had to wait to celebrate. She reminded herself that she had to say no to do this for Aya. Besides, they'd see each other tonight.

That cold feeling slowly changed into a cold sweat. What if she had a depression meltdown, complete with exhaustion and dissociation, out there? What if she had a panic attack? What if she got too ill to get herself back home?

Bugger it. She *had* to talk to Bill.

After a long, taxing walk, she passed through the ground-floor nail salon and then climbed up the shabby stairs to Muscles & Mitts. She smoothed her hair, knowing she looked terrible and hating herself as much for that as for everything else. Never mind, she reminded herself; this wasn't about her.

She walked into the gym, and a cacophony of noise hit her. People, mainly huge men, were skipping rope and punching either bags or each other. There was a lot of laughter and shouting, too. A shiver of not belonging ran down her back, but she shook it off. It wasn't like her to shy away from something new. Some of the boxers stopped what they were doing to watch her cross the crowded space. One of them was a tall girl with dread-locks. Next to her was a massive old bloke bellowing at her in an American accent. "Jenny! Pay attention for Pete's sake! D'you think I'm coaching you for fun?"

"No, Bill," she droned with an eye roll.

"Ah, yer killing me. We're here to do a job!"

"My fault. I distracted her," Gwen cut in.

Bill turned to her with a look of curiosity, not the unfriendliness that Gwen had dreaded. "Hey there. Who are you? You're way too skinny to be a boxer. Even a flyweight would eat you for breakfast."

"I'm well aware," Gwen said, good-naturedly. "I'm not a boxer, but I'm here on behalf of one. I'm Gwen, Aya's friend."

"Oh, right." He faced Jenny again. "Take a break and get something to drink, kid. Be back here in twenty minutes."

She ambled off, and Bill refocused on Gwen. "So, you're the Welsh chick that has Aya all dreamy, huh? I can see how you'd be her type. You're certainly a hell of a lot better than that bitch she dated before." He jolted as if the words coming out of his mouth had shocked him. "Shit! Man, I'm sorry. I never call women that. In fact, I tell my boxers off for doing it. It's just that she—"

"Deserves that particular slur? Nah, I don't agree. I think the comparison is unfair to female dogs."

He laughed. "Aya said you were funny. That's my favourite trait in a woman."

"I'm glad you approve of me as her new friend." Gwen

put emphasis on the last word. It had sounded as though Bill thought Aya and she were dating.

"It's not up to me to approve. She's a full-grown woman and makes her own decisions and choices."

"Yes, speaking of Aya's life decisions. I'm here to sound you out on something."

He squinted at her so much his face looked like a raisin. "Okay. What?"

"I know she's been sparring with Jenny."

"Mm. Jenny's a rising star, and Aya can teach her a lot. What about it?"

"That's just it. Aya is really enjoying helping her. It's raising her confidence and giving her purpose. As you know, it looks like she will be getting that admin job. However, that's in the morning. The rest of the day she's free and—"

"I'mma stop you there. Aya told me that you like to talk, and since I can be a bit of a blabbermouth, too, I think we better get to the crux of the issue before we yap the day away."

"Okay," Gwen said, trying not to bristle. "Go ahead."

Bill scratched his craggy chin. "You're suggesting Aya needs more work and asking me if she can coach Jenny, right?"

"Not exactly *coaching* her. I know that's your job," Gwen hurried to say.

"Yeah, but I'm old and slow. Aya isn't ready to coach someone trying to go pro, but she could be an assistant coach. Maybe I could scramble up enough money to pay her to train with Jenny for a few hours every day."

"Really?"

He held up a paw of a hand. "Like I said, *if* I can find

the money. I'll look into it and let you both know ASAP. How's that?"

"Brilliant," Gwen breathed. "I can wait. I mean, even if it doesn't pan out, I'm just so grateful that you tried. Aya loves boxing, and I know she misses doing it professionally. This could change her life."

"True. Anyway, I'd love to chat more, kid, but you need to skedaddle so I can find my fighter before she drinks a tonne of whey protein and can't box."

"Of course. Thank you for your time. It was nice meeting you."

"Likewise, Welsh chick. Take care."

Gwen left the gym, with its smell of leather, sweat, and menthol, behind her in a buzz of childish excitement. She might've just helped Aya with something that would mean the world to her.

Gwen checked her watch. Six thirty, and they had almost gobbled all of the Mexican food already. Well, she and Aya had. Charlotte ate like a bird and entertained them with stories of what had happened at the pub today.

Aya was belly-laughing at the crazy tales of a day shift in a Stoke pub. She seemed quicker to laughter than normal, like a weight had been lifted off that eye-catching chest. It was incredible what a job could do. Equally incredible was how radiant Aya was when she was happy. Her dimple was on constant display, and her body language was relaxed and open in a way that stole Gwen's attention.

As soon as they'd finished dinner, Aya stood and

brushed taco crumbs off her jeans. "I'm going to get something that I bought today."

Charlotte was packing away food containers. "Another indulging boost gift," she said from the corner of her mouth.

"You're just jealous," Gwen whispered back.

"Damn right. Although I did get a text from the egocentric, rugby-obsessed fireman. He asked for another date. He promised that he would treat me to a fancy dinner and then to a movie, so I'll be getting a little spoiled myself."

Gwen squinted at her. "The Charlotte I know doesn't give her precious time to some narcissistic bloke just because he buys her dinner. What else?"

Charlotte smiled. "He apologised, saying that he'd kept chatting about himself and rugby because I made him nervous. That I was the sexiest and most resilient woman he'd ever met."

"Resilient?"

She tucked a lock of hair behind her ear. "Yes, because of how I handle my family and our intolerant society in general."

"Nice! And?"

"And, he said that if I ever wanted someone to have a chat with my parents about accepting me as trans and as a woman, he'd love to help."

Gwen snapped her fingers. "Bingo. That would get him another date. Now I know why you mentioned Aya having a saviour complex," she whispered. "It sounds like you want a bloke who has one."

"I want a man who will stand by my side and speak up for me. Is that so wrong?" Charlotte said stridently.

"Absolutely not, love. You deserve that and so much

more." Gwen gave her a one-armed hug. "If this guy wants to fight in your corner, he sounds okay to me."

"Agreed," Aya said, walking back into the room with a smallish box in her hands.

Gwen's gaze was drawn to the package. It had been so long since she'd experienced curiosity like this, almost without any dampening depression fog.

Aya noticed and laughed. "Here. It's related to our first memory together."

Gwen opened the luxurious box without reading the text on it; she was too curious about this memory connection Aya had mentioned.

The box revealed a glass bottle full of whiskey-brown liquid. It wasn't whiskey, though.

Not in that small bottle.

Not with that golden deer head topper.

Gwen didn't need to read the label. "This is *The Tragedy of Lord George*."

"Yep, that cologne from our Chester trip. Before it all went pear-shaped when we found Susannah." Aya smiled a little. "Back when it was just you and me falling about in perfume shops."

"But this was so expensive!"

"It cost more than anyone should spend on stuff to smell good, yes. It's not just a perfume, though. It's a memento."

"Nonetheless, Aya. I'm insanely grateful, but can you afford this?"

"Sure. I still have some savings, and I'm getting a new job, remember?" They kept looking at each other until Aya grumbled, "Okay, I see you're not convinced. But I'm not taking it back! You deserve a treat and… you only live once."

Gwen surveyed the heavy bottle, contemplating how to ease her guilt over the cost. She looked back up at Aya. "Tell you what. Why don't we share it? I'd feel better about that."

Aya scratched the back of her head. "Um. Sure. I suppose I quite liked it. I'll definitely like smelling like you."

"Yes! I'd like to smell like you, too."

Abruptly, Charlotte laughed. They both turned to her, but she only shook her head before wandering out, muttering, "They have no idea, do they, Meatloaf?" towards the cage. Gwen couldn't make out the rest of the sentence, but thought she heard the words "in laugh." Or was it "in love?"

She ignored it, instead taking off the bottle's deer head topper. "Right. Come here."

Aya dutifully stepped closer. Gwen sprayed her left pulse point, then used her free hand to move Aya's head so she could spray the right pulse point without splashing that shapely jaw.

Aya sniffed the air. "That's nice."

Gwen breathed in, too, filling her nostrils with what her non-expert nose thought smelled like wood, sweet brandy, and her grandad's old shaving cream. Actually, it was the sort of cologne her granddad would've liked if he could afford it.

"Yes, it is," Gwen agreed. "Not as nice as you, though."

Close as she was, Aya's embarrassed expression was unmistakeable. "Not quite as nice as that day was," she mumbled.

"No, but a good reminder," Gwen answered, tentatively taking her hand. "And something to spur us on to have more adventures when I'm better."

Aya interlaced their fingers. "Absolutely. We should start with Chester. We'll go back and replace the bad memories of what happened with Susannah with good ones."

"I can't wait."

Gwen watched their hands. Thank goodness Aya didn't mind how touchy-feely she was; in fact, she'd quickly adjusted to it. Now, Aya squeezed her hand and Gwen found yet another reason to keep fighting that dark ocean looming behind her.

## Chapter Thirty-Four

# ROCK THIS

At that moment, in Gwen's cosy flat, with the cologne scenting the air between them, Aya squeezed Gwen's fingers and marvelled at their connected hands. Her breath had hitched when she dared to interlace their fingers, terrified that Gwen would think it was too intimate. Her fear had clearly been unfounded, as Gwen now squeezed back.

Out of the blue, another sensation pushed out the marvelling: a buzzing in her bum.

*What the hell is that?!*

She groaned. Obviously, it was her phone ringing on silent in her back pocket. She let go of Gwen and got the phone out. The call was coming from the self-defence instructor at the gym.

"Hello?"

"Hi, Aya. Sorry to bother you, duck, but I can't get hold of Bill. My class starts soon, but my babysitter hasn't shown up and I can't find anyone to look after my daughter tonight."

"Oh?"

*Please tell me she isn't asking me to babysit? I'd probably light the kid's hair on fire.*

"Yes. Anyway, I don't want to cancel the class on such short notice, so I wondered if you knew someone who could fill in for me?"

Seconds passed as Aya considered the confidence it would take her to hold a class. All the things she might say and do to make a fool of herself. How many of the class participants she could offend or confuse.

She noticed Gwen stealthily watching her and knew what she would say: "You know the moves and how to teach people. You can do this."

More than that, Aya knew that was true. In fact, she couldn't just do this, she could rock this!

"Yeah, I can recommend someone. Me."

"What? I mean that would be great, but would you be comfortable with that?"

Aya popped her neck and straightened. "Absolutely. I'll get going right away."

## Chapter Thirty-Five

# OPEN FOR HER

Gwen had some energy and strength the next morning. Breakfast finished, she stared at her phone. Should she call Aya and suggest what she wanted to suggest? The classic questions popped into her mind. What if she ruined her recovery? What if the energy drained and she had a breakdown while out? She ran a hand through her unwashed hair. She wasn't even in any state to show herself in public. Besides, what if Aya was busy?

On the table next to her lay the elegant box containing the overpriced perfume.

"You only live once," she said, echoing Aya's words.

She picked up the phone and made the call.

"Good morning, shug."

Aya's voice gave Gwen a helpful jolt. "Hi. How did the class go last night?"

"Great! I was going to text you, but I didn't know if you were sleeping. How are you, by the way?"

"I'm… not as bad as I have been. Which is why I'm calling. Do you have plans for today?"

"Nope. Have anything in mind?"

"I was thinking about what we said yesterday, about going to Chester."

"Yeah?"

"Mm. I wish I could go today. I need a change of scenery." Gwen toyed with the perfume box, feeling bad for once again complicating things. "The problem is that I'm not really presentable and I'm not sure I have the energy to be around people."

Aya hummed. "Well, there's an obvious solution."

"There is?"

"Yep. We take Janet to Chester and just drive around. That way you don't have to get out of the jeep, and no one will really see you."

Relief washed over Gwen. "Yes, that's a brilliant idea!"

"Cool, I can look for a boost gift for you there, too. Some exotic honey or something."

"No need. The trip will be my boost."

Aya hummed again. "You sure?"

"Positive. It'll be an adventure. There's no bigger boost than a spontaneous adventure."

"Okay, how about we go to a drive-through on the way and pick up hot drinks and snacks?"

"Perfect!"

"Right, I'll be over in about half an hour, gotta wait for the laundry to finish and then hang it. See you soon."

"Great. Thank you so much. I'll see you then," Gwen said and ended the call.

She brushed a few stray strands from her forehead. It was only then that she realised how badly she needed to wash her hair.

*Dammit. Do I have energy for that?*

Even if she stayed in the jeep, Aya would still see her. Besides, she wanted her hair to smell fresh. She got in the shower, planning how to do this using minimal amounts of her tiny allowance of energy.

When the hot water hit her skin, it relaxed her muscles, rigid from lack of use, and soothed her mind. She had soaked her hair and opened the bottle of vanilla-scented shampoo when her phone rang. She was going to ignore it, but it kept ringing. It could be Aya calling to cancel or something like that.

She put the shampoo back, got out, and grabbed her robe. When she located her phone, the caller wasn't Aya but the owner of the café, the wife this time.

Gwen answered it. About five minutes into the call she leaned against the wall and sank down to the floor. She was polite and didn't cause trouble; after all, she'd known this might happen and understood. She hadn't been fired, of course, but she might as well have been.

When the call ended, she covered her face and sobbed. There were no more silent tears, this was proper bawling her eyes out. She cried all the tears that had stacked up inside her until her wet face hurt and she had to crawl to get some tissue. Water had pooled where she sat, but she didn't care. She stayed in the puddle of shower water and tears as a new wave of crying hit.

When there was a knock on the door, Gwen considered not answering it. She had wanted to wash her hair to look her best for Aya. What would she look like now?

*She's seen you at your worst, remember? Open the damn door. It's Aya. Open for her.*

She dragged herself up.

Aya frowned when she saw her. "Gwen! What's wrong?"

"My boss called. They had to give my shifts to a new employee."

Aya burst in. "What?! They can't fire you!"

Gwen wrapped her robe closer around herself, seeking comfort. "No, they can't, and they wouldn't. They're just a nice, elderly couple trying to get by. But they talked about needing some sort of document from my doctor, then said they'd been forced to temporarily replace me."

Aya stepped farther into the hallway. "And when you come back, what happens then? Is this new person just hired during your sick leave?"

Gwen looked away. "I'm not officially on sick leave. That's what the document was for. I should've filled in paperwork to get sick pay and such."

"Why didn't you, shug?"

"I couldn't. It's... well, burying your head in the sand, even when everything is collapsing around you, is common with depressed people." Shame overwhelmed her. "I messed up, Aya, and now they're in trouble and disappointed with me. My boss sounded so upset on the phone, like she didn't want me back. This is one too many unofficial depression sick leaves. They'll ask me to quit this time."

"That's a lot of assumptions. Do you want me to call them back and get answers?"

"No." Tears lined her eyelids again, making it hard to see. "I want... I'd like you to..."

Aya moved closer. "What? Name it? I'll do anything."

"I'd like you to hold me," Gwen said quietly. She regretted it the second she heard the words resounding in the small hallway.

"Of course," Aya answered.

There was no hesitation or surprise. Aya simply closed the distance between them and wrapped Gwen in a tight, warm hug.

Gwen bent so she could burrow her face into the crook of her shorter friend's neck. She flung her arms around Aya and held on for dear life. Aya smelled fresh, of the outside air, but it was the underlying scent of her skin that calmed Gwen.

She cried, teardrops trickling down Aya's waxed jacket. She thought she was out of tears, but the last few weeks of desolation and numbness had apparently built up layers upon layers of them.

Aya simply held her, caressing her back in comforting circles. When Gwen got too embarrassed, she forced the sobs down and stepped back. She turned so Aya wouldn't have to watch her blow her nose and then muttered, "You know, I didn't even get the chance to wash my damn hair!"

Aya laughed softly. "Well, your hair isn't going anywhere, shug. You can wash it later."

"I wanted to wash it before we went out." Gwen held up a hand to stop any reply. "I know we said we wouldn't get out of the jeep. I still wanted it to be clean."

"Hey, I get that. As someone who works out in a grubby, old gym every day, I take great pride and joy in showering every bloody chance I get," Aya said with a chuckle.

Gwen tried to smile. "Well, I don't need a full shower. I washed this morning. I was going to clean my hair right before that call, but that went to hell. Now I'm bone tired."

Aya shuffled her feet. "Um, I... could help," she suggested hesitantly. "If you lean your head over the sink, I could wash it for you?"

"What? No. I couldn't ask you to do that."

Aya appeared more confident now, more convinced. "You didn't. I offered, and it would be kinda rude of you to say no." She grinned. "You know, it would be like questioning my ability to wash hair. I may be butch, but I do actually have more hair than you. I shampoo like a boss."

Gwen couldn't dispute that. She made a mental note to remember this moment so she could truly enjoy it when the depression retreated enough for her to laugh again.

"Then I won't say no. After all, I don't want to be rude."

"All right, one shampoo and conditioning treatment coming up!"

"My hair is short and oily enough to not need conditioner, so we can save time there."

"Cool!" Aya paused. "In that case, get that bottle of blue hair dye I bought. I read the instructions in the store. It seemed pretty quick and easy; I can dye your tips, then wash your hair."

Gwen staggered. "Y-you'd do that for me?"

"Sure, that's what friends do, right? Wouldn't Charlotte do that for you?"

"Yes, but we've known each other for ages."

"Well then, I need catch up by doing loads of intense friendship stuff. Go get the shampoo and the hair dye. I'll grab a chair from the kitchen for you to sit on."

She marched off, all resolution and practicality.

Gwen rolled her tense shoulders, trying to let go of all worries about being a bother. She'd let Aya make the decisions today.

It was only when the dyeing was done and Aya was massaging shampoo into her hair that Gwen relaxed. She took in the scent of vanilla filling the room, trying to calm her breaths. The sensation of practised fingers caressing her scalp and running through her tresses, was wonderful. She'd thought Aya would be awkward and want to get this over fast, but she took all the time and care in the world to make sure everything was done correctly and gently.

It was impressive that Aya not only managed to dye the tips without getting blue on anything else, but also managed to not get shampoo in Gwen's eyes. She did however, somehow, manage to flick some up into her own. This was followed by two minutes of her jumping up and down like a cartoon character and cursing the shampoo, the shampoo manufacturers, and the water that had caused the foam to splash. Then she'd laughed and said, "Sorry, sometimes the quick temper I inherited from my dad flares up. Never lasts long, though."

That was another memory that Gwen stored away for a day when she could laugh at it, like Aya had. She also stored it away to one day tease Aya about it.

When Gwen had tousled some hair products into her hair, Aya said, "That's all sorted, then. It can dry in the car, just get some clothes on. Unless you want to skip the drive?"

"No, I need the distraction."

"Brilliant." Aya clapped her hands. "Chester road trip time, guaranteed without getting out of the jeep."

## Chapter Thirty-Six

# MAKING HER STAGGER AND SWAY

The next day, Aya stood outside Gwen's door with a mind full of doubts. The road trip yesterday had turned out to be fun and laidback. Meanwhile, this was all too prearranged, she thought as she reconsidered the blanket and basket by her feet.

She stopped her brain and dredged up her newfound confidence. She could hold classes on a moment's notice, she could sure as hell get through this. She squared her shoulders and knocked.

Gwen opened right away. She was dressed. In actual clothes. Her hair was styled, too. And was that a little make-up? Gwen still looked as exhausted as a losing boxer after twelve rounds, but she was closer to resembling the woman Aya had first met in the café.

"Hey. Wow! You look healthier today."

"Thanks. You're flawless as always." Gwen took a step back to look her over. "Is this the first time I've seen you wear your hair down? I didn't realise how long it was. Or how shiny!"

"Don't change the topic. We were talking about how great *you* look."

"Right." Gwen cast her gaze down. "Thanks again. I've been less shattered. I've even done some boxing." To demonstrate, she shadowboxed in the cutest, most incorrect way, like a child pretending to be Muhammad Ali.

Aya swallowed her laughter while Gwen let her in.

"Brilliant, duck! I'm happy you're feeling better." Aya adjusted her grip on the basket and blanket. "I suppose that means I should've asked if you wanted to do this outside. Never mind, though; I brought it here now."

Gwen touched the blanket. "What's all this?"

"Um, since our trip to Chester yesterday showed that doing things without you needing to be in public worked, I figured we'd have a picnic. But indoors."

"A picnic?"

Suddenly defensive, Aya hurried to hang up her jacket so Gwen couldn't see her face. "Yes, that's a thing that people do, isn't it? Something friends do?"

Gwen came over to her. "Absolutely, it's a great idea. Thank you. I just didn't know you were the picnic type."

Aya went into the living room to put the basket and blanket down next to the sofa. "I like to eat and to be outside. That's a picnic. Well, I mean this one will be inside, but you get my point." Her discomfort echoed in her voice. She didn't want to be teased right now.

Without another word, Gwen kneeled in front of Aya and began spreading the blanket out on the floor. When she looked up, those beautiful and oh so expressive blue eyes made Aya stagger backwards. Only a step or two, of course. She was no weakling.

"Well? Are you just going to stand there, or are you

going to open that basket and help, woman?" Gwen asked with a hint of a smile and a quirked eyebrow.

Aya's mouth was dry. Strange.

"Yeah, um, I think I'm getting thirsty. I packed a bottle of cucumber water, but if you want your teeth-rotting honeyed tea, I can put the kettle on?"

"Water's fine. I'll fish out the cucumber and give it to Meatloaf."

Aya crouched next to her and began unpacking the contents of the basket. "I didn't buy plastic cutlery since we're trying to save the planet. Go fetch some forks, *woman*," she said, echoing Gwen's teasing from before.

Gwen bumped her shoulder with her own, making Aya sway until she stabilized on her hands and knees.

"What?" Aya said with a laugh. "Woman is the best title in the world, not an insult. Not when you and I say it, anyway."

Gwen bumped her again, more softly this time. "Agreed. We finally found something we won't quibble about."

Aya moved in closer, ready to shoulder-bump Gwen back. "What? You're not going to argue with me?"

"No. For once, you're not wrong. Besides, you're the one who usually argues."

Aya was about to dispute that when her phone rang from her jacket pocket in the hall. "I'll go get that. You fetch those forks."

"Fetch? What am I, a Labrador?" Gwen said before heading to the kitchen.

Aya found her phone, then froze and stared at the name on the screen. 'Tom from Explore.' This was the call.

"H-hello?"

"Hi. Is that Aya speaking?"

Her heart jack-hammered in her chest. "Yes. Hm. Yes, this is Aya Lawson. Sorry."

"Great, Tom Ballard here. I'm calling with good news. I'd like to offer you the position as admin assistant."

Aya put a steadying hand against the wall. "Really?"

"Yes. I take that as that you accept? We still need to iron out the details of your starting date and contract and such, but I wanted to call with the good news right away."

"Yes, I accept! Thank you for telling me." She swallowed. "Thank you *so* much."

"Thank you for fitting Explore's requirements so perfectly," he answered. "I'll call you tomorrow so we can discuss further if that's convenient?"

"Y-yes! That would be brilliant."

"Excellent. I'll ring again tomorrow morning, then."

"Yes, please do. I look forward to hearing from you. Bye." Aya hung up and then punched the air. "Gwen! I got the bloody job!"

Gwen raced into the hallway with a speed that Aya hadn't seen since their first trip to Chester. "Woohoo! I knew you would! Right, celebration time! I'm getting out a bottle of gin. And the chocolate biscuits. And Charlotte's fancy ice cream. Let's have every celebration we can think of!"

"Yes," Aya croaked, too lost for words to say more.

Her heart was so full; her mind was so giddy. She was going to celebrate her pants off!

Through the haze of joy and relief, she realised that Gwen's clanking in the kitchen was slowing down from its earlier speed. Her energy and positive emotions were fading.

*Oh, well. When Gwen's depression gets the best of her, we'll celebrate by resting together on the sofa again.*

After all, there was no bigger treat than seeing that pretty face relaxed in sleep.

---

In the evening, Aya was back home, watching TV with her parents. A text vibrated her phone, and Aya pulled it out of her pocket, happy to be distracted from the documentary about Plexiglas that her mother had decided they had to watch.

The text was from Gwen and read:

*Hey you! I was practising my right hook but it's rubbish and makes me nearly fall over. Am I just too weak or am I doing it wrong? xx*

Aya smiled at her screen for a moment before replying.

*Hiya duck. I'm sure it's not as bad as you think. I have an hour or so before I have to go spar with Jenny. Do you want me to drop by and give you some quick pointers? xx*

The reply came in fast, a resounding yes! Aya wasted no time; she texted back that she was on her way and said goodbye to her parents. It would've been nice if they had asked where she was going, but they just said goodbye and focused back on the documentary.

When she parked Janet on the road below Gwen's flat, a call came in. She answered it, and before she had time to say hello, Bill barked, "Where are ya, kid?"

She got out of the jeep. "I'm at Gwen's. Why?"

"You're supposed to be sparring!"

"No. We said 8:30." She checked her fitness watch as she walked. "It's 7:41 now."

"Oh." His accusing tone dissolved. "Shit. I must've gotten my times mixed up. Okay, forget it. See you at 8:30."

Aya was about to tease him for the mistake when he added, "Hey, you being at Gwen's reminds me: when you get here, we've gotta talk about something she and I cooked up."

"The two of you?" She stopped. "Can't you tell me now?"

"Well, I was hoping to tell her first since it was her idea, but I suppose I can start with you and then you can pass on the news."

When he'd finished explaining the offer and said good-bye, Aya whooped with triumph, hung up, and ran up the stairs to Gwen, not even caring that she left her hoodie in the car.

## Chapter Thirty-Seven

# HOOK AND HEAL

Gwen groaned. Good thing she'd called Aya. She was absolutely doing this hook business wrong. She kept flailing as if swatting a fly. Not that she needed a reason to be happy for Aya coming over. She'd missed her ever since they last said goodbye.

A knock on the door told her Aya had arrived. She tugged her tank top down where it had ridden up her stomach, fixed her hair, and pressed her lips together to make them less colourless.

As she opened the door, Aya—in only T-shirt and jeans—burst in and pulled her into a rib-crushing hug. Gwen was surprised by the embrace but enjoyed the living daylights out of it. Aya's body was solid with muscle but soft at its curves. The only thing softer was her smooth skin and that sleek hair of hers. Despite the autumn chill and her lack of jacket, her skin was hot. Had she run up here?

"Whoa! I, uh, what? Hi!" Gwen stammered.

Aya squeezed her hard enough to make her breathless

and then let go. She closed the door behind her and with a beaming smile said, "I know what you did, shug."

"Uh. We're not talking about my right hook here, are we?"

Aya laughed as she bounced on the balls of her feet. "No, Bill just asked me to be Jenny's assistant coach. I'll be training with her part-time, and actually getting paid for it! He said it was your idea?"

Gwen's stomach filled with butterflies. "Sort of, he still deserves all the credit. Oh, that's brilliant! I worried he wouldn't be able to find the money, that's why I didn't tell you about it."

"It's only small change at this point, but I'd do it for free anyway. I love the idea of helping another boxer. Getting to be part of that world still, you know?" Aya clenched her hands into happy fists, making the muscles dance under her compression shirt.

"Sure, but being paid for it means you now have two part-time jobs giving you almost a full-time wage, right?"

"Almost! It won't make me rich, but it'll be enough to start saving up for that deposit for a flat. Thank you again!"

Gwen didn't know what to do with this wonderfully ecstatic version of Aya, who was unable to stay still. Was this what Aya was like before she had to quit boxing and things started to go downhill for her? Or was this unguarded and uncool version of Aya a private one?

Gwen gathered her wits. "No need to thank me. Friends help each other, right?"

Aya shoved her hands in her pockets and glanced up through her jet-black lashes, looking so vulnerable that it pierced Gwen's heart. "I still want to thank you."

Gwen was warming up, inside and out. Breaking the emotional tension, she hooked a finger in one of the belt loops of Aya's jeans and pulled her farther into the flat. "You can do that by fixing my right hook. I'm starting to get into this boxing malarkey!"

*At least as long as I'm doing it with you*, she added inwardly.

"Come on then," Aya said, striding into the lounge and pushing the coffee table away to make more room.

Gwen took centre stage, breathed in, got in the right stance, and then attempted the right hook again.

Aya's mouth fell open. "Wow. When you said it was rubbish, I thought you were just putting yourself down. But, good god, woman, what in the name of every bloody oatcake in Stoke was *that*?!"

Aya looked so exasperated and shocked that Gwen couldn't help but laugh.

She flinched. Had she just laughed?

Clearly Aya was thinking the same thing; her theatrical grimace changed into something almost reverent. "Was that a real laugh or a faked one?"

"Real. I… I haven't done that for weeks." Her gaze became unfocused. That wasn't the only positive response she'd shown in the last few days, was it? A moment ago, she'd excitedly primped her hair because she wanted to impress her new best friend. Then she'd warmed at being able to help Aya with the coaching job. She put her hands to her chest as if she could touch the emotions as they returned to her body.

"Wow," Aya whispered.

"Yeah." Gwen exhaled shakily. "Well, I guess my right hook was good for something."

Aya smiled from ear to ear and nodded.

Gwen couldn't wait to tell Edward about this at their next session. In fact, she actually looked forward to her therapy work now. As Aya helped her get back into the proper boxing stance, she added *hope* to her list of returning emotions.

## Chapter Thirty-Eight

# SWEETHEART

It was a windy afternoon, but the sun was so high and proud in the sky that even the damn birds were singing its praise. A bunch of people got in Aya's way, university students by the look of them, and nearly spoiled her good mood. They were laughing and jabbering, a stark contrast to the peace and quiet between her and Gwen as they strolled along the canal path.

Gwen inched closer to her as the students passed. She'd always seemed like a people person; it was sad how depression had robbed her of that. Nevertheless, Gwen had not only dared to go out in public today, but even suggested it. That, Aya thought, must be an important step.

The students picked up their speed, shouting about needing to hurry back. It struck her that she and Gwen had all the time in the world, whether they wanted it or not. She surveyed Gwen, her thin shoulders slumped and her gaze on the ground.

*At least I start work tomorrow. She isn't so lucky.*

Nevertheless, Gwen was still happy for her sake. That

brought back a memory; Susannah's mocking tone when she talked about Aya's lack of employment. Susannah. It had been so long since Aya finally walked out on her.

Aya absently watched a narrowboat chugging past, her mind busy with the surreal concept of having dated someone like Susannah. Not because of how it felt then—the surreal idea of Susannah dating someone so beneath her, but because of how it felt now—that Aya would date someone so beneath *her*. Now she saw the real Susannah McVey. Charm, cunning, and a beautiful façade, but with nothing other than cruelty and selfishness rattling around underneath. Hollow like a cheap porcelain doll.

Susannah was the total opposite of the compassionate Gwen, who under her wonderful exterior had multitudes of thoughts, feelings, and memories. She was open and complicated like the universe.

It struck Aya that her parents were closer in temperament to Susannah than Gwen. They weren't ruthless like her, but they had little imagination, no need to analyse, no sense of adventure and wonder. They only wanted to do a good day's work, watch some TV, and then go to bed. Perhaps have dinner and drinks with the neighbours once a month.

There was nothing wrong with that, in fact they were probably happier than she was, but perhaps it was why they'd never understood her. They had never understood why she threw herself into boxing instead of getting a sensible job; why she daydreamed and obsessed; why she wanted to travel. Why she'd rather be alone than pass the time with people who didn't understand her.

She wasn't alone anymore, though. Was she? The wind caught some of Gwen's hair and blew it into her face, the tips of blue caressing her rosy cheekbone.

Aya brushed them back before she had time to consider if she should. "Having fun? Well, no, this isn't fun. No, that came out wrong. I'm having fun with you. I meant that this isn't exactly a barrel of laughs. I mean—"

"If I was enjoying the walk," Gwen said. "No need to explain."

"Phew," Aya said on an outbreath.

Gwen gave her a hint of a smile. "I am. I can't believe I'm saying this, since I'm not an outdoorsy person, but it's actually nice to get some air and daylight."

"I know what you mean. It's a pretty day, despite the cold wind."

Gwen buttoned up her coat and squinted up to the sky. "I wonder what countries this wind has swept through before blowing over us."

"The weather report said it came from the east. So Scandinavia? Russia?"

Gwen leaned her head on Aya's shoulder for a second. "Maybe even your Japan?"

"Maybe."

They walked in comfortable silence, watching pigeons settle on the window of a derelict pottery.

Gwen yawned. Was she bored with her company? She wished she could make sure Gwen had as good a time as she was.

"So, um, I'm sorry that I couldn't think of a boost gift today." Aya put her hands in her jacket pockets. "Like I've said, I'm better at planning outings than presents."

"Your presents have been perfect! Not that you have to give me any. As I've mentioned before, being with you is a boost," Gwen said, her raspy voice warm. "This is a nice outing, isn't it? Look at this ridiculously pretty day with the birdsong, autumn leaves blowing in the wind, and sunshine reflecting off the water. We've even got cute ducks." She pointed to a flock of birds swimming along the canal.

"They're geese," Aya mumbled, unable to keep from correcting her.

"Huh?"

"Geese, not ducks."

"Fine, Ms. Know It All." Gwen gave her a pointed look with an amused eyebrow quirked. "Anyway, what were you thinking about before? You were smiling."

"Honestly? I was thinking about Susannah."

Aya froze as the words fell out of her mouth. Was that the wrong thing to say? Susannah was still a sore point, right?

"I've thought about her, too." Gwen wrapped her arms around herself. Was it because she was cold, or perhaps because she wanted to be held? Aya would gladly help but didn't want to interrupt as Gwen continued. "It's hard not to think of her when she was what brought us together, right? Or rather, the pining over her did. You and I obviously had different reasons for lusting after her, but do you know what I think connected your yearning to mine? What they had in common?"

Aya thought for a second. "No."

"We were drawn to her confidence. She was so comfortable in her own skin. So confident that it brimmed over into arrogance, sure, but super confident, nonetheless. We both wanted that for ourselves, I think."

"That's probably true, yes. Susannah is pathetic, but her belief in herself and how she learned to handle the world? That I still envy. There's stuff there that a lot of us women need to learn." Aya bent to remove two fallen leaves that had stuck to the top of her boot. "You're definitely right about us being more attracted to her confidence than to the real her." She caught Gwen's eye before adding, "The fact that she was *massively sexy* didn't hurt, though."

Gwen laughed. It goose-pimpled Aya's skin. How she'd missed that sound!

"You'd know more about her sexiness than me. Was she… you know?" Gwen gave her a quick, suggestive glance.

It took a while before the penny dropped for Aya. "Are you asking what I think you're asking?"

Gwen had an air of innocence. "Of course not. Asking if she was good in bed would be highly inappropriate."

"Yeah, it would," Aya agreed with a grin. "And yes, she was. Well, she was great at foreplay and receiving. Not so great at giving, if you know what I mean."

"Ha! Well, there's a surprise," Gwen drawled.

"I know. I should've guessed. She once said that giving head, to either men or women, gave her migraines."

"What?!" Gwen said with an incredulous laugh. "Okay, so I don't know anything about men in bed, but what about the other million ways to make a woman climax?"

"She never mentioned them. I don't get it. Making a woman come is the best thing in the world!"

A grey-bearded dog walker appeared from a side path. He gaped at Aya as if he had actually caught her in the act, not just talking about it.

Gwen laughed again, watching the man rush past them. "Oh, Aya. You have the best timing, sweetheart."

A tingle ran through Aya at that word. *Sweetheart.* Man, her rep as a tough loner was in tatters. Not that anyone knew but her. Not that anyone cared. Gwen certainly didn't concern herself with reputations or with trying to be tough or cool. She was too busy living her life. Aya wanted to learn how to do that. Wanted to be surrounded by it.

Gwen, unaware of Aya's admiration, strolled along before stopping to hug her arms around herself again.

"You cold?" Aya asked.

"Yes. Maybe it's because I'm not used to being out of the house. Or that the sunshine fooled me into thinking only a T-shirt under my coat would be okay."

"Probably both. Also, you're recovering from lack of sleep and food. Here," Aya said, taking her knitted scarf off and handing it over. "Put this on."

Gwen did, with a soft "thank you."

"You're *so* very welcome."

They locked eyes until Aya got too self-conscious. "Hm. Where to now? I mean, do you want to keep on the canal path?"

"No. Change of scenery. Let's pop into the park!"

With that, Gwen veered a hard left onto the side path. Aya stopped in her tracks and turned as well, as thrilled with Gwen calling the shots as she was with her never being predictable.

Everything now, even a simple trip to the park, was exciting.

*Chapter Thirty-Nine*

# HANDSOME, PRETTY, OR HOT?

Gwen sat in the waiting room. Her therapy session should've started by now, but Edward was running late. She texted Aya.

*Thanks for the walk yesterday. And for the dinner and movie afterwards. Clearly it was a good formula because I actually got a good night's sleep last night. And guess what? I drew a little while having breakfast! xx*

A reply came in after only a few seconds.

*That's great! It's nice that you give me credit for that, but your recovery is all down to you, shug. Sorry to change the topic but can you believe I'm at work now? My first day. It feels so weird. I can do this, right? x*

Gwen wrote back:

*Absolutely. You can do this in your sleep. They'll give you all the info and training you need. Other than that, you're smart and hardworking. You've got this! xx*

Aya's reply took a little longer to come in this time.

*I'm not so sure, but I trust your opinion. Anyway, it could be worse. A few weeks ago I would've been convinced that I COULDN'T do this. Shit, they're calling me. Gotta go. See you later. xx*

Gwen replied with wishes of good luck. Then she too was called into an office. She wished it was work in her case, but then, therapy was more important right now. She had to get her mind working better. Then she could think about work.

An hour later, Gwen walked out of Edward's building, thinking about what had been said. Her throat constricted. He'd talked about her clear improvement for the first part of the session. Then talk had turned to her insecure job situation and how she hadn't looked into what paperwork she needed to fill out, what her employers needed to send her, and so on. He voiced worries about her financial situation, pointing out how dire it would be if she kept burying her head in the sand.

She couldn't argue. Her savings were running out. She was okay for food and rent, but how would she keep affording things like her Photoshop subscription? Even if she managed to draw again, she'd struggle to keep up with her commissions without it. She'd have to downgrade to cheaper software.

She'd discuss it with Aya and Charlotte later at lunch, maybe even force herself to ask for help with the paperwork.

However, when the three of them sat in Gwen's kitchen, Charlotte had another topic in mind. She put her salad down with a miserable expression. "I don't know how to say this, so I'm just going to spit it out. I think it's time for me to move out."

"What?! No," Gwen whinged. She hated whining, but it had come from the heart before she had time to stop it escaping her mouth.

Charlotte put her hand over Gwen's. "Love, it's time. I need to get back to my own flat. Besides, you're doing better."

"Yes," Gwen had to agree.

Charlotte bit her lip, as if trying not to smile. "Also, you don't need me keeping you company when you have handsome Aya here every hour of the day."

"Not every hour," Aya groused.

"Well, every hour you're not at the office or the gym," Charlotte amended.

"I'm not handsome," Aya grumbled further.

"No? Do you prefer pretty? Or hot?" Charlotte said with half a grin. "I mean, I can see that you're attractive. I'm straight, not blind." She turned to Gwen. "Maybe we should ask you. Is Aya handsome, pretty, or hot?"

Gwen made a point of avoiding looking at Aya. She had a feeling that Aya was doing the same. Charlotte opened her salad with a hint of a smirk.

Gwen slumped in her seat. Not because of the attractiveness discussion, she could simply ignore that, but at the thought of being alone in the flat. Even so, she couldn't be selfish and ask Charlotte to stay. It was time.

"You're right," Gwen said. "You should get back to your own space, especially for when you want to bring blokes home. I'll miss you, though."

"We'll still see each other all the time, duck," Charlotte said, patting her hand on the table. "I'll move out in a couple of days, then?"

"Yep! I'll help," Gwen said, making a concerted effort to not sound sad.

Something was waved in front of her face; she moved back enough to see that it was Aya's sandwich.

"Want a bite? It's wholegrain with egg and turkey for a huge protein hit. Great for building muscles to help someone move. And to throw a proper right hook," Aya said with a wink.

Gwen couldn't help but laugh before she took a big bite, making sure to snag Aya's fingers with her teeth.

Aya drew her hand and sandwich back. "Ouch! She bites! You have to stay, Charlotte. I can't be left with this bitey monster."

"Nope. I've done my part. Now, she's all *yours*," Charlotte said, busy skewering a piece of lettuce on her fork.

"Oh." Aya stopped with the sandwich in the air. "Okay."

Gwen leaned closer. "I promise I'll keep my biting to a minimum."

Aya only gave a quick nod, blushing. Gwen smiled at her, and Aya returned it, showing that sweet, little dimple.

There was a sudden soaring in Gwen's chest.

Aya was tight-lipped as usual, but now Gwen understood. There was communication in that silence, true emotion that was shown with body language and looks. Not with words, which could be faked or be simple politeness. How had she not fully appreciated Aya's silences before? She had thought she wanted someone who kept up constant conversation like she did. Now she saw the beauty of Aya's expressive silences, of how she only said the words that mattered. It wasn't something she'd ever adopt for herself, but in Aya, it was perfect.

Aya blinked, and affection flashed in her dark eyes. They still echoed the shy smile on her lips.

The soaring in Gwen's chest grew.

Maybe Charlotte moving out wasn't the end of the world after all. Maybe being *all Aya's* could be kind of nice.

## Chapter Forty

# HOLD HER. KISS HER

Aya touched her damp hair as she took the last steps up to Gwen's flat. She'd done a terrible job of drying it after training with Jenny. She'd hurried out of the changing room, as always far too eager to see Gwen.

She was let in and hugged before Gwen walked to the kitchen, saying, "Come on in. I'm just finishing up cleaning Meatloaf's cage."

Aya stopped in the hallway. "Okay, should I take my jacket off or are we going straight out?"

Today's, or rather tonight's, boost gift was a drive up to Mow Cop. Gwen had never seen the view from the castle ruins over most of Staffordshire and Cheshire. It was particularly pretty at night when the stars watched over the two counties and all was quiet.

There was a click of a cage door before Gwen came back into the hall. "I'm so sorry, but I'm exhausted. The cage cleaning and adjusting to all the changes lately have knackered me. I'm not back to my normal energy levels, so helping Charlotte move, even though I didn't do as much as she and you did, combined with the stress over the sick-leave paperwork…" She trailed off.

Aya immediately took her jacket off and hung it up. "Say no more. A night in, it is."

Gwen held a hand to her chest and chewed her lower lip, like a child worried about being in trouble. "Are you sure? I don't want you to get bored with me not being able to do much."

"Treasure, I could never get bored with you."

Gwen knitted her brows. "Treasure?"

"What?" Aya said defensively.

"Nothing," Gwen said, her tone warm. "I just like that you called me treasure. It's cute."

Aya couldn't remember the last time she'd felt this much like a right pillock. "Well, I mean, you're very precious, right? I think so. I mean, you are. So, it's not strange to call you that. I think."

*Stop babbling, Lawson.*

Gwen leaned against the wall, a smile tugging on lips that were no longer pale or parched. "You can call me anything you like, sweetheart. Anyway, let's change the topic to something that makes you more comfortable: boxing. Since we're going to be in, would you fancy doing a bit more practice with me?"

"I'd love to!"

"Wonderful."

The smile on Gwen's lips grew and now reached those expressive eyes. How had Gwen described their colour? Sapphire blue. Yes, that made sense, sparkling sapphires. Mesmerised, Aya moved towards her, drawn to the sweet woman in front of her like a moth to a flame. What was she doing? What did she want to do when she reached Gwen? The answer came as a bolt from a clear sky. She wanted to hold her. To kiss her. To touch those rosy lips to her own.

Aya stopped dead. What the hell was she doing? Why was she lusting after a friend? One who was in recovery and needed support, especially now that Charlotte was gone? Gwen needed her. There was no way she was taking advantage of that. Aya buried any lust or attraction down deep and said, "Right, we shouldn't stand about, then. Let's get boxing."

## Chapter Forty-One

# ACTION

The next morning Gwen woke up to her whole body feeling different. A pleasant heat and humming coursed through her. She soon remembered why. She'd been having a wet dream! For the first time in months, she was *aroused*. She laughed with relief at that her body and mind were reconnecting. Life thrummed through her again in the shape of all of the emotions, and now she could add lust to that list. In fact, it was thrumming between her legs very nicely right this moment.

She slid her hand down her stomach and into her damp curls while trying to remember the dream. There had been a woman, seated with her in an otherwise empty train carriage. She couldn't quite remember what the train, or the woman, looked like. She winced. It hadn't been Susannah, had it? After all, Susannah had been the focus of Gwen's erotic dreams over the past year.

No, there hadn't been that sensation of a distant crush and an unreachable goddess. This dream was based in real emotion. A real connection. Just as much lust and passion as in the Susannah dreams, but so much more *potent*.

Gwen focused on that feeling, closed her eyes, and let her hand between her thighs do the rest. She was out of practise, meaning she had to keep fighting thoughts that wanted to pop up and interrupt the action. Her mind circled around how ridiculous it was that she'd thought it was Susannah in her dream. Everything surrounding Susannah had been a faint echo of real emotions. Even the pick-me-ups that she'd gotten from seeing Susannah paled compared to, for example, the ones she got with Aya.

Everything was better with Aya. She was the perfect friend. The perfect woman. Strong in body, spirit, mind, and heart. Honest, kind, interesting, and so damn sexy with that enticing dimple. Not to mention those steady hands with thick veins that ran up trim wrists. Or that long, shiny, soft, midnight-black hair. That sharp jawline. That smooth skin. That muscular but lean build, with sculpted pecs showcasing soft breasts, and the waist tapering into solid hips and a buff bum. Aya could've been sculpted out of clay by a particularly good artist. Her body wasn't just aesthetically pleasing; it was primed for action. The raw power in that body was balanced with such tender movements. Tender like when she touched Gwen.

Gwen's eyes snapped open just as she realised two things. One: that she'd been taking note of Aya's body more than she had realised. Two: that she was nearing orgasm while thinking about Aya. Worse, it was thinking about Aya that was bringing her close to the edge. She gasped with realisation, and then gasped even louder as her climax erased all thought.

## Chapter Forty-Two

# ONLY ONE SLIGHT TOUCH

That night Aya warmed up with some jumping jacks and windmills and watched Gwen mimic her movements. Her hostess had wanted more boxing practise, and Aya wasn't going to argue. It was nice to show her expertise and coach a student, without the pressure and seriousness that prepping Jenny for a professional boxing career involved. Not to mention that being in Gwen's company was her favourite thing these days. It was like coming home.

Aya did one last windmill and motioned for Gwen to stop. "Okay. We're warmed up. Get in the ready position, and we'll work on your offence first. I think you're okay with hooks, so let's focus on jabs, uppercuts, and cross punches."

Gwen pouted. "I can't just keep doing hooks?"

Aya shook her head with a chuckle. "No. Why did you zero in on that particular punch anyway?"

"Because it had a fun name, I guess? I liked the pirate connotation."

Aya put her hand over her eyes, chuckling again. "Well, you're doing this for fun and exercise, so you can stick to any punch you want, but only doing hooks will get dull pretty quick."

"Fine. We'll do some jobs, upper crusts, and cross stitch."

"Stop taking the mick," Aya exclaimed, almost able to hide her smile. "We'll start with jabs."

Gwen adjusted the straps of her red tank top and moved her feet into position, Aya standing next to her. They went through the checklist of forming the correct stance for jabs.

"Ready," Gwen called in triumph. "Time to jab it up!"

"Almost. You need to pull your right shoulder back and move the left one forward more. That way your body becomes a narrower target for your opponent."

Aya demonstrated the proper positioning and waited while Gwen drew her gaze over her body.

"Got it. Like this," Gwen said, casting her left elbow out to the side.

"No, that's too much. Also, your right one has to be tight by your side. But not glued to your ribs—you still have to be able to move it at a moment's notice."

"Okay," Gwen said, unsure. She tried to correct the posture and almost ended up where she'd started.

"No, it's too much in the other direction now, treasure. Hang on, I'll show you."

She stood right behind Gwen and took a gentle hold of her elbows, placing them correctly. Gwen swayed a little but then solidified into the pose. She smelled of that vanilla shampoo of hers. She must've showered just before Aya arrived.

Aya let go of her elbows but didn't move away. While she was there, she might as well make some more corrections. After all, how was Gwen going to be able to swing properly if her stance wasn't solid?

"You need to soften your knees more for stability."

Gwen bent more at the knees, making her closer to Aya's height. Gwen's bum brushed Aya's pelvis as she crouched down. Aya distracted herself from the sensation by leaning her head over Gwen's shoulder to check that she was still keeping her chin down. She had a tendency to lift it, exposing it to blows.

When Aya peered over Gwen's shoulder and down her front like this, she noticed that the vanilla scent wasn't coming only from her hair but from her chest and neck, too. Soap? Lotion? Perfume? Aya hurled the thoughts away. She couldn't let herself think about what had touched Gwen's naked body. She had to focus! What the hell had she been doing? Oh right, correcting posture.

"Good! Try to balance your weight in the centre of your body," Aya said, still looking down from the shoulder to see all of Gwen's front and check that she obeyed.

*Bloody hell. That tank top really doesn't cover much.*

It didn't help that Gwen was breathing hard and fast. The quick movements of her chest kept drawing Aya's attention against her will.

Aya cleared her throat. "Great. Now keep your eyes ahead, on the target of your jab."

Gwen moved her head forward.

"No, shug, not your entire face. You need to keep your chin down, remember? Just set your gaze."

Gwen shifted, bringing their bodies closer but also edging out of the proper stance. "Sorry. I'm getting a bit nervous all of a sudden."

"I can tell. Your left elbow is in the wrong place again."

Aya grasped the offending elbow to return it to where she wanted it. This time, though, she was so much more aware of Gwen's heated skin. Her fingertips couldn't help but brush the rose-petal softness of the sensitive inside of Gwen's forearm.

It was only a second of caressing, nothing as long-lasting or as intimate as their hugs or when Aya washed Gwen's hair, but it was enough. Somehow, that little touch stood out like a bright red rose in a field of dull snow-drops. They moved apart as if they'd both been electrified. Gwen turned and they stared at each other. Aya searched those wide, blue eyes, trying to figure out if Gwen had sprung away because she was shocked or offended.

Her stomach ached. Was it too much to hope that Gwen hadn't noticed the touch going from platonic boxing corrections to something more intimate? It had only been a moment after all, the tiniest fragment of time. One slight touch.

Gwen smiled bashfully, then scratched the back of her neck as she mumbled, "That tickled. Sorry for jumping away."

She wasn't sure if it had tickled or if Gwen was politely making up an excuse. She wanted to kick herself. Not only was Gwen her friend—and vulnerable during her recovery—she was also her student right now. It was morally wrong to caress someone while you were doing manual corrections. Sure, Gwen was so physically affec-tionate that they touched each other more than Aya remembered from her other few friendships in life. This touch, however, had been different. So wonderful, but so dangerous.

She tried to calm down. Gwen looked fine. In fact, she appeared to be back to normal. She had picked up the glass of water off the coffee table and smiled at Aya between sips.

*How can she be so carefree when my world just got upended by... A. Single. Damn. Touch?!*

Gwen tilted her head. "You okay? Want some water?" She held out the glass.

"Y-yes, please." Aya moved closer, as carefully as if she were nearing a dangerous animal. She took the glass and drank.

Gwen was still smiling. She snagged her lower lip with her teeth and watched Aya through her lashes. They were darker today, she realised. Was she wearing mascara? How had Aya not noticed before?

Aya drank some more water, buying time while trying to figure what to do and say next.

Gwen was still giving her that doe-eyed expression and biting that lower lip. Was she suddenly shy? Uncomfortable? Or could that be... some sort of subtle flirtation?

All of this was too confusing for Aya. Normally she'd ask Gwen to interpret the situation for her, but as Gwen *was* the bloody situation, that idea was off.

Silence poured into every inch of the room. How long had they been staring at each other? Aya noticed that the glass was empty and put it down.

Gwen's throat bobbed as if she had swallowed something big. "So, now what?"

Aya shifted her footing. "Um. I don't know. We might want to call it a night?"

"Yes! Good thinking. We should do that because..." She trailed off as if she'd lost the rest of her sentence.

"Because we..." Aya tried to help, but her brain wasn't giving her a single excuse as to why they should separate. She'd only arrived about fifteen minutes ago.

"Because, um…" Gwen gallantly tried again.

They weren't keeping eye contact anymore. In fact, they'd both become fascinated by their feet. Or maybe the floor. It was a nice carpet after all.

Aya's stomach clenched again.

*Say something! Even if it's one of those old pick-up lines you memorised. Just anything! Act the tough butch that you're supposed to be and fix the situation.*

"Because I have a cramp in my left leg!" Gwen blurted out. It would have been more convincing if she hadn't rubbed her right leg as she said it. She spotted Aya watching the leg being rubbed and shouted, "I meant right leg!"

"Oh, no. That's bad," Aya answered feebly.

The situation would've been funny if it wasn't so bloody mortifying.

Aya edged her way towards the hallway. "Yeah, so, uh, cramps are the worst! Um, make sure to eat something salty and drink some water. Oh, and do the stretches I've shown you!"

"Yes, that might help," Gwen said.

"Yep. That'll do it," Aya needlessly agreed as she kept moving towards the much-desired door to freedom.

When she was out in the hallway, she grabbed her jacket without pausing to put it on and shouted, "See you tomorrow."

"Sure, see you tomorrow," Gwen called from the lounge.

Aya slammed the door and ran down the stairs. Gwen always came to the door to see her off. Was she staying in character and pretending to have a cramp? Was it a symptom of the shyness/discomfort/weird flirting from before? Or was Gwen offended by the fingertip brush? Aya had no clue. She nearly missed one of the steps in her hurry and decided to take the lift the rest of the way. She could use the time to try to get her head screwed back on.

---

Aya stayed unsteady in mind and body for the next couple of hours. She walked around in a daze, half of the time daydreaming about rose-petal soft skin, the other half, worrying a hole in her gut over having upset Gwen. It was a damn good thing that she wasn't meant to be in the gym tonight.

She was making an evening coffee for herself and her dad when her phone beeped. She quickly put the mugs down and checked the phone, heart pounding. Yes. It was a text from Gwen.

*Hi. Sorry that it all got a bit abrupt earlier. I had a great time and I think I'm learning a lot. Could we try again? It doesn't have to be right now, of course. Unless you want to? I know you're free tonight but maybe you don't want to see me right now? I'd totally get that. xx*

Aya didn't have to think. She shouted to her dad, "You'll have to make your own coffee. I'm going to Gwen's." Then she picked up her keys and ran to the jeep.

---

When Gwen opened the door, she was still dressed in that

damn, skimpy, rose-red tank top and black leggings. Aya brushed down her hoodie, wishing she would've changed into something more flattering.

Gwen stood aside to let her in, saying, "Guess what!"

"What?" Aya asked. She was about to hang her jacket before she remembered that in her haste, she hadn't put it on. No wonder she was cold.

"I 've been drawing some more since you left. I don't know why, but I was really inspired. And best of all, I just got a commission from a writer that I really admire!"

"Oh, cool," Aya said, following Gwen into the kitchen.

"It really is. I've been a fan of hers for ages. We're connected on both Twitter and Tumblr, but I never expected her to hire me to draw one of her characters."

"That's brilliant! You'll have to show me who she is later. For now," Aya licked her lips, nervousness shooting through her, "did you want to do some more training?"

Gwen drained a mug of what was probably tea. "Yes, please. Maybe another type of punch?"

"Um. Sure. What about an uppercut? Let's try a left one. You need to work on your weaker side."

"Yes, Miss Lawson," Gwen droned in the obedient but bored voice they'd all used with teachers when at school. Then she smirked.

Aya crumpled her brow and pointed to Gwen. "None of that cheek, young lady, or I'll make you stay after class."

"That's a rubbish threat, considering I love spending time in close quarters with you," Gwen said with a beaming smile as she headed into the living room. "So, what's the posture for an uppercut?"

"With this one you need to think about shifting most of your weight to your back leg."

Gwen tugged on her earlobe, an adorable frown of confusion on her features.

"Just get in the ready position and we'll go from there," Aya said, unable to hide her smile.

Gwen did as asked, glancing over at her for approval.

"Cool," Aya said. "Now, you have to really anchor with your back leg for a powerful uppercut."

Gwen leaned back as if there was a bad smell in front of her.

Aya crossed her arms over her chest. "Not that much. You can't reach your opponent now."

"Well, excuse me for not knowing what you're on about. Show me instead of standing there complaining," Gwen said with an exaggerated pout.

Aya pulled off her hoodie, adjusted her Muscles & Mitts T-shirt, and demonstrated the posture. Gwen copied it but was still leaning back too much with her legs too far apart.

"Hm. Better, but you sort of look like you're trying to do the splits. Also, your back is tilting backwards too much. The bend needs to come from your knees and hips."

Aya grasped Gwen's shoulders to tug her torso forward, like Bill had done with her when she was learning. However, on those occasions, she had never stood with her legs *this* far apart. Or been so thin and tall. Nor been so unbending during the manoeuvring. Gwen being all these things, and never very balanced, meant that the movement unsteadied her completely. She surged forward, making them collide. Luckily, Aya stood secure and caught her.

Now Gwen was in her arms, her entire body weight

held in Aya's embrace, her hands clutching Aya but her mouth showing a graceful, calm smile.

A quick memory of when she had carried Gwen from the floor blinked into her mind and then back out. This was so entirely different. Back then, Aya had been helping Gwen and was in complete control. Now, even though Gwen was the one off-balance, Aya felt that all the decisions were in Gwen's hands. Aya watched the left hand nimbly gripping her bicep. Those fingers were so creamy white, smooth and long. Gwen's hands weren't clumsy and calloused like Aya's boxer's hands, which only punched and lifted weights. These beautiful, agile hands created things. Right now, they were creating all sorts of sensations in Aya. Admiration, affection, arousal.

Gwen remained smiling in her arms, leaning towards the ground but clearly unafraid. She trusted Aya to hold her up. Then those jewel-blue eyes moved, and Aya traced her gaze. Gwen was staring at her lips. Aya's chest tightened. When had she taken her last breath? She inhaled, sounding like a drowning person gasping in a breath.

*Well, that's an attractive noise, you pillock.*

Gwen's right hand, formerly gripping Aya's shoulder, moved to cup Aya's cheek. "Are you okay?" she whispered, as if a louder voice would shatter the moment.

Aya nodded, too fast and too desperately to be convincing.

"It's all right," Gwen whispered with all the certainty that Aya didn't feel.

She lost herself in those safe, blue eyes and slowly began to relax. She'd learned to trust Gwen's assessments. It was okay. Everything would be all right as long as Gwen was with her.

Gwen with the kind face and that sweet, upturned nose.

Gwen with the soft hand that still cupped her cheek, the thumb rubbing comforting circles on it.

Gwen with those lips that had been pretty even when pale and parched, but now, had bloomed into an inviting rosy sheen. They drew her full attention, hypnotising and appearing to pulsate with life.

*You're hallucinating because you're not breathing properly. Get yourself together!*

Aya forced herself to take a deep breath, filling her chest and belly. As she did, she had to adjust her slipping grip on Gwen. Something which only brought their bodies closer together. Those rosy lips were so close now. They called to her. In this moment, they were Aya's whole world. Nothing else mattered.

Before she could think it through, her own lips had sought them out and connected with them. Gwen's lips were warm and yielding, like her whole body, still resting in Aya's embrace.

It was an honour to be allowed kiss her, to hold her. To have Gwen trust her like this. To share this perfect, intimate moment. This perfect kiss, all tingling warmth and bliss. How could she be this lucky?

Then Gwen's hand on Aya's bicep tightened and Gwen disentangled herself, getting to her feet. She stood and backed away.

Alarm bells blared in Aya's mind. That sent a clear message. Gwen hadn't wanted to be kissed. Not by Aya? Not now? Not like this? All of the above?

Panic made Aya want to throw up. She had risked everything. She needed Gwen, and now she'd lost her. She knew this had been too good to be true. Of course she would do the wrong thing and ruin it, like she always did. And for what? Because she couldn't keep her hands, or rather her lips, to herself.

Disgust and anxiety made her nausea worse. She put a hand to her stomach. "Sorry. I-I have to go."

She ran out before Gwen could answer. If Gwen didn't speak, nothing was definite. Nothing bad could be said if Gwen couldn't say it. It wasn't logical, but it was all Aya had.

She switched off her phone as she got into the jeep. She would discuss this with Gwen, of course, but not now. Now all she could think to do was escape by driving home as fast as she legally could.

## Chapter Forty-Three

# LOVE-STRUCK

The next morning dragged, mainly because Gwen couldn't get Aya to reply to her texts or voicemails. Granted, Aya was at work now, but she could still check her texts occasionally.

Gwen rubbed her forehead. Maybe her messages asking Aya to get in touch had been too vague, but she couldn't be honest and say that she'd loved the kiss. Loved it so much that right after it, she'd gotten to her feet to be in a better position to kiss Aya again. And again. And never stop.

She couldn't be honest because Aya had looked horrified by the kiss and run off.

No, Gwen had to be vague. She had to play it cool until she knew how Aya felt. If Aya regretted the kiss, then one of the most important friendships in Gwen's life was at stake.

To make things more complicated, Gwen couldn't stop worrying about the consequences. If Aya said she liked the kiss as well, if there was a chance of romance between them, questions would have to be asked. Was Aya prepared to date someone with a debilitating mental illness? Was it fair to ask Aya to live with that sort of burden? Were Gwen and her recovering mind even ready to be in a relationship again? Was Aya?

The memory of Sarah, the woman she was set to marry until Gwen's depression got too much for her, kept rearing its ugly head.

*Aya isn't Sarah. She's much more stable and steadfast.*

Gwen managed until eleven-thirty, then her desperation for answers got the better of her. If Aya wouldn't, or couldn't, give her answers, she had to find the person who knew her best and maybe could answer for her. Bill.

Gwen steeled herself to leave the flat and then headed for Muscles & Mitts. It had been a mild, sunny morning, so she chose a knitted sweater instead of her coat. Ten minutes into the walk, though, the sky arched grey and overcast above the city, mirroring her wretched mood and making her reconsider her outfit. She picked up her speed.

When she entered the gym, weaving between a woman pummelling a speed bag and two blokes skipping rope, she saw Bill.

He was inspecting the men with the skip ropes and bellowed, "I told you those shoes were too slippery" as one of the men fell. After checking that the guy was okay, Bill looked up and spotted Gwen.

He nodded at her and came over. "Hey, kid. You looking for Aya?"

"No, I know she's still at Explore. I wanted to talk to you."

"Me?" He knitted his bushy, grey eyebrows.

"Yes. I need to talk to you about Aya. Or rather, ask you about her."

"Okay, shoot. I've known her since she was a teenager, and she's as much of an open book now as she was back then."

Gwen decided to start with the obvious. "I think I've fallen in love with her."

He threw his fists above his head. "Boom, there it is! I've been waiting weeks for you two to stop thinking you were just friends. So, what you want to ask me is if I think she's in love with you, too?"

"No. That's probably a question I need to take up with her. As soon as she starts replying to my texts," Gwen grumbled. "What I wanted to ask you, as someone who probably knows her better than she knows herself, is," she hesitated, fidgeting with her sleeve, "is if she's equipped for a relationship with someone who will at times be a burden."

"A burden?"

Gwen wanted to sink through the floor but pushed herself on. "I don't know if she told you, but I have clinical depression."

"She did. She talked about how impressed she was with your moxie, you know, when it comes to coping with it."

"That's nice," Gwen said vaguely. "She's very supportive and the best friend anyone could ask for. However, it's a whole other thing when you're in a full-time relationship with someone who has a different brain chemistry."

Bill rubbed his huge chest pensively. "Hm. Well, I'll tell ya three things." He held up a huge finger. "Aya, or anyone worth your time, would never think of you as a burden."

He waited until she reluctantly nodded, then held up a

second finger. "Aya's strong and flexible. She can handle anything if she's got someone who believes in her and reminds her to believe in herself. During her boxing career, with all the pain and pressure—and of course growing up with absent parents who I honestly believe didn't want kids—she's lived through a lot of crap. She's a tough cookie. She can take whatever your depression might throw at her."

Gwen's racing mind came to a screeching halt. That was true, wasn't it? Aya was a fighter who wasn't put off by hardship. She'd spent a life fighting for her parents' love and never gotten it.

*Can I really let my depression rob her of my love, too?*

He held up a third finger. "Finally, the most important thing, Aya's love-struck for you." He stared her right in the eye. "She'd fall to pieces if you didn't let her love the hell out of you."

Outwardly, Gwen lurched a little. Inwardly, a shaft of sunlight was cracking through the cold unease in her chest and spreading bright, heated bliss. "I… I'd like to be the person who reminds Aya to believe in herself."

He knitted his brows again. "Well, kid, why the hell are you telling me? Go tell *her.*"

Gwen beamed. "I will. I'll go right now."

"No, hang on for a sec. I wanna talk to you about these 'boosts' that Aya has been giving you."

Hiding her impatience, Gwen replied, "Sure, what about them?"

"The idea stuck in my mind." He scratched his cheek with the air of a man formulating his thoughts. "When Aya told me about them, I started thinking about my life. I figured the woman I loved and the job I loved almost as much were my boosts."

Gwen must have looked sceptical because he held up a hand. "I know, I know. Those are things that I love and that make my life worth living, not the boosts you were talking about, right?"

"Right." She searched for the words to explain. "My pick-me-ups, or boosts, have more been like, um, moments of joy. Little treats or even surprises that pop up in a normal day."

He pointed a finger at her, all enthusiasm now. "Yeah! That's what I figured, too, and that was when it hit me. What we're talking about here, kid, is romanticising the small things in life."

"The small things?" Gwen asked, smothering the wish to shut him up so she could run to Aya.

"Uh-huh. Like treating yourself to a great piece of pie. Or catching a movie you've been dying to see." He scratched his cheek again. "It's about the treats, but most of all it's about how you take them when they arrive, how much you enjoy them! They're something to look forward to and to really enjoy the hell out of when you get 'em, right?"

"I suppose so, yes."

He nodded as if they were now in some sort of conspiracy or club. "There you go. Well, my boost for today is gonna be leaving work ten minutes early so I can go see the woman I love." He eyed her. "Speaking of which, why are you here? Go see the woman *you* love, kid. Go get 'er!"

Gwen didn't argue; she thanked him and hurried out.

Not only had her doubts been doused by Bill, but she'd also gotten some perspective when she was finally out of her flat and her own cage of a mind. No matter how afraid she was of getting into a relationship and what it could do to her mental health, no matter how she worried if Aya would be able to handle her and her illness full time, it was with her as Bill said it was with Aya - She was love-struck and there was no fighting it.

## Chapter Forty-Four

# HER HEART ON HER SLEEVE

Aya stepped out of the office and into Hanley, the town functioning as Stoke-on-Trent's city centre. It had been a sunny morning when Aya arrived at this busy side street. Now the sky was filled with massive, grey clouds, heavy with rain. It explained why there wasn't anyone around; everyone was taking shelter. Aya pulled up the hood of her jacket, getting ready to sprint through the pending rain. She turned, though, at the sound of footfalls pounding the pavement and saw Gwen stop in front of her, clasping her side as if she had a stitch.

"Gwen! Are you okay?" Aya scanned her knitted jumper and light trousers. "You're not dressed properly. It'll pour down any second."

"No time," Gwen stopped to suck in a breath, "to get changed. Bill said to hurry," another gasp for air, "to you."

"Bill? What does he have to do with this?"

"He said I should go get you," she said, breathing almost back to normal.

"*Get* me? What, like fetch me? Has something happened to him?"

"No, he's fine! He just wanted me to tell you that I want to be with you and take care of you, that you are worth any risks, and to…" Gwen took a long inhale and bit her lip before finishing with, "…to do this, I suppose."

She leaned in and quickly touched her lips to Aya's, then stood back with her hands clasped.

Aya wasn't quite sure what the statement, or the peck, meant. Considering how touchy-feely Gwen was, it could mean 'we're really close friends so a little kiss is fine, don't worry about last night'. Or it could mean 'I enjoyed the kiss and want to date you'. There was no way around it. As much as it pained Aya, she'd have to come right out and ask.

"Was that like a… *friend* kiss?"

Gwen fidgeted with her hands. "If you want it to be."

The blood rushed in Aya's ears. "And if I want it to be more?"

"Then you better give me a kiss that shows that it's more," Gwen said quietly.

Aya closed the gap between them, put her hands on Gwen's waist, and, with her heart pounding like a drum, let herself be drawn to those rosy lips again.

How could she convey all her love and appreciation in one kiss? Would that be open-mouthed? Should she press their lips together hard or go in gentle and sweet? Before she had time to decide, her mouth was on Gwen's. Gwen parted her lips and unlocked Aya's. From there, their lips clasped each other in every possible formation.

Aya's hands were less certain. They kept moving from Gwen's waist to her hips and back again, barely clutching her, as if Gwen was as fragile as spun glass. Gwen was having none of that. She put her hands over Aya's on her waist and squeezed. That was all the direction Aya needed. She grabbed Gwen and pulled her close with all the craving she'd been burying for weeks. She didn't know you could need someone's touch like this, need that physical connection like you did air or food.

The kiss intensified, tongues touching and exploring mouths. Gwen's hands stroked her neck and threaded into her hair. Aya was thunderstruck. It was as if beneficial electricity buzzed through Aya's veins and into her heart, making it pulse faster and stronger, growing her heart to twice its size to fit all the love she was generating.

Only when her teeth knocked into Gwen's did she stop the kiss. "Oops. You okay?"

Gwen nodded. She was breathing fast, her eyes lidded and her mouth ajar. Aya could've sworn she was high on something.

"That," Gwen panted, "certainly wasn't friendly."

"No," Aya replied with an incredulous laugh.

Gwen placed her forehead against hers. "Now what?"

Aya knew what had to come next, but it frightened her. She remembered asking Susannah out. As nerve-wracking as that had been, she could fall back on silly pick-up lines and over-the-top flirting. At the time it had been extremely important to her, but deep down she'd known that if she messed it up, she'd leave, go home to Stoke, and life would carry on.

This situation, though, this woman, *had become her home.*

The stakes were so much higher. This time, she wasn't gambling with her self-esteem; she was gambling with her heart and her newly rebuilt life. There was no pick-up line that would do. No suave comment. No joke. There was only her heart on her sleeve.

She braced herself. "If you think it's a good idea, could w-we start dating?"

Gwen pressed their foreheads together closer. "It would risk our friendship."

"Yeah, it would. Sure, if the relationship goes to hell, we'd still try to be friends. But it wouldn't be the same, would it?"

"No," Gwen whispered, moving their faces apart. "On the other hand, will our friendship be the same after that kiss? Hasn't everything already changed? Hasn't it… deepened?"

That current of electricity buzzed through Aya again, singing in her blood. "Absolutely."

"I think we have to try dating, then. I sure as bloody hell want to," Gwen said with a beaming smile. Aya couldn't take her eyes off that smile, that mouth which was heaven to her.

Aya wanted to shout with joy. Instead, she pulled Gwen flush against her for another kiss. That was when the skies opened. They kept kissing, and the rain kept worsening. Somehow the sprinkling of tiny raindrops felt like a celebration to Aya, like confetti on newlyweds outside a church.

Aya's mind half focused on the incredible kiss and half mocked her soppy imagination.

*What the hell has happened to me?*

Gwen broke the kiss to give an exulted laugh. She whirled around in the rain, hands held out and face to the sky. Aya watched the rain streak her mascara, but she clearly didn't care. Gwen Davies didn't care what people thought about someone dancing in the rain and taking up the whole pavement. Nor how her makeup looked. Nor if her clothes were ruined. She was savouring her happiness with every fibre of her being.

Aya shivered, as much due to the chilly rain as from being awed by the sight.

*Oh, yeah. That's what happened to me. Gwen happened to me.* She laughed, too, and watched the woman she adored dance, brimming with pride and affection.

*Thank god she happened to me.*

## Chapter Forty-Five

# THE MILLIONTH SESSION AND THE FIRST DATE

Gwen glared at her watch. She wanted to spend every second with Aya, talking to her, kissing her, touching her. Most of all, she wanted to focus on their first real date tonight.

Not happening, though. She had to focus on herself as well, on her recovery and her future. She was a grown woman and had learned the dangers of being swallowed whole by a relationship.

So here she was, in her therapist's dingy chair for the millionth time, telling him about how being hired to draw art for her favourite writer had meant a lot of internet buzz, not to mention new commissions.

"Most of all, though," she said, "I'm excited about November suggesting—"

"November," Edward interrupted. "That's this favourite author of yours?"

"Yes. November Jones. I'm excited about her suggesting we work together. She mentioned an idea for a web comic."

"A comic book?"

"Yes, but they're posted online. I mean, they can be in book form, too, but that'll come later. If we get it right and it sells well, there could be a whole series."

"Good, good. That would bring some income. Maybe you could sell merchandise then, too?" Edward said with his first real smile of the session.

"Um. Yes, perhaps."

His smile dissolved. "I'm sorry to be crass here, but your financial situation needs cash flow."

"I know," she bit out. "Most comic creators don't make a fortune, though. I'll have to have another source of income. Anyway, one thing at a time." *Time for a topic change*, she decided. "Like with Aya. Tonight is our first date, and I'm trying not to get ahead of myself."

He started making notes. "Ahead of yourself as in expecting sex?"

"Ahead of myself as in proposing marriage."

He nearly dropped his pen. "Oh."

"That," she said with a laugh, "is how we lesbians, or rather all sapphics, tend to operate. We bring a spare key on the first date. Keep up, Edward."

"Right. Of course. Carry on."

Gwen sat back. "Well, I know what I'm doing for the date. I'm giving her a little bright-spark moment, or boost, or whatever you want to call it."

"That's great." He gave her a searching look. "Speaking of those, I hope you're finding some of those for yourself and not relying on a romantic partner to provide what appears to be vital to your mental health."

Gwen crossed and uncrossed her legs. "Um, shouldn't I rely on her? After all, we're dating, so she'll be my team-mate in life. You have to lean on your teammate at times, right?"

"Lean, yes. Utterly rely on, no."

"Okay. Makes sense. I'll find the balance there."

"I'm glad to hear it. Striving for balance is crucial. Especially for those of us with mental illnesses."

"Us?"

He gave a curt nod. "I have OCD. Not the worst case I've encountered, but not the lightest case either."

Unconsciously, he reached down and tugged his sock further over his trouser leg. Gwen wanted to smack herself. All this time, she had been making fun of a trait that was a symptom of his condition!

*I suppose you really never know about a person's life until you look closer.*

Edward wasn't merely some neurotypical, conventional academic with bad fashion sense. He could relate to her more than she'd realised.

She sat up straighter, determined to take him more seriously. "Thanks for telling me."

"You're welcome. Now, should we talk about how you're going to keep your improvement stable, despite financial troubles and the overwhelming rush of hormones falling in love brings?"

"Yes," Gwen said, opening an entryway in her defensive wall. "I promise not to change the topic this time. Let's do it."

---

The evening finally settled and Aya knocked on her door, just like she'd done countless times. This time, however, was immeasurably different than all the rest.

Gwen rushed to the mirror to tousle her hair and check her makeup, then ran to the door. Aya was wearing her hair down, skin-tight grey jeans, and a burgundy cashmere jumper that fit criminally well. All her clothes hugged her as tightly as Gwen wanted to hug her. Aya put on the black peacoat she'd been holding. She was nervous, judging by her darting gaze and jerky movements.

"Hey gorgeous," Gwen said.

Aya blinked repeatedly. "Hey... uh, bugger me, I don't even have a word to describe how great you look."

"Thanks," Gwen said, subtly tugging her wide-necked blouse down to show off her collar bones. And her cleavage, of course. She didn't wear this strapless, push-up bra for nothing.

Aya cleared her throat and bolted forward to pull Gwen into a quick hug. She hoped Aya could smell their shared cologne on her.

"No need to come in," she said, grabbing her winter coat off the hook. "We're heading straight out."

"Okay? And you can't tell me what we're doing, shug?"

"Nope. Surprise adventure."

"Fine. Can you at least tell me if were walking there or if we're taking Janet?"

"We could walk since it's unseasonably warm tonight. It'd be faster if we drove, though," Gwen said as she locked the front door.

Aya pushed the lift button. "Janet it is, then."

Gwen stood next to her, expecting to wait for the lift while stealing glances at this sexy woman. Aya had other plans. She pushed Gwen up against the lift door and kissed her, deep and hard.

Gwen dropped her coat but didn't much care. She needed her hands to hold Aya flush against her. She felt Aya's heart pound through her sweater. Or was that her own heart echoing into Aya's chest?

The lift arrived with a *ping*. That sound might as well have been a microwave beep denoting that her libido was ready and bubbling over.

Aya moved away. "Sorry. I couldn't resist you."

"Oh… please don't resist me," Gwen said, clearing her throat and trying to clear her dizzy head. "Feel free to not resist me at any time during tonight."

Staggering, Aya picked up Gwen's coat and handed it to her. "You dropped this."

"Right. Thank you. So, um, what were we doing again?"

Aya grabbed the wall. Clearly Gwen wasn't the only one whose blood flow had gushed from her brain down between her thighs.

"The lift," Aya finally said.

"What? Oh yes, we were getting in the lift."

"We can't be all over each other like that for a while. Not if I'm going to be able to drive us to this mystery location."

"Noted. We'll slow down and keep ourselves to ourselves for now."

They got into the lift, both smiling.

---

Gwen noted that Aya's shoulders were up by her ears. She knew the feeling. Their conversation on the way over had gone from tentative to strangely polite small talk. It was palpable in the tense air just how much this date meant to both of them.

Gwen put her hand on her chest, unsurprised to find her heart pummelling against it like a moth trapped in a jar. *God, I hope she likes her surprise.*

Finally, they arrived at a field outside of Stoke. It belonged to her awful Coffee4U co-worker Dave. Gwen had sought him out, told him off for giving out her home address to Aya, and then blackmailed him into lending her this field. It belonged to his parents, but he and his mates set up movie nights here in the style of an American drive-in, with picnic blankets instead of cars, throughout summer.

On this quiet, autumn evening, it was set up only for them. Three blankets to sit on and then one each to cuddle up with. Next to them waited an ice bucket filled with Aya's favourite brand of beer. Behind that was a big Tupperware box of Aya's favourite sandwiches and another filled with sweet and savoury snacks.

Aya took it all in. "We're having our date here?"

"Yep. Unless you think it'll be too cold?"

"Not with all those blankets and our coats. Or with this hot company I've got."

Gwen gave her a wink, trying to cover up the fact that any compliments after her self-hating down phase meant so damn much to her, especially coming from Aya. "I wanted to arrange that outdoors picnic we talked about, but with an added bonus."

Aya smiled, almost shyly. "Is the bonus that we get to watch a movie?"

"Yes, but not just any movie. Guess what we're watching."

The smile morphed into puzzlement. "What?"

"That boxing biography you told me Susannah refused to take you to."

"No!" Aya breathed.

"Yep. I bought a digital copy, and it's ready to be projected onto that screen. Our own little cinema."

Aya opened her mouth, but no words came. Instead she whooped and picked Gwen up to spin her round in celebration.

Flying through the air, Gwen craned her head to kiss Aya's soft hair. Only the hair—she didn't dare get embroiled in one of those insane make-out sessions again. They'd never get to the movie, and she knew how important it was to Aya.

When her feet were back on the ground, she said, "Come on, let's feed those muscles of yours and get the movie going."

Gwen started the projector the way Dave had showed her. She peered up at the twilight sky and begged the weather to stay nice.

She sat down as the movie started and was handed a sandwich and tucked into her blanket by Aya. They ate and watched, sitting so close that they kept bumping each other with elbows and hands. Aya's body was stiff. Gwen didn't blame her; despite the cosiness, the mood was strange. It felt loaded with too many expectations and too much fear of screwing this up.

About half an hour in, there was a scene where the boxer ran through the landscape, set to atmospheric music. Gwen used that moment to ask, "Enjoying the movie?"

"So much! I can't believe I missed it at the cinema because Susannah was such a selfish cow."

Gwen snorted a little. "She was, wasn't she? God, I can't believe you let her treat you like that."

"What?" Aya said.

Her tone sounded a little short. Gwen assumed it was because she was focused on the movie, where the dialogue had just started.

*I'll just quickly explain and then let her get back to enjoying the movie.*

"I just meant that it still surprises me that you didn't tell her to buzz off sooner. You're a clever woman, you *know* you could do so much better."

Aya shifted and grimaced as if she'd eaten something sour. "Well, not everyone can be as insightful as you." A muscle bounced in her cheek before she added, "And I guess you're suggesting that you're the 'so much better,' huh?"

Any cosiness drained from the air between them. It sunk through the blankets and deep into the ground. Aya's short tone hadn't been because she was focusing on the movie, then. Why was she so prickly and rude all of a sudden?

"Hey, no need to be like that," Gwen said, trying to be the calm one.

"And there's no bloody *need* to keep rubbing my bad taste in women in my face!"

"Whoa. I meant no offence. If I was claiming you had bad taste in women, I wouldn't be doing myself any favours, would I?" Recrimination had snuck into her tone. How could it not when this touched a nerve, when she knew deep down that she wasn't good enough for Aya?

"We should stop talking about this. Watch the movie," Aya snapped, facing the screen.

Gwen considered that, her heart thumping. But being quiet and letting this fester was a ridiculous idea. No, she had to explain what she'd meant, and they had to clear the air.

"Look, I know you only stayed with her because she was a symbol for your fight to regain your confidence. You saw that she wasn't good for you early on. You just didn't want to believe it."

Aya kept her gaze on the screen, that muscle in her cheek still bouncing. "Thanks for telling me what I did and how I felt."

"Well, someone has to, because you have no clue, do you?" Gwen sniped.

Aya moved away from Gwen before roaring, "Would you stop being so superior and know-it-all and just watch the bollocking movie like I asked you to?"

Gwen pulled back. "Did you really just shout at me? Over something like this?"

Aya threw her arms out in a gesture of exasperation. "Do you even know how to be quiet? The chatterbox thing is all very charming when we're not trying to focus on something, but right now you need to sh—"

Gwen stabbed a finger towards her. "Do *not* tell me to shut up, Aya Jane Lawson. I've had enough of that throughout my life. I'm damn well not putting up with it from someone who's meant to care about me. Especially not on a date!"

"Then maybe we should end the bloody date," Aya said through gritted teeth.

"Yeah. I think we should."

"Great," Aya growled as she stood. "Come on. I'll drive you home."

Gwen crossed her arms over her chest. "I can walk."

"Just get in the bloody jeep," Aya said and marched off.

Gwen considered throwing a sandwich after Aya but stopped herself. Sadness was replacing her anger. She had inadvertently pushed Aya's buttons, and she'd done it on a night when Aya had clearly been nervous and insecure. It didn't excuse it, but it did explain it.

*Shit. Why did we have to talk about Susannah?*

She got up and followed Aya. She wasn't giving up on this night, or on their budding relationship.

*Chapter Forty-Six*

# UNDRESSING HER

When Aya had walked Gwen to the door of her flat, she had decided she wasn't going to come in. She was going to watch Gwen slam the door, glad to know she was home safely even if Aya was furious with her.

Why was she so furious with her? Aya closed her eyes, trying to sort her feelings while Gwen unlocked the door. It was because she'd tried so hard to be perfect for this amazing woman and then Gwen's comments had highlighted how stupid she was. She'd felt pitied. And patronised. Now, regret took over. She'd been channelling her dad back there on the blanket, temper flaring, shouting, and then shutting down the conversation.

*Why was I such an arsehole? I should've told her how I felt. I'm so bloody awkward!*

She opened her eyes and saw that Gwen was in her flat. Good. Now she could escape and hide until she could calmly figure out how to explain her feelings and apologise. Maybe even get an apology back.

"Ah, bollocks!" She heard Gwen shout.

"What's wrong?" she said, worry creeping in.

"I must've left Meatloaf's cage door ajar. She's not in her cage. Come in and close the door!"

Aya didn't question the order. As she rushed into the kitchen, Gwen was switching the light off in there.

She turned to Aya. "She's not in this room. The only door that was open was the one to the living room. She must be in there."

"Okay," Aya said, unsure of what to do.

"Could you help me search for her? Please? It's not a big room, it'll be quick."

"Sure." She sought Gwen's flitting gaze. "Hey. Don't worry. We'll find her."

When in the living room, Aya concentrated on the task at hand, pushing her anxious hurt down deep.

Gwen switched on a wall light, even though the purplish glow of twilight and the full moon bathed the room in lilac and silver. Perfect light to see an orange fluff ball on a beige carpet.

Gwen squirmed. "I do have to find her. B-but it's not the end of the world if we don't. There are no exposed cables in here, and the other doors are closed so she's safe at least."

"It's okay. We'll find her. Little beast is probably under the sofa," Aya muttered, throwing her coat on the table.

They got on their hands and knees, but the sofa was too flush to the ground. Gwen lay flat on her stomach to look. Aya followed suit.

"Can you see her?"

Gwen hummed. "There's something over there."

"Where?"

Gwen got back on all fours and went to point to where she'd meant, right as Aya thought she spotted movement on the other side and leapt to investigate. They collided, Aya hitting her head hard against Gwen's shoulder. She put her hand out to push the shoulder away but didn't touch something hard. She got a handful of something round and yielding. She looked to her hand and so did Gwen. Yes, of course. Of course she would be grabbing Gwen's boob. That was exactly how her damn night was going.

She was about to retract her hand when she heard Gwen weakly stifle a moan. When Aya searched her features, she realised that this definitely wasn't an offended face. Nor was Gwen moving away. She was leaning in.

A moment passed in thick, meaningful silence, as all of Aya's emotions and thoughts clicked into place.

A sensual but cautious smile tugged at Gwen's lips. "Do you... want to move that hand?"

"Do you want me to?" Aya asked in a strangled whisper.

"Absolutely not."

"Good," Aya breathed. "Because I really don't want to either."

Another beat of silence. Their gazes stayed locked.

"Gwen, I'm sorry for shouting and for being cranky and for ending the date. I shouldn't—"

"Shh," Gwen said. "I know. We both acted badly and we'll discuss that in a moment. Right now, I need your hands on me. *All* over me."

Arousal flooded her without mercy, bringing back the urgency built up by every daydream and wet dream about Gwen.

"Get up," Aya said. "Please," she added.

They stood, facing each other. With reverent hands, she took Gwen's blouse off. When only a bra stood between her and a topless Gwen, her hands began to tremble.

*Bloody hell, you'd think I'd never undressed a woman before.*

Aya got herself together and unhooked the strapless bra and let it fall to the floor, next to the blouse.

The curvature of Gwen's pale breasts, with tips as rosy as her lips, nearly undid Aya. How could anything be that pretty? How had she known Gwen for months without being allowed to put *those* in her damn *mouth*? She pulled Gwen to her by the waist and bowed so she could kiss those taut nipples, deep and hard, then placed kisses all over Gwen's chest and shoulders. She wanted to kiss every sweet inch of Gwen but didn't have the patience to remember what parts her mouth had already mapped.

Gwen growled, deep in her throat. For a moment Aya thought she was angry about the fight again. Her worries calmed as Gwen said, "This is taking too long. Get your clothes off," before starting to pull off her own trousers.

They quickly but clumsily undressed, both staring at the parts of the other's body that was being unveiled.

Aya took Gwen's hand and guided her down onto the thick carpet. She didn't dare suggest pausing to go to the bedroom, didn't dare break the spell. Gwen sprawled out as if she'd planned to make love here all along.

The wall light barely reached them on this side of the sofa, meaning the curves and planes of Gwen's body were painted in silver shadows by the full moon. Aya sucked in a breath. The beauty almost hurt, especially as Gwen smiled and the moonlight reflected in her gleaming eyes.

Aya's apprehension had transformed into affectionate passion before, but now, oh now, she became all languid arousal. The sight of Gwen brought back the persistent tug in her lower abdomen, which had first shown up when they kissed by the lift earlier. That tug now went all the way down between her thighs and spread soaking, red-hot heat.

She had to know if Gwen was as turned on as she was. She trailed her hands up Gwen's thighs, signalling to her what she wanted. She moaned when Gwen complied and parted her legs, her folds opening up like a pulsing, pink rose, revealing wetness and the hardness of her clit. Aya wasn't the only one *desperate* for this.

Her fingers needed to explore all of it. They glided, dipped, and came out coated with liquid as thick as the honey Gwen had in her tea. Aya put them into her mouth. She had to learn what Gwen tasted like. Sea salt and spice filled her mouth, sweetened with something that echoed the scent of Gwen's skin.

"You taste too good not to eat," she murmured before diving down between those long legs. She tried to be as methodical and skilful as usual, but it was impossible. Her feelings for Gwen had undone all of her expertise. All she could do was hope her mouth would know what to do. It clearly did as it wasn't long before Gwen's back arched off the floor and she keened loud enough for it to echo off the walls.

When Gwen was finished, Aya kissed her way up her pubic hair and onto her belly, wiping her face at the same time as she got to kiss more of that soft skin.

Gwen grasped for her. "Let me hold you." The words sounded soul-baring, almost broken. Aya happily moved up Gwen's delicate frame and nestled into her embrace. Their bodies lay hot and flush against each other as Aya nuzzled into her beautiful swan neck, feeling the rapid speed of Gwen's pulse.

Her own heart was pulsing as hard, but so was everything between her thighs. She couldn't wait any longer. She positioned her pussy on Gwen's thigh and began to move her hips, the much-needed friction making her groan.

Gwen gave a little laugh, as much sinfulness as pure joy.

"Mm, that feels so good," Gwen moaned. "Congratulations. You guessed my biggest kink on the first go. Maybe it doesn't actually count as a kink but I," she gripped Aya's arse, "absolutely love tribbing. Not as much as I love you. But close."

Aya froze. Not only had Gwen mentioned having *kinks*, she'd professed her love! Just like that. This woman was so damn free and open.

"I think I… No, I know that I… love you, too," Aya said softly, feeling as vulnerable as a newborn kitten.

Gwen connected their gazes and caressed the hair out of Aya's face. "Then get on your back, sweetheart. Let me show you what my love feels like in action."

Aya slowly moved off, grieving the loss of Gwen's body against hers. She didn't have to miss it for long. Gwen soon draped herself over her, placing a hand between Aya's legs. Its fingers knew what they wanted and how to drive Aya out of her mind. They moved expertly around her clit, as if they'd done so a million times before. Aya had one hand on Gwen's back and the other entwined in her short hair, keeping Gwen tightly on top of her.

She could hear her own groans turning into needy whimpers.

Gwen kissed her ear as her fingers kept circling and rubbing. Then she plunged them deep into Aya, making her cry out with the pleasure of it.

Aya was so close to climax. All she needed was the right pressure on the right spot. Gwen's fingers danced over that spot inside her, never lingering. She kept her thrusting light and teasing while she kissed the column of Aya's throat.

Aya's inner muscles tightened to the point of pain. She had to be brought over the edge *right now* or she was going to howl like a goddamn wolf.

"Either stay on my G-spot or move to my clit, just bloody well get me off!" Aya grunted through gritted teeth.

Gwen lifted her head to look into Aya's eyes. "I'll give you anything if you order me in that tone of voice," she said hoarsely.

"Then stop talking and make me come. Right fucking now!"

Gwen applied her other hand to Aya's throbbing clit. A couple of seconds of that was all it took. Aya blinked away dots of lights and shut her eyes tight against the onslaught of pleasure as she came.

When she returned to her senses, Gwen's head was resting on her chest. Not right on the tattoo between her breasts, but to the left, as if listening for a heartbeat. Her fingers were on the tattoo, though, caressing the wisps of smoke with reverence.

With tired, affectionate movements, Aya craned her neck to kiss the top of the blonde hair, smiling as she spotted the blue tips that she'd helped dye.

"Gwen," she said, still slightly out of breath, "I'm so sorry for our fight. I overreacted to what you said. I mean, I always say the wrong things and mess up, but blowing up like that was crap even for me. I suppose..." She brushed some stiffness from hair products out of Gwen's hair while searching for words. "I suppose everything was intensified because I so desperately wanted the date to work out. You mean the world to me, and I was so scared of ruining it that I, well, ruined it."

"It wasn't just you. I don't why I phrased it so clumsily or why I kept babbling when it became clear that I was speaking out of turn. I guess I was nervous, too. So nervous that I ran my mouth without thinking. I apologise from the bottom of my heart."

Aya ran her finger along Gwen's cheek. "The high stakes got the better of both of us, huh?"

"Mm. The best thing about our friendship was that we were so relaxed and honest with each other. We should try to keep that in our relationship."

"Yeah, we'll just add romance and sex."

"Agreed," Gwen said with a relieved laugh.

*How do we do that? Hm, some friendly teasing might be a good start.*

Aya knew exactly what banter to go for. "I suppose we should also add tribbing, huh?"

Gwen sat up with a flirty expression and playfully slapped Aya's abs. "Are you slut-shaming, or rather, trib-shaming me?"

"Hell no, I loved it, too, shug. I want to do that in all its variations."

"That can be arranged! But let's do it on the bed. As comfy as this carpet is, we're not twenty-one anymore." She stretched, popping her back as proof of her point.

"Sure. Hang on. What about finding Meatloaf?"

Gwen winced. "Ah. Yes. About that. Um, you know how I blurted out that there were no exposed cables and the other doors were closed?"

Aya sat up. "Yeah. That was a bit weird."

"Yes, well, that was because I didn't want you to worry when we didn't find her."

"What do you mean?"

"I mean that Meatloaf is safely asleep in her cage. Saying that she escaped was a white lie. I needed a reason to make you come in, so we could talk and clear the air before that little misunderstanding became a big thing."

Aya stared at her for a few seconds and then cackled. "You clever minx! Brilliant. Come here."

Gwen did, first kissing Aya's lips and then her neck, then down to her breasts. She planted a gentle kiss on the tattoo next, her fingers following where her lips had gone, caressing the black lines of ink. "Can I ask about this? It's incredible. What is it?"

"It's an enenra, a Japanese smoke creature taking human form. I got it to honour my Japanese heritage about seven years ago." Aya looked away. "I wanted it to be something I could talk to my mum about, but she just said she hated tattoos."

"I'm so sorry. Well, I love it, just like I love every other part of your body." Her delicate hand slid down Aya's torso to rest on her hip, right where she'd gotten a bruise the day they fell in the perfume shop in Chester.

Gwen tilted her head to the side. "Why did you pick the… Nenra, was it called?"

"Enenra. I was young and thought it was cool, being a monster made of smoke and darkness. And well," she coughed in an embarrassed manner, "an enenra is only meant to be seen by those pure of heart, and I'd broken up with a girl who cheated on me. At the time I sort of only wanted pure-hearted women to be able, or rather allowed, to see it."

"And you just let *me* see it?" Gwen said, teasing sneaking into her tone.

Aya wasn't rising to the bait. Both she and Gwen knew that for all of her faults, her heart was certainly pure. "Mm-hm. And you're one of the few lovers who took this much interest in it. Most women just accept that it's from Japanese folklore, and that's it." Aya made herself say the rest, wanting to be open with Gwen. "They don't really see it and how important it is to me."

Gwen was quiet for a while. The dim light and earnestness made her eyes darken to a deeper blue. "*I* do. I want to see all of it and all of you. Inside and out. If your mum won't help you connect to your Japanese heritage, you and I will figure it out together. If that's okay with you?"

In answer, Aya pulled her into a long kiss. She tried to pour every ounce of gratitude, adoration, and vulnerability she could into it. Sealing their bond in the best way she knew how.

After a while, Gwen moved back a hairsbreadth. "So, you still want to go to bed with me?" she whispered against her lips.

"More than ever," Aya replied hoarsely, standing and giving her lover a hand up. When they were face to face, Aya knew the kiss hadn't been enough. Gwen deserved more. Aya would need to do the hardest thing: put it all into words.

"Gwen?"

"Yes?"

"Thank you."

"For what, sweetheart?"

"For making me clear the air right away and for, well,

wanting to stay with me. For falling in love with me. For needing me. For choosing me."

"I should be thanking you," Gwen whispered. "I'm not an easy partner to have. Everyone who came before you gave up and left."

"Well, I don't want easy. It's overrated and usually hides something rubbish. Give me complicated and meaningful any day." Aya felt her grin go from ear to ear as she decided to break the serious mood. "Anyway, we should go *thank* each other in bed."

"Yes!" Gwen laughed. "You go ahead, my love. I'll be right there. I'm just going to grab our clothes. I want to get my knickers before I forget that I threw them into the damn bookshelf!"

Ecstatic, Aya sprinted for the bed and jumped into it, breathing in Gwen's scent on her bedding. Soon she heard naked feet quickly padding to the bedroom and realised that the source of the scent, the most incredible person on this whole bloody earth, was about to join her. Her Gwen. Gwen, who, for some reason, loved her back.

## Chapter Forty-Seven

# EPILOGUE

Gwen shifted to get comfy in the jeep's front seat. Six months. She put down the notepad where she'd been drawing Aya's tattoo and the impressive abs it led into. How had it already been six months since their pining over Susannah brought them together?

Half a year, containing enough drama and growth for a decade. She was as grateful for these six months as she was that her depression was in an up phase.

"Can you believe it's been six months?" Gwen shouted, trying to be heard over Donna Lewis' "I Love You Always Forever."

"What? Sorry, I have to switch this off," Aya said and pushed the off button.

Gwen couldn't blame her. They'd listened to it four times in a row, partly because it was Gwen's favourite song and partly because Aya knew her girlfriend loved it when she sang the part about "the most unbelievable blue eyes I've ever seen" to her. It was sugary sweet, but in Gwen's experience, life was bitter. She'd take all the sugar she could find.

With the music off, Gwen tried again. "Can you believe we've been together for six months already?"

"Seven."

"Uh-uh. Wrong, sweetheart. Tomorrow it'll be exactly six months."

Aya kept her eyes on the road. "Nope. Seven."

Gwen sighed. "I'm not doing this with you. Not today. Today, nothing can shatter my good mood."

"Ha! Give me time and I bet I can shatter it like a shatter expert."

Gwen shook her head. "What does that even mean? You're impossible, you know that? Luckily I know how to *handle* you." She put her hand on Aya's thigh.

"None of that, duck," Aya said. "Not while I'm driving."

"Fine. Fancy pulling over at the next unoccupied lay-by?"

Aya swallowed visibly. "Yes, but we're not going to."

"Oh? We're not? Want to give me a reason?" Gwen purred.

"Just because we shag like champions doesn't mean we should do it all the time."

"Shag like champions?" Gwen questioned, laughing.

Aya shrugged in her embarrassed way. "Yeah. You're the best lover I ever had."

"Really?" Gwen thought back to the pining that had brought them together. "Better even than the *exciting Susannah*?" she asked acerbically.

"God, yes." Aya paused to switch lanes. "Whoever came up with the cliché that sex in a good relationship with a caring partner is worse than sex with a hot hook-up needs to have their head examined. You're smashing in bed!"

"Same," Gwen said, mollified. "You're smashing in every way. I mean, look at you."

Aya snorted.

"No, I mean it! You're taking time off from two jobs that you love just to drive all the way to Cilcain and meet my family!"

Aya's forehead creased. "There's nothing smashing about that."

"Maybe not to you," Gwen said, leaning over to kiss her cheek. "Anyway, I'll get to return the favour when we go to Shirahama and hopefully find some of your relatives."

*Hopefully they'll give a damn, since your parents don't.*

Aya's forehead creases doubled. "Yeah. A Japan trip is a bit pricier than a drive to Wales, babe."

"We'll get there, one quid at a time. Being back at Coffee4U and working on the comic with November Jones means I'll be earning more soon."

The creasing smoothed, and Aya beamed. "Yeah. That's true. I'm so proud of you." She nodded towards the notepad in Gwen's lap. "Did you only draw my body parts today, or did you actually work on any of the panels for the comic?"

Gwen smiled as well. "Mainly your body parts. I've been drawing your amazing enenra again! If you want any other tattoos, I'd love to sketch them out for you and come with you to the tattoo parlour."

"That's very sweet. But," Aya's face grew stern, "you changed the topic. I know your tricks now, I won't fall for that. Answer the question. Did you work on the last of the panels before we left?"

The comic was almost finished. The last panels she had to colour and shade were coming along well. Well, except for the heroine's shoulders. Why was drawing shoulder musculature still so hard? Aya's shoulders were frequently in her sight, in her hands and, on good days, under her mouth.

"Yes, bossy, I did the lion's share. I just need to do the final touches on the last panel when we get back. Then it's off to November Jones for checking and then to the publisher."

"Brilliant!" Aya roared. "Everything that woman writes sells like ice lollies on a hot day. I'm sure it'll be a success. Either way, as I said before, I'm bloody proud of you."

Gwen was pretty damn proud of herself, too. She had a job, a girlfriend, a purpose in the form of an art project that stimulated her head and heart. Her mental health was good right now, and when it worsened again, she would have a good support system in Aya, Charlotte, and Edward. Well, also November and Aya's Bill and Jenny too now, she supposed.

They might be on their way to see her biological family, but she was very satisfied with the chosen family she and Aya had collected. It helped them both more than any blood-related people ever had.

She brushed a strand of loose hair away from Aya's face. "I'm proud of you, too. You're so much more confident these days."

"Thanks. It's my new moisturiser," Aya said with a grin.

Gwen shot her a look. "Oh, yeah? It has nothing to do with how Jenny is telling everyone far and wide, including BBC Radio Stoke, that she owes her success to her cool role model and training coach?"

Aya showed off that dimple in another grin, one which

faltered as she stared at something on the dash. "Um, treasure? Don't kill me, but we have to stop."

"Okay. Sure, but why? We've only been driving for like twenty minutes."

"I may have been overly optimistic again."

Gwen followed her gaze to the petrol light flashing angrily on Janet's dash. "*Really?*" she grumbled. "I told you to fill it up when you went shopping yesterday."

"Yeah. I didn't think I'd need to. It's fine, though. There's a services in two miles."

Gwen shook her head with a laugh. "Well, I suppose I could use another cup of tea."

---

A little later, they sat in a café with hot drinks and the peace of mind that Janet was refuelled.

Aya ran a thumb along the side of her mug. "You know, this reminds me of when we drove to Chester that first time. When we drank mochas and bonded over pining over Susannah."

Gwen sat back. "I hadn't thought about that, but yeah, it was a services much like this one."

"That's because it *was* this one."

"No, you're wrong again, babe. That one was smaller."

Aya took a sip of her coffee. "Nope. It was this one."

Gwen scanned the place and reluctantly admitted to herself that Aya was right. "Weird. I totally remember it being smaller."

Aya chuckled. "Me too, actually. Is this where I say something cheesy about everything seeming smaller before you came into my life?"

"No. It's not," Gwen monotoned.

Aya shrugged with a pleased expression.

"It is weird, though," Gwen said. "We started out as strangers. Then became rivals over the same unattainable woman. Then we stopped talking. Then we became friends, and now I'm introducing you as my girlfriend to my family."

"It's been a journey, shug. I credit your idea about having a boost every day for a lot of it. It gave me a way to get to know you."

"Mm." Gwen tapped her mug. "You know, I think Bill was right about the bright sparks. You can find them in everyday life if you try. Like this extra cup of tea. Or the jolt I get when someone compliments my art."

"Or being with me?"

Gwen stopped the movement of her fingers. "Babe, you're not some little boost. You're thrill and safety, support and challenge. Your love infuses every part of my life, improving everything it touches."

"Ooh, so poetic."

Gwen laughed. "Drink your coffee and shush."

Aya laughed, too, before leaning in for a quick kiss. Then they settled back into silence and people-watched. A brutish man eyed them, and for a second Gwen wondered what it would be like to not have to consider homophobia when you kissed in public. She fixed the thug with a glare, and he looked down. She sipped her tea.

Aya swallowed a big gulp of coffee and said, "I think it's healthier, you know."

"What? Coffee?"

"No! The way we live now compared with back when we stopped here on that Chester trip."

Gwen took another sip. "Well, of course it is. We were both miserable."

"Let me finish," Aya whinged. "You know how hard it is for me to put stuff into words."

"Sorry. Carry on, sweetheart."

"When we were crushing on Susannah, we were both trying to escape reality and pining over a fantasy."

Gwen smiled. "More like a mirage, I think, but I get your point."

Aya waved that away, warming to her subject. "It wasn't about wishing to be with her, but what we wished our lives were. You used her as inspiration to create art, but always for others, never daring to make something for yourself, or not thinking you deserved to." She paused, frowning for a second. "Me, well, I was living in the past, thinking that if I got some made-up *win*, I'd feel as confident as I did when I boxed."

"We were just trying to survive," Gwen countered. "Using fantasy to fill in the gaps where real life disappointed us."

Aya shot her an annoyed look. "Sure, and that's fine. In small doses. For us, it… I don't know, it took over our existence, making us invest more time and effort in daydreams than into our lives. You know what I mean? You're right, we were just surviving. Not living."

"Now who's being poetic?"

"I'm just saying that Bill talked about romanticising the little things in life, right?"

"Yes."

"I think we need to take it a step further," Aya said, voice rising. "Romanticise our whole damn lives. And if there's nothing to romanticise, we should change it."

"Easier said than done for most people, love. They need their uninspiring jobs to pay the bills. Or maybe they can't change things because of their health."

Aya sat forward, radiating fervour. "Then do one little thing! Start at the gym. Buy a self-help book. Date someone new. Start singing in the shower. Anything to make your life feed your soul."

"Love being in Stoke-on-Trent instead of just dreaming of moving to Chester?" Gwen suggested.

"I know you're joking, but yes. Stoke-on-Trent can be pretty, it can be cultural, and it has heaps of interesting history, just like Chester. We just have to search for it and appreciate it."

Gwen tapped her fingers against her mug again, mulling that over. "So you're saying that loving something is better than pining for something?"

"Yep. And that goes for people, too."

Gwen thought back to when she pined over Susannah. Then to their whole lives, as they were then, and as they were now.

She smiled at Aya. "Okay. This time, you're definitely not wrong." Then she kissed her, long and heartfelt, romanticising over and loving every second of it.

# ABOUT THE AUTHOR

Emma Sterner-Radley, a Swedish romance and fantasy writer, got a degree in Library and Information Science because she wanted to work with books, and being an author was an impossible dream, right? Wrong. She's now a writer and a publisher. (But still a librarian at heart.)

She lives with her wife and two cats in England. There's no point in saying which city, as they move about once a year. She spends her time writing, reading, daydreaming, exercising, and watching whichever television show has the most lesbian/sapphic subtext at the time.

Her weaknesses are coffee, sugary snacks and small chubby creatures with tiny legs.

www.emmasternerradley.com

# ALSO BY EMMA STERNER-RADLEY

## LIFE PUSHES YOU ALONG

**Zoe's on autopilot. Rebecca is stagnating. When change comes knocking, will they open the door?**

Twenty-something Zoe Achidi feels safe in her unchallenging life in a London bookshop. Bored, but safe.

Her only excitement comes from pining over frequent customer, Rebecca Clare, unobtainable as this beautiful businesswoman in her forties seems.

One day, Zoe's brother and her best friend bring Zoe and Rebecca together.

While they connect, and it turns out Rebecca is also bored with her life, their meetings remain all business. When things take a turn for the worse, life pushes along.

But will Zoe and Rebecca end up being thrust in the same direction?

If you're looking for an age-gap romance that will inspire you to shake up your life, then look no further.

Take the leap with Life Pushes You Along by Emma Sterner-Radley

# ALSO BY EMMA STERNER-RADLEY

## LONG-DISTANCE COFFEE

New York personal trainer Erin Black lives a solitary life plagued by insomnia. Isabella Martinez, a former CEO turned writer, is stuck in a platonic relationship in Florida with her baby boy.

One sleepless night on social media, they strike up a conversation that changes their lives and makes them question everything. Over midnight cups of coffee, they try to resist the powerful chemistry that builds between them. They soon discover their connection could be the key to unlocking their personal issues.

Questions remain though. Are they more than friends? Could they be right for each other? And if they are, how will they handle a relationship a thousand miles apart?

A sapphic romance about closing the distance.

# ALSO BY EMMA STERNER-RADLEY

## GREENGAGE PLOTS

**Two women. One plot. Six thousand interfering islanders.**

Katherine "Kit" Sorel is new to the cosy but quirky island of Greengage. When she tries to use her talents for plotting to help a friend, she soon discovers that on this British island—anything can happen.

Kittens can race, fruit can be sexy, wheelbarrows can be menacing, and straight women might not be so straight after all.

In the end, Kit needs to solve the problems of those around her while finding her home. She's certainly not looking for love. But is it looking for her?

Escape everyday life, take a trip to a British cosy island by picking up a copy of Greengage Plots.

Printed in Poland
by Amazon Fulfillment
Poland Sp. z o.o., Wrocław

49992426R00209